Kate Kingsley has lived on both sides of the Atlantic, spending time in New York, London, Paris and Rome – so she's more than qualified to chronicle the jet-set lives of the YOUNG, LOADED AND FABULOUS girls.

Kate also writes for magazines such as *GQ* in New York, where she's had the enviable task of interviewing fashion designers like Paul Smith, and celebrities like James McAvoy. She's currently hard at work on her next book about the YL&F crew.

Check www.youngloadedandfabulous.co.uk regularly for news of Kate Kingsley's next fabulous book.

Young, loaded and fabulous

Too CRUEL for SCHOOL

KATE KINGSLEY

headline

First published in Great Britain in 2011 by
HEADLINE PUBLISHING GROUP

2

Cataloguing in Publication Data is available from the British Library

ISBN 978 0 7553 5984 4

Typeset in New Baskerville by Palimpsest Book Production Limited,
Falkirk, Stirlingshire

Printed and bound in Great Britain by
Clays Ltd, St Ives plc

Headline's policy is to use papers that are natural, renewable and recyclable
products and made from wood grown in sustainable forests. The logging and
manufacturing processes are expected to conform to the environmental
regulations of the country of origin.

HEADLINE PUBLISHING GROUP
An Hachette UK Company
338 Euston Road
London NW1 3BH

www.headline.co.uk
www.hachette.co.uk

Chapter 1

The antique sofa in Alice Rochester's bedroom groaned as Jemimah Calthorpe de Vyle-Hanswicke flopped on to its spindly frame.

'St Cecilia's is totally going to kick me out on Monday and then I'll be an outcast for the rest of my life!' Mimah moaned, her voice muffled by the couch's lilac silk cushions. 'I'll be the most disgraced person in London. Everyone will be bad-mouthing me – I should probably just curl up and die right now.'

'Mmm. Yeah.' Alice glanced at her watch. Typical. Mimah always chose the most inconvenient times to sink into her moods. Like right now, at quarter to ten on Saturday night, when Alice had thirty seconds to get her out the door, into a black London cab, and on their way.

'OK; that's it.' She clapped her hands. 'Get up. I'm not wasting my entire weekend sitting at home. Plus, you need cheering up. We're going to Kiki Club.'

'Kiki's?' Mimah grimaced. 'You're joking, right?'

Alice was never what you'd call a sympathetic friend, but she could at least be making a bit more of an effort tonight. Tomorrow was Mimah's last official day of suspension from

St Cecilia's boarding school, and her future wasn't exactly looking rosy. A week ago, she'd been caught carrying drugs in the woods near school and had been dragged off to the headmistress's office for a serious showdown. '*Suspension with the possibility of expulsion*' had been the verdict, accompanied by a storm of reproaches like 'severely disappointed', 'betrayal of trust', and, Mimah's personal favourite, 'disgrace to your parents and friends'.

Mimah sighed. It was all so unfair. For a start, she hadn't even been taking the drugs. She'd never even *intended* to take them; she'd just confiscated them from her fourteen-year-old sister, Charlie, who'd stupidly stolen them from their mum's medicine cabinet. But, in a moment of heroism, Mimah had decided to swallow the blame. Surely it was better to save her little sister's future than her own?

Or maybe not. Maybe heroism was an overrated concept.

A bundle of beige cashmere landed in Mimah's arms.

'Coat,' Alice said. 'Put it on. Hat. Scarf. Bag. Let's go.'

'Who lit a fire under your arse?' Mimah protested, as she was practically shoved out the front door of the Rochesters' magnificent Kensington town house, through the garden, and into the street, which was lined with bare December trees. 'And by the way, did you hear me agree to come to Kiki's? I thought we were staying in with a bottle of wine and a stack of rom coms.'

'Boring,' Alice snorted. 'Change of plan.'

'In your head,' Mimah retorted. Then her eyes widened. 'Unbelievable!'

'What?'

2

Mimah pointed at Alice's outfit. 'I should have known you were never staying in with me. I mean, an Hervé Leger bandage dress? Yeah, great TV-watching gear.' She gestured at her own black leggings and belted shirt. 'This just proves I can't come – I look like someone's household staff. Ugh, I am so not in the mood for a bar packed with random people. I'm going home.'

'No!' Alice hailed a passing taxi. If Mimah took off now, all her plans for the evening would be ruined. She'd spent most of the past few days coordinating every last detail for tonight, and she did not intend to look like a fool. 'Your outfit's super-chic. I mean, yeah – haven't you heard? Grunge is back. Now get in. You have to.'

'Why?'

'Because I said so, silly. Pretty please, Mimey? Kiki Club coconutinis on me . . .'

'Oh, wonderful,' Mimah grumbled, ''cause there's nothing a coconutini can't fix.' But arguing was futile – when Alice had her heart set on something, only a miracle could change her mind. So Mimah slumped back against the cab's grey leather seat and tried to relax. It didn't work – obviously. Nothing was comforting enough to distract her from Monday's impending doom: not the familiar rasp of the taxi's diesel engine; not the tones of Laura Marling drifting from the driver's radio; not even the holiday lights twinkling overhead like necklaces against the night sky.

'Who are you texting?' she asked suddenly. Alice had slipped out her phone and was covering the screen as she typed.

3

'What? No one,' Alice said, shoving her phone back in her pocket. She craned her neck at the web of electric stars winking over Sloane Square, clearly straining to change the subject. 'They always do a stunning job on the Christmas decorations in our part of town, don't they?'

Mimah shrugged. 'I guess.'

'Not that it's surprising. After all, families like ours wouldn't stand for it if they didn't. Shit – can you believe Christmas is in less than four weeks? And it's less than three weeks till we're out of school! I can't wait.'

'Yeah. Me neither. If I still have a school to be out of.'

'Babe, could you stop being such a downer?' Alice kicked Mimah with one of her green patent leather wedges. 'Look on the bright side: whatever happens, you're still invited to come to Jasper's ski chalet for New Year.'

'Wow, thanks. And there I was, assuming that if I got expelled I'd be dumped by all my best friends and barred from every guest list.'

'You know that's not what I meant.' Alice rolled her eyes. 'I was only trying to be encouraging. Come on, Mime – you're almost seventeen – you've got to stop allowing every little thing to get you down.'

Mimah clenched her teeth. Perhaps she should point out that the threat of being expelled from one of England's oldest and most exclusive boarding schools was hardly a 'little thing'. But no – there was no point. Alice wouldn't get it; she'd never had to deal with anything adverse in her life. Literally the worst thing that had ever happened to her was having bad sex with her boyfriend, Tristan

Murray-Middleton, a couple of weeks ago. And bad sex wasn't exactly unusual – especially when it was your first time.

Mimah sneaked a glance at her friend. 'So . . .' she began, unscrewing the cap of her lip gloss, 'how come you didn't want to see Tristan tonight?'

'Huh? Oh . . . 'Cause I wanted to see *you*, babe.'

'Yeah, right, suck-up. How's T doing?'

'Fine, I guess'. Alice picked a piece of invisible fluff off her Aubin & Wills coat. She hadn't seen Tristan since she'd visited him in hospital last weekend, just after he'd been injured in a terrifying rugby accident. 'I mean, he's recovering from concussion and a broken collarbone – it's not like he's gonna go climbing Mount Everest any time soon. Maybe he'll think twice before he plays rugby again.'

'Sure he will,' Mimah snorted. As someone who was majorly into her sports, she knew exactly how Tristan felt about his. 'Seriously, though, the Paper Bandits argument – are you over it?'

Alice shrugged. The Paper Bandits were Tristan's band, and he was their lead singer. Obviously Alice was proud to have a boyfriend with star quality – but not when it blinded him to everything else. Like, how important *she* was. Which was precisely what had happened a couple of weeks ago: straight after they'd had sex for the first time, T had started acting like he cared more about his band's success than about the fact that Alice had just lost her virginity. And that wasn't just hurtful – it was humiliating.

'Actually, I'm still quite pissed off,' she sighed, biting

her lip at the memory. 'I mean, can you blame me? What kind of guy pays more attention to his guitar than to his girlfriend?'

Mimah smirked. 'Every single seventeen-year-old guy I know?'

'Whatever.' Alice allowed herself half a grin. 'I suppose I can't hold it against him for too long while he's in a sling, anyway. How bitchy would I look if I was nasty to an invalid? I'd be like, *persona non grata*.' Flicking her long, dark hair, she sneaked a glance towards the front seat. Hopefully the cab driver had heard that little Latin gem. It really was impressive what a private school education could do for your vocabulary.

Mimah clicked shut her Lulu Guinness handbag and leaned closer. The tiny mole under her left eye drew level with Alice's face and made it look like she was winking. 'OK, babe, you know what I really want to know.' Her look was expectant. 'Spill it.'

'Spill what?'

'Hello? In bed . . . I mean, T's practically immobile – it's gotta be bizarre, right? Tell me everything! Have you two done it again?'

'Maybe.'

'OMG, that *totally* means you haven't.'

'No! It means, "shut up and mind your own business." Just 'cause you don't have a boyfriend, you don't have to, like, live through *my* love life.'

'Come on, Al – don't be mean. I know it wasn't great the first time, but you were a virgin, and—'

6

'Shut *up*!' Alice's face was as red as a hot coal. 'Would you mind not informing the cab driver about every secret of my sex life?'

Luckily, before things could get any more excruciating, the taxi swung into a side street off King's Road and rumbled to a halt.

'Kiki Club, haunt of the rich and famous,' the driver announced, switching off his meter with a flourish.

Alice gazed at the carved palm trees heralding the entrance to the bar, at the caffeine-buzzed paparazzi drooling for a celeb sighting, and at the crowd of pretty young things jostling inside the velvet ropes. Swallowing, she checked her watch again. Tonight better go well – and she meant that about more things than one.

Chapter 2

'Why did I agree to this?' Mimah scowled under her blunt black fringe. She batted a dangling palm frond out of her eyes and trailed Alice through Kiki Club, trying to avoid the hula-skirted waitresses balancing trays of blue and orange cocktails as they weaved between the bamboo tables.

'C'mere, pretty lady,' mouthed a floppy-haired boy whose jeans were hanging off his boxer shorts. He stumbled into Mimah's path, gliding towards her in time to the sultry Buddha-Bar-style lounge music. His eyes were half-closed, either because he was under the mistaken impression that this was sexy, or because he was too wasted to keep them open. 'Yeah, baby, want a snog?' he whispered, shimmying closer, his head bobbing on his skinny neck.

'Fuck off,' Mimah snapped. She shoved the boy's pink-shirt-clad chest and watched him flail backwards into a row of carved tiki masks. *Bullseye.* Mimah smirked. Obviously all that lacrosse she'd been playing was toning up her arm muscles.

Her shoulders drooped. Lacrosse – yet another thing she shouldn't be thinking about. After Monday, there wouldn't be any more school sports. No more captaining the Lower-Sixth team. No more rowdy coach trips to away matches. No more galloping down the groomed St Cecilia's fields, her yellow and grey school scarf tailing out behind her. Mimah put her hands to her face. Suddenly, Kiki Club felt like a cage: cramped, hot, full of screeching inmates. She needed some air. Or, at the very least, a drink.

'Whoo!' Alice cried. She bumped Mimah with a skinny hip. 'Babe, stop acting like a corpse and dance. Hey – I wonder what's back here?'

'Who cares?' Mimah shrugged. Alice was heading straight past the bar towards an artfully ripped skull-and-crossbones flag. Behind it, there seemed to be some kind of hidden private lounge.

'Doesn't this look mysterious?' Alice brushed her hand over the flag so that the candlelight glowing through it shimmered on the wall.

'Um, no? It's just a VIP room. I need some booze. Come on.'

'Hmmm, I don't know . . .' Alice scratched her chin. 'I kind of want to stay here. I think it looks like a . . . *pirate shiiip!*' she bellowed, practically howling the last two words.

Mimah leapt into the air. 'What the hell—'

'*Surprise!*'

The flag flew aside and a crowd stampeded out, sloshing tropical cocktails, waving streamers and cheering at the top of their lungs. In the lead was Alice's best mate, Tally Abbott, strands of her white-blond hair whipping back towards Sonia Khan, who was pumping her arms like a crazed marathoner, trying as hard as she could to get to the front. Behind the girls burst Tristan Murray-Middleton, Seb Ogilvy, Jasper von Holstadt, George Demetrios and Tom Randall-Stubbs – the Hasted House gang.

'Smile, babies,' Sonia said, whipping out her state-of-the-art video camera. Sonia's life ambition was to storm Hollywood and be the best director the universe had ever seen. Shame her only projects so far amounted to stalkerish home videos of her friends, and an unfinished documentary about the Paper Bandits.

'Group hug!' George roared.

Mimah gasped as she felt her feet leave the floor. 'Help! G-guys, seriously. It's awesome to see you but . . . I don't get it. It's not my birthday. I-Is it?'

'Duh, silly,' Alice laughed, elbowing her way into the middle of the group. She smacked a kiss on Mimah's cheek. 'But it *is* your last night out before judgment day, and I wanted to make it special.'

'Ali, you mean this was *your* plan?'

'Of course it was Al's plan!' Tally butted in. She passed Mimah a coconut with a fat pink straw sticking out of it. 'Do you think anyone else would have been anal enough to organise this? Ow!' she giggled, as Alice's Marni wedge landed on her toes. 'So, come on, Mime, how surprised are you? On a scale of one to ten.'

'Twenty. I almost died of shock.'

'Perfect. Now at least if you get chucked out on Monday, you'll have happy memories to keep you warm. Enjoy your last night out as a St Cecilia's girl, OK?'

Alice rolled her eyes. But before she could tell Tally to shut up a familiar chuckle sounded behind her.

'Good old Tals and her natural tact,' commented a boy's voice.

Alice's body stiffened like a tripwire. Tristan. This was only the second time they'd been in the same room since their argument a couple of weeks ago – and that argument had been so bad it had almost been a break-up. Her eyes flew towards his – but just as their gazes met, Dizzee Rascal blasted over the speakers.

'Tune!' hooted Jasper. 'Dance with me, people.' Grabbing Tally, Mimah and Sonia, he leapt on to one of the VIP couches and cocked his houndstooth fedora at a jaunty angle. 'Rando,' he bellowed, 'get up here!'

'Budge over, then.'

Alice watched as Tom Randall-Stubbs hopped up on to the cushions next to Tally and swung her in his arms.

'Wheee!' Tally shrieked, kissing him.

Alice folded her arms. Those two had been seeing each other ever since Rando's country house party a couple of weeks ago, and it was sort of weirding her out. Not that she could explain why. Maybe it was because Tally had always sworn to date other men rather than boys their age. Or maybe because it was strange to see people splitting into couples – people who weren't her and T, that is. It changed everything when your friends paired off – for a start, they had different loyalties than before. Yeah, you could go on about 'mates before dates' as much as you wanted but, when it came down to it, that wasn't the way things went.

'Hey.' Tristan grazed her arm. He was smiling cautiously, shifting from one foot to the other. 'Looks like your surprise was a success.'

'I guess.' Alice flicked a strand of her long, chocolate-brown hair.

'Cool. So . . . how're things?'

'Fine.'

'Cool.' Mentally, T kicked himself. Why was 'cool' suddenly the only adjective in his vocabulary? 'You look . . . nice.'

'Thanks,' Alice murmured, lowering her eyelashes. She brushed his sling. 'How's the shoulder?'

'It's sore. But getting better.' Tristan swallowed. Alice was wearing some sort of sweet, delicious perfume that was making his blood throb. He could feel it rushing towards that crucial point in his trousers, pulsing until he thought he might burst. He and Alice had only had sex once, back before he'd cracked his collarbone, but he'd been thinking about it ever since. He'd thought about it all last week at home while he was lying on the couch, watching crap daytime TV and trying to recover from his rugby injury. He'd thought about it while he was choosing which polo shirt to wear out tonight. And he was thinking about it right now. Alice's outfit . . . Her dress was so tight it looked like she'd wrapped herself in rubber bands. There was no way she'd be wearing it if she wasn't thinking about sex. Maybe he could get her to stay at his house tonight so they could do it again. That is, if she wasn't still pissed off from their spat about the Paper Bandits.

12

'Hey, are we OK?' T murmured.

Alice shrugged. 'Yeah. Of course.'

'Good. Then come here.' He pulled her into a kiss, breathing that perfume, sliding his hand down her smooth back, over the slight curve of her bum.

'Get a room!' jeered a voice in his ear. George Demetrios nudged Jasper. 'Bloody smug snogging couple. Hey, Jas, don't these lovebirds make you sick? Bet you wish you'd kept Dylan Taylor around at times like this.'

'Why would I wish that?' Jasper asked.

'Because, knobhead, girlfriends are basically sex on tap. Especially Dylan. At least, from what I've heard . . . I mean, how could she not be with boobs as big as—'

'Shut up!' Jasper rammed George against the wall. 'Why do you always have to be so vulgar?'

''Cause I'm not totally *gay* about girls. Got a problem?'

'OK guys, break it up!' Seb Ogilvy jumped in brightly. 'Where is Dylan tonight, anyway?'

Jasper shrugged.

'Dunno,' George grunted.

Alice flicked her hair. '*I* know where she is. She told me. She's at home, helping her sister pack for school. It's Lauren's first day at St Cecilia's tomorrow. Remember?'

'How could I forget?' grumbled Sonia Khan. 'Just what our school needs – another tacky Taylor. 'Cause, you know, one just isn't enough.'

Tristan ran a hand through his public-schoolboy quiff. 'Come on, Sone, Dylan's not tacky. She's just different. She's American. They've got a different style over there.'

Alice pursed her lips. She was mostly over the fact that T had had a fling with Dylan last summer, before Dylan had moved to London and enrolled at St Cecilia's, but he didn't have to defend her. T was always doing that – speaking up for people, trying to understand them, being sensitive. That'd been his thing ever since he was a kid.

'Oh, puhl-ease,' snorted Sonia. 'Look, T, I know you're trying to be nice, but get real. Dylan looks like an ad for breast reduction. Plus, she dances like a stripper. And, anyway, I'm the one who lives with her. You should see her underwear. So. Slutty.'

'Oh, god, don't tease me,' George Demetrios pleaded. 'Slutty underwear? I think I'm falling in love.' He nudged Tristan, and the two of them cracked up.

'Ugh,' Alice groaned. 'Why are boys so repulsive? I'm getting drinks.'

'See you in a bit, babe,' T called after her, still laughing. 'Oh, and bring me a beer!'

'Vodka Red Bull,' George guffawed.

'Whisky,' Seb cried. 'On the rocks!'

'Nice try,' Alice flung over her shoulder as she headed for the bar. It was seething with punters, but she had no intention of waiting around. Queueing was for losers. Standing on tiptoe, she glimpsed a familiar shock of dark brown hair.

'Rando!' she yelled, and launched herself forward.

Tom Randall-Stubbs's head jerked round. He had two drinks on the bar: a vodka, and a bright pink frozen daiquiri with cherries and strawberries stuck around the edges of the glass.

'Al, hi,' he said, a smile brightening his features. Alice felt her own smile bubble up to meet it. There was something so infectious about Rando's grin – maybe it was his dimples. Or his cute pointy teeth. Or the fact that it just made him look so eager and boyish.

'What's up with the champion party organiser? Can I get you a drink?'

'Sure, thanks,' Alice said. 'mojito, please.'

'Done.' Rando tossed his messy brown hair out of his blue-green eyes. 'Hey, guess what I bought today?'

Alice shrugged. 'Your very first hairbrush?'

'Nope – my plane tickets to Jasper's place in Val d'Isère for New Year. You coming?'

'Of course. I can't wait.'

'How about Tristan? Will he be able to ski?'

'No. But he's still coming – he wouldn't miss it. The von Holstadts have such an awesome chalet. Well, actually, two chalets – one for the parents and one for us.'

'I know – I used to go there with Jasper and Aunt and Uncle von Holstadt when I was younger.'

'Oh. Yeah.' Alice pretended to rearrange the bracelets round her wrist. She hated being shown up. 'Well, our New Year's trips aren't like some lame family holiday. I mean, no offence or anything.'

Rando shrugged. 'None taken. I think.'

'All I mean is – we party. We stay up all night, every night, playing drinking games. Last year, in "Truth or Dare", Sonia had to make naked snow-angels in the front garden. The neighbours' huskies started barking at her while she was doing it and all the security lights went on. She was so mortified.'

Rando burst out laughing as he handed Alice her drink. 'I wish I'd seen that. The most adventurous Jas and I ever got when we went there as kids was playing sardines. Ever play?'

'OMG, yes. I'm so terrified of that game.'

'Same! It's like, when you're the last person left and everyone's hiding together, secretly making fun of you? Awful.'

'Totally. That's, like, my worst nightmare.'

'Can I make a confession?' Rando said.

Alice slid her straw between her lips, looking at him from under her eyelashes. 'Sure. Go ahead.'

'Once, when I was eight, I got so terrified playing sardines in the dark, that I wet myself.'

'Gross!' Alice burst out laughing. 'I can't believe you just told me that.'

'I know! I must be drunk. You have to promise not to tell anyone.'

'Don't worry,' Alice grinned conspiratorially. She took a sip from her glass. 'Your wimpy secret is safe with me.'

'Oops. Uh . . .' Rando pointed. 'You've got a bit of mint leaf on your cheek.'

'Oh, shit, where is it? Here?'

'No, a bit to the left. Um, no, right. No, down a bit. Hang on – here.' Reaching up, Rando brushed the sprig away, his fingertips skimming Alice's olive-hued skin.

'Thanks.' Her cheek reddened in the wake of his fingers.

She swallowed. 'So . . . Who's this for?' she asked, prodding the frozen daiquiri in front of Rando. 'Get yourself a nice girly cocktail, did you?'

Rando glanced down. 'Oh, shit, I'm an idiot. That's for Tally. I should have brought it to her ages ago. The ice'll be all melted now.'

'A diluted drink will probably do Tally good.' Alice's heart was beating unnaturally fast. She reached again for her mojito.

'Hey,' said a voice in her ear. Tristan's arm slid round her waist. 'There you are. I've been looking for you everywhere. Hey Rando – thanks for taking care of my girl.'

'No worries,' Rando grinned, picking up Tally's drink.

'Listen, babe.' T nuzzled Alice's neck. 'My shoulder's hurting. Shall we go back to my house?'

'Oh . . . I don't know. I should probably stay. After all, I did organise this party . . .'

'Please? My place will be more fun than here, I promise . . .'

'Oh. OK. Sure.' Alice downed her drink and leaned back against Tristan's strong, warm chest. 'See you soon,' she called, turning over her shoulder to wave. But Rando had already disappeared. Craning her neck, she caught a glimpse of his navy blue jumper as he wove his way back towards Tally, through the crowd.

Chapter 3

Tristan drew his lips away from Alice's and traced his hands down her naked body. She was lying across his rumpled duvet, her arms thrown above her head.

'It's too dark,' he murmured. 'I want to see every inch of you.'

'Babe!' Alice blushed. 'That's embarrassing.'

'No it's not. Let's get a candle.' He nudged her. 'You go.'

'Why don't *you* go? You're the one who wants one.'

'I would, but my shoulder . . .'

'Oh, OK.'

Alice shrugged and rolled off T's double bed, tiptoing across the wooden floor, her inky hair flowing down her bare back. She probably shouldn't admit it, but she was almost glad for the interruption. She wanted to have sex – of course she did. But she was nervous – maybe because the only other time she and T had done it, it hadn't been great. Maybe she just needed to relax. She felt her way to the other side of Tristan's familiar bedroom. His lair, at the top of the Murray-Middletons' Holland Park town house, had always been a boy's idea of paradise. It occupied its very own floor and was stocked up with all the latest gadgets. Mixing decks. A keyboard. A state-of-the-art film projector. Two computers. Three guitars. A Wii. Radiohead posters and Arsenal season tickets were stuck to the walls.

When T and Alice were younger, they used to spend hours up here, playing video games, cooking up practical jokes to play on the nanny, building fortresses out of cardboard boxes and T's mum's expensive silk shawls. Each corner had its own special memories. Smiling, Alice plucked a fig-scented candle off the windowsill and peered out at the grasping branches of the old oak tree in the garden. Six years ago, T had decided it would be a really clever idea to sneak out of the house. He'd crawled out the window and swung from the treetop, cackling softly as he prepared to drop on to a lower branch. Instead, he'd fallen and broken his arm. Alice smirked, glancing at him across the room. But as her eyes fell on his sling, almost identical to the one he had to wear back then, her stomach dropped.

Was it weird that the two of them were still up here all these years later – the same people, the same place, just doing different things?

Alice lit the candle and placed it on the bedside table, sucking in her breath as its light flicked over Tristan's skin. Everyone looked good in candlelight, but no one had ever looked as hot as T did right this second. His arm muscles glowed caramel. His hazel eyes flickered with pinpricks of flame.

'Come here,' he whispered.

19

Alice pressed into him, undoing the buttons of his shirt, yanking it down.

'Ow,' he yelped. 'My shoulder!'

'Sorry.'

'Urrrgh.' T rocked back and forth. 'It's really sore.'

Alice rolled her eyes. Boys were so pathetic with pain. 'Sorry,' she whispered, still trying to sound sexy. 'Do you want to stop?'

'No.' T kissed her. 'Let's just forget about my shirt. Help me with my jeans?'

'Sure.'

Alice took a deep breath. Not only was T behaving like a pathetic invalid, but she was having to act like his nurse. As she pulled off his trousers, Mimah's words kept popping into her head: '*He's practically immobile – it's gotta be bizarre, right?*' Alice swallowed. Tonight she was obviously going to have to go on top. What if she did it wrong and rebroke T's collarbone? What if the angle made her look fat? Maybe she should point out that T probably shouldn't be having sex in his condition at all.

But before she could say a thing, her gaze fell on his chest, rising and falling, rippling and relaxing. She knelt over him, letting her hair tumble on to his face.

Afterwards, Tristan held her nestled against his good side, a smile glimmering about his lips. He stroked her hair. 'That was amazing.'

'Mmm.' Alice's face was buried in the pillow.

'You OK?'

'Yeah.' She shifted to pull the covers up to her chin.

20

Something crackled. 'Hey, what's this?' she asked, sliding a piece of paper from under the duvet.

'Huh? Oh!' T sat bolt upright. 'Nothing. Give it.'

'What is it?'

'Nothing!'

'Yeah, right. If it's nothing then I guess I'll just read it.'

'Don't!' T sighed. 'Fine. It's a song, OK? I just . . . don't want you to read it.'

'OK . . . Can I ask why?'

'I made this resolution not to show you my stuff anymore.'

'Oh.' Alice felt like her stomach had been hit with a rugby ball. 'Why would you do that?'

'Because. The way you reacted to the songs I wrote you before – you hated them. We almost broke up over it, and it sucked. But I can't just not write music – it's practically what I live for.' T stretched out his hand. 'So just give it to me and I'll put it away.'

Alice passed him the paper in silence. After a moment, she shook her head. 'This is crazy. What kind of girlfriend and boyfriend are we if you can't share what's important to you? Please sing it to me. I won't react how I did before.'

'Al, babe, I promised myself—'

'Well, now *I'm* promising you . . .' Alice gave a wheedling smile. 'I won't do anything mental. Come on – your other songs just took me by surprise. The first time I heard them was when you sang them in front of an audience. This'll be different.'

'Look, I believe you.' Tristan sighed. 'I'd just prefer not to get into that whole thing again.'

21

'Why? Is that song about me?'

'It's . . . Well, it's kind of . . . Let's forget it and go to sleep. OK?'

'Oh. OK.' Frowning. Alice let Tristan kiss her forehead. She watched as he turned on his side, the paper still in his hand.

After a few minutes, his breathing evened out. Raising herself on her shoulder, Alice crept her arm over his sleeping form and gently tugged the paper from his fingers. Lifting it towards the window, she let the moonlight illuminate the words.

THE MORNING AFTER

In the morning
At the first light,
I rush to find my jeans.
I say, 'Last night –
What a dumb fight.'
But
'I'm sorry,'
Is what I mean.

At the noon bell
During lunch break
I eat a plate of baked beans.
I have a headache.
I say, 'Pass the cake.'
But

Too Cruel for School

'I'm sorry,'
Is what I mean.

When the sun sets
In the red sky
I ask: 'How's your day been?'
I plead, 'Don't cry.'
I say, 'I'm just a guy.'
But
'I'm sorry,'
Is what I mean.

Tristan's breathing was peaceful, but Alice lay sleepless next to him, staring at the shadowy forms of his bedroom. The song was clearly an apology for the way he'd acted after they'd first made love. So why couldn't he share it with her? Why couldn't he just say the words? She gazed at the Radiohead posters on his wall, at the collection of incense he kept to mask the smell of cigarette smoke and weed from his mum, at the old oak tree, full of childhood memories, swaying in his garden. She knew Tristan Murray-Middleton better than anyone in the world – and yet sometimes it felt like she didn't know him at all.

Chapter 4

'What number was it again?' Dylan Taylor asked.

Her voice bounced off the lilac walls of Locke House, sounding way too loud in the bizarrely silent corridor. It was five o'clock on Sunday afternoon, dark outside except for the garden spotlights glowing on the pathways, and cold. Most pupils hadn't yet returned from their weekend escapes.

'Room twelve.' Dylan's fourteen-year-old sister, Lauren, was gnawing her fingernails. 'I hope it's nice. What if I have to spend the rest of the school year living in a hell-hole?'

'As if. It's not like the girls here would put up with bad accommodation.'

'Yeah, but I'm turning up in the middle of a term. What if all the real dorms are full? What if they just, like, shoved an extra bed in the broom closet or something?'

'Then at least you'll have your own room.'

'Oooh, here it is, number twelve!' Lauren squealed, halting in front of a dark wooden door. She bounced on the soles of her feet, seeming to forget her freak-out of the second before.

Dylan smiled. That was so Lauren. Her sister always made her think of a flying bird, her thoughts darting and changing so abruptly you didn't know where to look. 'So . . .' She took a step forward. 'Are we going in?'

'No, no, wait!' Lauren grabbed her hand. 'I have to prepare. Let me open it.' Closing her eyes, she gave the door a shove.

'Hey, not bad!' Dylan said, peering over her sister's shoulder. 'I've never seen a Year Ten dorm before.'

'Not bad? It's a million times nicer than I thought!' Lauren skipped into the room, her gaze bounding across its four single beds – two near the window and two near the door. Each bed was raised off the ground, with a set of shelves and drawers fitted underneath, and a bulletin board and reading lamp fixed overhead. Three of them were covered in bright duvets and fluffy pillows and flanked by walls full of photos. One, nearest the door, was empty.

Lauren cast a glance at her suitcase, which was squatting in the middle of the room where the school porter had left it. 'As soon as I do a little decorating, my corner will look great. I wish Mom was here to help me unpack, though. Too bad she had to go away on that book tour with Vic.'

Dylan clenched her teeth. She hated it when Lauren referred to their mother's new fiancé as 'Vic'. Victor Dalgleish was a sleazy, second-rate media personality who'd stolen their mom away from their dad. He lived in a Fulham bachelor pad full of leather sofas and bottles of cologne. And the only nickname he deserved was 'Ratface', because it accurately described his looks. Victor had recently written a tell-all book about his tacky life as a quiz-show host, which he was off promoting all over Europe. Dylan couldn't believe there were people who'd pay money to read his egotistical crap.

She dragged the suitcase towards Lauren's bed. 'Look, there's no point wishing Mom was here. That's the whole reason she sent you to this school in the first place – she wanted to rush off and follow "*Vic*", and she had nowhere else to dump you.'

'Shut up – you don't have to put it like *that*.' Lauren had never shared Dylan's negative opinion of their mother's new love life – or of their move to England. 'It's just . . . Dilly, I can't believe I'm actually at boarding school in the English countryside. This is like something out of a movie. That old courtyard we walked through – what did you call it?'

'Quad.'

'Right, Quad.' Lauren shut her eyes as she said the word, as if she was memorising it for a test. 'That place is awesome. They must have, like, an army of gardeners to take care of all the ivy on the buildings. I can't wait to have classes in there!'

'Lessons,' Dylan corrected. 'English people call classes "lessons".'

'Whatever. Everyone'll know what I mean. They'll probably think my accent's adorable.'

Yeah, right, Dylan thought. If her own experience of starting at St Cecilia's back in September had been anything to go by, 'adorable' was the last word the Year Tens would use to describe her sister. Especially her sister's chirpy personality. But she couldn't blame Lauren for not getting it; she'd never told Lauren how Alice Rochester had treated her when she'd first arrived. Or how some of Alice's friends, such as Dylan's dorm-mate, Sonia Khan, still treated her. After all, who wanted to admit they'd been bullied – especially to their little sister? It was way too humiliating. And anyway, maybe Lauren would be fine. Maybe the Year Tens hadn't honed their bitching skills quite as sharply as the Lower Sixth.

'So, who do you think my room-mates are?' Lauren asked. She was eyeing a state-of-the-art MacBook Air, and a cluster of designer handbags hanging from a hook on the wall.

'Let me check.' Dylan poked her head outside the room. 'Miranda Coombes. Portia Mehew-Montefiore. Georgina Fortescue,' she read off a stencilled plaque near the door. Her eyebrows knitted together. Georgie Fortescue – wasn't that the wolfish-looking blonde girl who was always hanging out with Mimah Calthorpe de Vyle-Hanswicke's younger sister, Charlie?

'Oh my god!' Lauren squealed.

'What?' Dylan ducked back inside the room.

'Look!' Lauren was giggling at a small cupboard in the wall. 'You'll never guess what's in here. A sink! In a bedroom!'

'Oh.' Dylan rolled her eyes. 'Whatever.'

'But how weird is that?'

'Babe, all the dorms have sinks in them. It's some kind of English thing. They have a hand-washing fetish or something.'

'Or . . .' Lauren grinned. 'If you were a boy you could pee in the sink instead of using the bathroom. Think the girls ever do that?'

'Gross!' Dylan's blond hair bounced as she laughed. 'I bet Sonia does. I bet she sneaks over for a sly pee in the middle of the night when I'm sleeping. She probably needs it, with all the water she drinks.'

Dylan's smile faded as she pictured her room in Tudor House, with Sonia's rows of Evian bottles all lined up on their own special shelf, as if by some creepy robot. Dylan sighed. She still got butterflies in her tummy whenever she came back to school after a weekend in London – not that it was nearly as bad as before. Stepping into the dorm she shared with Sonia used to feel like descending into hell. But now Alice Rochester was being nicer to her. Alice had even invited her to Mimah's surprise party on Saturday night. It was possible that things were looking up – except for the situation with Jasper . . . Dylan bit her lip. She'd thought things were going so well with Jas – and then he'd suddenly dumped her the week after they'd had sex. She shook her head to get rid of the thought and caught sight of Lauren, transfixed by a photograph on the bulletin board above one of the desks. 'What are you staring at?'

'Huh?' Lauren's face was dreamy. 'Oh, nothing. Just . . . this boy . . . Isn't he cute?'

'Let's see.' Dylan crossed the room. The photo was of

Georgie Fortescue with her arms around two people. One was Mimah's younger sister, Charlie. The other was a tall blond boy, whose handsome face was just growing out of its babyish phase. He had soft almond eyes and a smile full of charm. Something about the jut of his cheekbones sparked a flash of recognition.

Dylan examined the caption under the photo.

'*Me with Charlie Calthorpe de Vyle-Hanswicke and Hugo Rochester.* Whoa.' She raised her eyebrows. 'It must be Alice's younger brother. I think he goes to Hasted House.'

'Hmmm? Whose brother? What house?' Lauren giggled. 'He just looks so ... cute. And friendly. And gorgeous. Don't you think?'

Just then, a shout came from the front garden. Lauren glanced out the window. 'Oh my gosh, people are arriving! Dilly, you should go. I don't want my big sister hanging around when my new room-mates arrive.' She fluffed her blond hair and pouted like a starlet. 'I gotta make a good impression.'

'OK, I'm leaving.' Dylan zipped her coat. 'Oh, by the way, L?' she said, pausing by the door.

'Yeah?'

'Just ... play it cool. Don't start firing questions about that Hugo Rochester guy. And don't, like, spread your stuff around the room too much.'

'What are you talking about? It's *my* room.'

'Yeah, well, it's also Portia and Miranda and Georgie's room. And there are rules – and etiquette.'

'Etiquette?' Lauren snorted, unzipping her suitcase. 'Oh,

please. What is this, finishing school? You told me to bring
cool stuff to lighten the place up. My roomies'll love it.'

'Yeah. I hope so.' As Dylan shrugged, turning to go, the
door flew open, smacking her right in the forehead.
'Owww,' she groaned, reeling.

'Oops,' giggled a short brunette.

'Oh god, that hurt.' Dylan checked for blood. 'Shit! I
think my eye's swelling up.'

The brunette snickered even harder, gasping for breath.

A switch flicked in Dylan's head. 'What the fuck is so
funny?' she snarled. 'What's your fucking name?'

'Minky,' replied the girl. 'Well, Miranda. Miranda
Coombes. Not that it's any of your business.'

'*Excuse* me?' Dylan shrieked. Red rage blinded her.
Dizziness rattled her brain. 'You just fucking hit me with
a door, you bitch. How about saying "sorry"? How about
shutting your mouth, you stupid, ignorant little sh—'

'Dill,' Lauren's voice squeaked, reaching through the
fog of temper. 'Stop. Please?'

Dylan glowered. Minky Coombes shrank backwards.

Lauren bit her lip. 'Dilly, please. Don't. Don't . . . you
know.'

Dylan sucked in a breath. Her shoulders sank. It was all
just too familiar.

'Yeah. I know,' she murmured, slipping into the hallway.
No. No way was she letting that old demon come back to
haunt her again.

Chapter 5

Click. Click. Clickety. Click. Click. The secretary's fake gold bracelets knocked against each other as her wrist flew across the leather-bound notebook on the desk outside the Headmistress's office. Mimah dug her black-painted nails into her palms. She glared at the secretary's nameplate: *Mrs Cushings.* Ugh. Mrs Cushings was probably one of those irritating old biddies who referred to their bracelets as '*bangles*'. As in, '*Are my bangles bothering you?*'

'*Yes!*' she wanted to yell. '*Yes, they fucking well are!*'

Mimah stared at the fine old polished floorboards. Her eyes moved to the fringe of the oriental rug, then to her mother's soft brown leather boots. *Tap. Tap. Tap. Tap.* Her mother's foot drummed a bass line for the clicking bracelets. Mimah knew Mummy was just as anxious as she was that Mrs Traphorn might kick her out of St C's for good. Her mother's life had crumbled enough already, and this might be the final straw. The future wasn't too bright for a poor little rich kid who got expelled from one of England's most venerable schools. And the immediate future was especially dim. Mimah shut her eyes. Last week had been miserable: sitting at home for seven days in her mother's Victorian

31

mansion while her mother self-medicated with whisky and tranquillisers, the windows closed, the curtains drawn – just as they had been for the past six months, since the morning Mimah's father left. No wonder Charlie had started behaving badly. Not that stealing prescription drugs from your mother was ever anything but stupid.

Footsteps sounded within the Headmistress's office. A hand opened the carved wooden door.

'Mrs Calthorpe de Vyle-Hanswicke, hello. Do come in.' Mrs Traphorn shook hands with Mimah's mother. She turned and, as an afterthought, tossed Mimah a curt nod. 'Jemimah.'

Mimah felt sick. She'd never realised it before, but Mrs Traphorn looked exactly how a Headmistress would want to look if her intention was to inspire terror in every living creature. She was at least six foot tall. Her grey hair lived in a perpetual bun at the back of her head. Her calf-length skirts and sturdy, low-heeled shoes left you in no doubt that what she meant was business, and business her way.

'Have a seat.' The Trap pointed to two empty chairs on one side of a dark wooden table.

Mimah gulped. On the other side, the Headmistress was taking her place among three familiar figures, introducing them to Mimah's mother. There was Mrs Hoare, Mimah's horrendous Housemistress. The Ho despised Mimah's entire gang. She'd been the one to catch her with the drugs in the first place. Next was Mr Vicks, the Head of Physics. He'd told Mimah only ten days ago that she stood a chance of being accepted to read Natural Sciences at Cambridge.

He was probably seething with disappointment. Next to Mr Vicks sat Miss Colin, the lacrosse coach. There was hope, at least. Colin would support her. Mimah was St C's star player.

'You all know why we're here,' the Trap began. Her voice was regretful: bad sign. 'Jemimah, you've been at St Cecilia's for over five years, and the Calthorpe de Vyle-Hanswicke family has been affiliated with the school for generations. But our policy on drugs is intractable: they will not be tolerated.'

Next to the Trap, Mrs Hoare sniffed and narrowed her eyes: bad sign number two.

'However,' the Trap went on, 'as a venerable English institution, St Cecilia's believes in allowing the accused to defend themselves before pronouncing a verdict. Jemimah, do you have anything to say?'

Mimah blinked. Anything to say? What, besides, 'I beg you! Don't expel me!'? Would it be too pathetic if she got down on her knees? Kissed the Trap's hem? Mimah swallowed a smirk. Why was it that she always had the urge to pull ridiculous stunts at moments like this?

Mrs Traphorn raised her eyebrows. 'Jemimah?'

'Um, please,' Mimah began. She had to say something. 'I know how this looks.' She glanced at Mrs Hoare, who seemed to be staring at her right down her flared nostrils. She looked at Miss Colin, whose arms were crossed tightly across her pink and white tracksuit.

Mimah's words congealed in her throat. Yes, she did know how this looked – or rather, how *she* looked to *them*:

like a bored, spoilt rich kid who didn't give a toss about rules or consequences. Everything was always exactly how it looked, as far as adults saw things. They didn't know anything about taking the blame for your sister to protect her from all the mistakes you yourself had made. Or about living in a dark, musty, lonely house with a pill-popping mum. Or about watching your dad, your hero, melt like a waxwork before your eyes.

She set her jaw. 'You know, I don't really have anything to say.'

'Jemimah!' her mother whispered.

Mrs Hoare bared part of an incisor. Oh, she was so clearly loving this.

'Except,' Mimah continued loudly, 'that I'm not a kid anymore. Teachers at this school are always telling us to behave like adults, so you can trust us – but you don't *treat* us like you trust us. I had a reason for carrying those pills. I can't tell you what that was and I'm really sorry. But if you want to trust me, now's your chance. Yes, Mrs Hoare caught me carrying prescription drugs that weren't mine outside the school grounds – but she didn't see me taking those drugs and she had no evidence that I was going to. I'm telling you with absolute honesty that I wasn't. If you want to punish me for being off school grounds without permission, that's totally fair. But please don't expel me for using drugs that I was never going to use.'

Mimah's mother was staring at her. She looked pale – mortified. She'd probably been expecting some sort of grovelling apology.

Someone's chair creaked.

A throat cleared.

The room was suddenly stifling.

'Well, then . . .' Mrs Traphorn said slowly. 'If that's all you have to say, I'll ask the teachers for their verdict.' She turned to Miss Colin.

Mimah permitted herself a smile. Good – Colin had always liked her. A strong start.

But the Games teacher met her look with a stony face before turning to the Headmistress.

'Mrs Traphorn, it's true that Jemimah has always been one of the most talented athletes at St Cecilia's. My teams would certainly suffer without her presence. But I can no longer have a girl like Jemimah representing the school at matches. Her recent behaviour goes against everything that school sport stands for: honour, integrity, good clean fun. I move for Jemimah's immediate expulsion, in order to set an example for the rest of the pupils at the school – particularly the younger ones. We need to be their moral compass at times like this.'

Mimah's cheeks were burning. Miss Colin's refusal even to address her directly was making her feel like an insect.

'Mr Vicks?' came the Trap's voice.

The Head of Physics ran a hand through his thinning hair. His bushy eyebrows beetled together. His voice came out deep and authoritative. 'In my opinion, drugs should absolutely not be tolerated.'

Mimah shut her eyes. Shit. She was done for.

'But,' Mr Vicks went on, 'Jemimah was caught with her

mother's prescription medication, which isn't strictly illegal. She swears she wasn't planning to take the pills. Why should we, as teachers, help destroy a seventeen-year-old's future? I believe in giving pupils a second chance. Mimah is a gifted Physics student – one of the most gifted I've ever seen. If she's allowed to remain at St Cecilia's, I'll tutor her for Cambridge. I'll also supervise a suitable punishment for her infractions – I have just the thing in mind.'

Mimah's heart beat a tattoo of fear. Seriously? Mr Vicks was actually on her side? Then her eye caught the Trap's stern expression as the Headmistress made a note in Mimah's school file.

It wasn't over yet. The score was tied one all. The Trap's would be the final word. No prizes for guessing what that would be.

Chapter 6

A gust of wind snatched the trail of smoke from Tally's cigarette and dispersed it into the freezing air, rattling the leaves of the bushes where she huddled next to Alice.

'Since when did England become the Arctic?' Alice shivered. 'My feet are turning into ice cubes. I should have worn those extra-thick cashmere socks Daddy bought me last winter in Zurich.'

'It's not that c-c-cold,' Tally insisted, her teeth chattering. 'Anyway, it's better than being in lessons.'

'Duh.' Alice peered down the hill at the Great Lawn, the rolling carpet of grass, criss-crossed with paths and dotted with bare trees, that was the social hub of St Cecilia's. It was Monday morning, and she and Tally had decided to ditch their first double-lesson of the week – English with Mrs Hoare – because, right at this second, the Ho was holed up in Mrs Traphorn's office, deciding Mimah's fate. They couldn't possibly work at a time like this. Plus, what was the point of turning up to a lesson just to listen to a boring supply teacher?

'Supply teachers are just regular teachers who aren't good enough to get a proper job,' Tally had sniffed as she and

Alice crept over to their smoking spot near the gardeners' sheds. It was pretty safe to sneak a fag here: if any of the gardeners caught you, all you had to do was flash a smile (and some leg) and you were safe.

Alice snuggled into her faux-leopard coat. 'I wish they'd hurry up and finish the meeting. Mimah can't be expelled! We've all been together since we were, like, twelve. Let me know as soon as you see her leave Quad.'

'OK! Now can we please talk about something else? This Mimah situation is way too stressful.'

'Fine.' Alice flicked a dried leaf off her arm. 'How's Rando?'

'Amaaazing.' Tally hugged herself. 'He's so different from other boys. It's like, he really cares about me – he doesn't just want to get my pants off.' She giggled coyly. 'Not that I'd be complaining if he did. In bed, he's incredible. Every time he touches me I want to moan.'

'What? Why?' Alice sputtered on her cigarette smoke. 'What does he do?'

'I can't tell you that! It's private.'

Alice stared at her friend. Tally usually dished every detail of her hook-ups – what the hell could be so different now? She knew she should say something – agree, maybe, as if Tristan's touch had the same effect on her. As if their sex life also happened in some intense, enchanted world.

'We had such a good time on Sunday, too,' Tally was saying. 'Daddy and Evil Stepmum were away for the weekend so we spent all morning in bed. Then I took him to the Coronet cinema in Notting Hill Gate. I showed him how to sneak in without paying.'

Alice shook her head. 'What's up with you and the whole "not paying" thing?'

'Babe, what do you mean? It's all about the thrill.'

'Yeah, but what's so thrilling about a free film when you can afford to buy the whole cinema?'

Tally curled her lip. 'Come on, Al. The money isn't the point. It's just so fun – defying authority.'

'Well, excuse me if I still don't get the excitement – we defy authority enough already. I mean, we're skiving off school right now, aren't we?'

Tally ashed on to the frozen ground. 'Whatever. Anyway, we were talking about Rando. So, after the film, he took me back to his place and he played piano for me – some bit of classical music. You'd probably know it, but I've got no idea about that sort of thing. OMG, he is so talented, it's incredible. It's like, T takes all the credit for the Paper Bandits, but Rando could totally be the star if he wanted. He's way too modest, though.'

'Excuse me, but are you implying that T's some kind of spotlight whore?' Alice stamped her cigarette into the ground. 'I seem to remember that the whole band thing was his idea in the first place. T loves *music*, not fame.'

'OK! All I'm saying is that he's not necessarily the most talented band member.'

Alice glowered at the ground. This was absurd – she felt like she was in some kind of battle of the boyfriends. Why the hell were she and Tally even talking about this?

Ping ping.

She grabbed her iPhone. 'Oh. My. God.'

'What? What?' Tally tugged Alice's coat sleeve, clearly happy to forget their spat.

'It's Jasper.'

'What does he want?'

'Here.'

'*Yo,*' Tally read off the screen. '*Can we talk about Dylan? UR in with her now, right? Is she seeing anyone else?*' Tally's big sea-grey eyes widened even further. 'Jasper cares if Dylan's seeing someone else? Do you think he wants to get back together with her?'

'Who knows? I doubt he has much of a chance, after he dumped her so rudely.'

'You gonna tell him that?'

'Hmmm.' Alice tapped her foot. But before she could answer, her phone pinged again. 'Whoa, since when did Jasper get so desperate? He's supposed to be a manwhore.'

'It's not Jasper. It's George Demetrios.'

'Oh, great. That idiot probably wants help learning to tie his shoelaces. Read it to me.'

Tally was staring at the screen. 'Um . . . babe? Maybe you'd better read it yourself.'

'Why?'

''Cause it's, like, unbelievable?'

'Just read it!'

'OK! Chill. "*Hey Al*",' Tally began, putting on a stoned George-Demetrios-style voice. '"*So now that Dylan's rolling solo, think she'd want a piece of Demon Demetrios pie?*"'

Alice's mouth dropped open. '*What?* Give me that!' She stared at the phone. 'Is he fucking joking? I can't believe

40

this is happening. How can all the boys like Dylan? She's totally stealing our men!'

Tally giggled. 'Um, Al? We both have boyfriends – and their names aren't Jasper von Holstadt or George Demetrios.'

'So what? Hmm . . . Help me think.'

'About what?'

'Ohmygod – yes!' Alice grabbed Tally's arm. 'How brilliant would it be if we played Jasper and George off against each other and didn't tell Dylan?'

'What's the point of that?'

'Come on, Tals – it'll make Dylan look like the biggest slapper ever. We'll make it look like she's leading on two poor, lovesick best friends – they'll all think she's a total bitch.'

'But, Al, *why*? I thought you liked Dylan now.'

Alice shrugged. 'I don't like anyone who thinks they should get all the guys. They're *our* boys. We need to put her in her place.' Swiping her phone from Tally, she tapped furiously at the screen, a sly smile creeping over her face.

'Hey, look.' Tally had tensed and was pointing at the Great Lawn. 'There's Mimah. I think the meeting's over.'

Alice almost dropped her phone. 'Run!' she ordered. 'I have to be the first to get the news!'

Chapter 7

By the time Alice and Tally stumbled, out of breath, on to the Great Lawn, Mimah was deep in discussion with Sonia outside the Tuck In, St Cecilia's shiny new glass-enclosed café.

'Oh, no!' Tally gasped.

'What?'

'She hasn't gone inside – she's just standing out there in the cold.'

'What does that have to do with anything?'

'Hello? It probably means she got expelled and isn't allowed in school buildings anymore. I bet the security guards are coming to escort her off the grounds any second!'

'Stop being so dramatic,' Alice panted, worry clouding her face. She pounded up to Mimah and Sonia. 'So? What happened?'

'I'm—' Mimah began, but Sonia shoved her aside.

'—not expelled!' Sonia practically bellowed. She gazed adoringly at Alice; news like this was definitely worth a scrap of praise. 'She's being punished. She has to do community service and report to crazy Mr Vicks once a day. Oh, and she's kicked off the lacrosse team. But she's back at school.'

'Brilliant!' Alice squeezed Mimah's arm. She wasn't one of those sappy cuddly people, or she might have bundled Mimah into a hug like Tally was doing right now.

'Congrats, babe!' Tally gushed. 'I've never been so relieved, ever.'

'Me neither, I can't believe it,' Alice said. 'Well, I mean, I knew no one from our gang would get expelled, but still – you had me worried. What's this crap about community service, though? Stupid Hoare – I bet that was her idea.'

'Nope,' Mimah grinned. 'It was Mr Vicks. He saved me.'

'Mr Vicks? But that freak's favourite hobby is catching people when they try to sneak out of school. Since when does he stand up for rule breakers?'

Mimah shrugged. 'I guess since he decided I was prime Cambridge material. He's the only one who fought to let me stay. They're making me volunteer as a maths tutor at the Hasted Community Centre once a week.' She smirked. 'I'll be teaching retarded townies how to do algebra and trigonometry and shit.'

'Total shag,' Sonia snorted.

'Well, maybe,' Alice said, 'except that helping those less fortunate than yourself always looks good on UCAS forms. That's why I make a point of being Mummy's right-hand woman when she organises her spring charity ball every year.' She checked out her reflection in the Tuck In Café's glass doors. 'Come on; coffees on me.'

But Sonia darted inside first. 'No, I'll get them!' Smiling to herself, she pushed towards the counter. Doing favours for Alice Rochester was one of her prized pastimes. 'Double-skinny-latte-cappuccino-café-mocha-black-coffee-chocolate-croissant-non-fat-yoghurt!' she called, struggling to be heard over the scream that had just arisen from the Lower Sixth tables.

'Mimeeeey!' cried Flossy Norstrup-Fitzwilliam, her blond curls springing up and down in excitement. 'What's the scoop?'

'You in or out?' yelled Farah Assadi. Her smoky eyes blazed with curiosity.

Even Mimah's dorm-mate, Gabby Bunter, the most pathetic girl in the year, was staring at Mimah, her shoulders hunched over her iced bun.

'In!' Mimah declared.

Sonia sighed as a cheer almost deafened her delicate ears. Whoever had designed the Tuck In obviously hadn't been to an all-girls boarding school, or they might have realised that glass and steel don't provide satisfactory acoustics for caffeine-buzzed pupils catching up on gossip over Break. She hurried over to their gang's regular table, where Alice was gossiping with Bella Scott.

'Hey, girlies,' she trilled.

'Oh, hi.' Bella threw Sonia a glance, then turned back to Alice. 'Anyway, it's just so difficult and—'

'Ahem!' Sonia cleared her throat loudly. 'What are we talking about?'

'Nothing.'

'Bella's trying to decide who to invite to her dad's Christmas party this year,' Alice said, taking her cappuccino and *pain au chocolat* off the tray.

Sonia's eyes lit up like birthday candles.

'Oh. Christmas party?' she echoed innocently, like she had no idea what Alice was on about. As if. Bella's father was Sir Lucian Scott, the world-famous British film director, and Bella was always jetting off to the Oscars and the Golden Globes and to Cannes. It was enough to make you sick. Some people (such as *herself*, thank you very much) had to work their way up from nothing. Sonia's parents had zero contacts in the film industry. Apart from buying her a £10,000 digital video camera, they'd done absolutely nothing to help her career. That was why she just had to get invited to Sir Lucian's party this year. The director's annual Christmas bash was legendary. Hollywood players were always there in hordes. There was only one problem: the last time Sonia had seen Sir Lucian, she'd had a run-in with him over her disastrous school fashion show. If she didn't get a second chance to impress him, she just might die.

'So . . .' Without looking up. Sonia examined her perfect nails. 'Who are you gonna invite?'

'Dunno.' Bella tucked a strand of auburn hair behind her ear. 'Daddy says I can have twelve invitations, so I'm trying to choose six St C's girls and six Hasted House boys. It's horribly difficult.'

Sonia nodded sympathetically and eyed her non-fat yoghurt. 'I'm sure you'll choose the right people. You know,

45

the ones who care about you the most.' She stared into Bella's face, blinking her long eyelashes. 'By the way, honey, I got you a treat – just for you.' She nudged her snack towards Bella. Her tummy was rumbling, but art was worth any sacrifice.

'Ugh, rank.' Bella made a retching sound. 'Don't you know I despise yoghurt? I mean, thanks Sone, but are you trying to make me sick?' She rolled her eyes at Alice. 'As I was saying, everyone wants invitations this year. It's going to be impossible deciding who to invite.' Sighing, she prised the lid off her hot chocolate. 'Could you pass the sugar?'

'I'll do it, I'll put it in for you!' Sonia yelped, bolting for the sugar shaker. As she lurched for Bella's cup, her long manicured nails clipped its rim.

'Watch it!' Bella cried, as her drink teetered and splattered on to the table. She scrambled backwards. Torrents of hot chocolate streamed towards her lap. 'Help! It's gonna stain my new Marc Jacobs coat! Daddy will kill me.'

Suddenly, a hand shot out of nowhere.

'I've got it,' cried someone. A wad of newspaper landed on the spill, soaking it up just before it gushed over Bella's military-style tweed jacket.

'Ohmygod,' Bella gasped, slapping her hand over her heart. She blinked. 'Dylan? I didn't even know you were there. H-how'd you do that?'

Dylan grinned. 'I have hidden talents, I guess.'

'Yeah,' Sonia muttered. '*Very* hidden. So hidden they're fucking invisible.'

'You're a lifesaver,' Bella declared. She tugged a chair in between Sonia's and her own. 'Have a seat.'

'Thanks!'

Sonia stabbed one of the blueberries in her yoghurt and glowered. Stupid Dylan Taylor and her stupid grinning face, always ruining everything. Always loitering where she wasn't wanted.

Someone was hovering at her shoulder like a mosquito. 'Excuse me . . .' began a timid voice.

'Yeah?' Sonia snapped.

'Sorry,' stammered a slim blonde girl. 'I . . . I'm . . .' She was wearing a shiny new school uniform and was clutching a strawberry smoothie. She looked like she was about fourteen. And she had a familiar creamy complexion and berry-blue eyes. Sonia snorted.

'Hey, roomie,' she sneered in Dylan's direction, 'looks like your clone's here.'

'Lauren!' Dylan exclaimed. 'Oh. Hey.'

'Hi, Dilly. Can I sit with you?'

'Oh. Um . . .' Dylan shifted. There were no assigned seats in the Tuck In, but everyone knew the hierarchy. She glanced across the table. Alice Rochester was stirring her coffee, eyebrows raised.

'The Year Tens sit over there, sis. Look, Georgie Fortescue has plenty of room at her table. You have to make your own friends.' Twisting a piece of her thick, straw-coloured hair, Dylan turned back to her group.

Lauren sloped away, her gaze sneaking across the room to Georgie Fortescue's sharp, bony profile. All of a sudden, tears pressed behind her eyes. Throwing her unopened smoothie in the nearest bin, she fled the crowded café. If she'd known boarding school would be like this, she never would have come.

Chapter 8

'Just look at that footwork!' Tristan gloated, tackling Seb and racing down the field with the football. 'Bravo! He's a champion, even with one arm in a sling.'

'Illegal!' Seb called. 'You elbowed me.'

'Nice try,' T grinned. Flopping down on to the ground next to Rando, he reached into his coat pocket for a spliff. It was lunch break, and he and his two band-mates had sneaked off for a smoke in one of the hilly fields bordering Hasted House. The sunwarmed winter grass crackled under his back. Clouds scudded across the sky. T let his eyes sink shut. He loved these pale winter afternoons, when every ray of sunlight was like a drop of gold.

'Give me a toke, mate,' Seb said, collapsing next to him.

Tristan handed him the joint, softly humming part of a new song he was writing for the Paper Bandits.

'Nice tune,' Rando remarked. Drowsily, he tapped out a drumbeat on the ground. 'Got any words?'

'Not yet. But here's the idea: I write so many songs about girls, I thought we could have one about friendship. You know, like how loyal your mates are. Bros before hos.' Tristan paused. 'Do you reckon it might sound a bit . . . gay, though? We don't want people to think we're homos.'

Seb swallowed. 'Um, no. Sounds fine. Uh oh,' he added, squinting across the fields. 'Look. Someone's coming.'

T sat bolt upright. Two people were approaching over the grass. 'Bury the weed. Quick!'

'Hang on. We're not sure they're teachers yet.'

'Oh, we're not *sure*? Good point, let's wait till we're all exchanging pleasantries before we hide the drugs.' T rolled his eyes. His dad would go apeshit if he got caught smoking a spliff. Lord Cecil Murray-Middleton had spent most of last Saturday lecturing anyone who would listen about Mimah's drug bust – how it was not only a disgrace to her family, but a disgrace to their entire social set. 'Disgrace' was one of Lord Murray-Middleton's favourite words – along with 'discipline' and 'success'. Tristan's dad was an eminent politician, and had had T's life mapped out from before he was born: Hasted House, followed by New College, Oxford, followed by a stellar political career. It wasn't that these things were beyond Tristan's reach, if he put his mind to them; he usually managed to achieve whatever he wanted. But unfortunately for his dad, what he wanted was to be a musician.

'I'm not sure those *are* teachers, actually,' Seb said. He was still squinting down the field. 'They look a bit small.'

'Could be Mr Harper,' Rando suggested. 'He's practically a midget.'

Suddenly, Seb laughed. 'For fuck's sake, it's only Hugo Rochester and Felix Hedley-Bunk. You paranoid loser,

T. You were totally just shitting yourself about a couple of Year Tens.'

'At least I'm not a loser on the football field,' Tristan shot back. He returned Hugo's wave. 'All right, you two. What do you think you're doing, skiving off school?'

'Just following your excellent example,' retorted Hugo Rochester, flashing a cheeky grin. Alice's fourteen-year-old brother looked exactly like his mother, with almond-coloured eyes and flaxen hair – the opposite of Alice's olive complexion.

Felix Hedley-Bunk pulled a plastic baggie of weed out of his sock. 'Skin us one up,' he said, handing it to Hugo. Everyone knew that Hugo Rochester was one of the best rollers in the school. He'd been personally taught by Tristan last year.

Tristan raised his eyebrows. 'Shouldn't you be going a bit easy on the illegal substances, Bunkers?' he asked.

Felix shrugged. 'Why? What do you mean?'

'Um, let me think. The fact that Mimah Calthorpe de Vyle-Hanswicke almost got expelled on your account? Nice way to repay her. She took the blame for you and her sister once – who's gonna do it next time?'

Felix's face clouded, but only for a second. 'Nice one, T,' he chuckled. 'Trying to be all moral. Look at you lot – you've been sneaking out of school for years, and nothing bad's ever happened to *you.*'

Tristan sighed and took a puff on his spliff. The kid had a point. But still – now that he was in the Sixth Form, shouldn't he be setting a good example, or something?

'You lot coming to Shock Box on Saturday?' Felix asked.

'Yeah,' Rando said. 'I'm meeting Tally there.'

'And I,' Tristan said, nudging Hugo, 'am meeting Alice.'

Hugo groaned. 'Oh, gross. Can we please not talk about the fact that you're dating my sister? It's way too weird. You guys have been friends my entire life. What the hell made you want to start going out with her? Wait, don't answer that.'

Tristan laughed. 'I think you need a girlfriend, too, Hugo – it's about time. And, as your big-brother figure, I'm appointing myself to help you get one. So, who do you like?'

Hugo turned red. 'No one.'

'Go on – don't be lame.'

'No one!'

'For fuck's sake . . .'

Felix elbowed him. 'Aw poor little Hugo-wugo's embarrassed to tell us who he's in love with. Come on Hugo-wugo.'

'Shut up. Anyway, who says I want a girlfriend?'

'Oh, please.' Tristan leaned back on his hands. 'Come on, I've got Alice, Rando's got Tally, Felix has Charlie . . .'

'*Seb* doesn't have a girlfriend.'

'True!' T kicked his best friend. 'Seb, how'd you like a lady in your life? How about Sonia? We can work on that at Shock Box.'

Seb took a deep breath. But, before he was forced to answer, shouts came from across the field.

'All right, losers!' George Demetrios waved. Behind him

jogged Jasper von Holstadt, and – Seb's heart raced – Tom Huntleigh.

Tom was totally Seb's type. He was tall and athletic, with close-cropped strawberry-blond hair and blue eyes that made him look like a Norse god. Seb's tummy fluttered whenever he thought of how he and Tom had snogged the other weekend at Rando's country house party. OK, so the kiss had only lasted a few seconds. And it had happened during a game of Spin the Bottle. And Tom wasn't gay. But it had been Seb's first ever kiss with a boy, and he couldn't get it out of his head: the firmness of Tom's muscles next to the softness of his mouth; the strength of his arms under his flimsy T-shirt.

'Good call, bringing a football,' Tom said, as he reached the group. 'Anyone for a bit of two-on-two?'

Seb jumped up. 'Me!'

'I'll play,' Jasper added.

'Me, too,' George Demetrios said. 'Great – Jas and Seb versus me and Tom. You two are going down!'

George kicked off. Seb chased him down the field, stealing the ball and pivoting back.

'Sneaky move!' Tom shouted, launching himself into Seb's path.

Seb felt his feet tangle. The ground gave way, grass raced towards his face, and something heavy thudded on top of him.

'Erg.' He tried to move. It was Tom. Tom's limbs weighed against his – leg to leg, chest to chest. His heart thumped. He could smell Tom's deodorant and the saltiness of his skin.

'Seb?' came Jasper's voice. 'Hello? Seb? Are you concussed? Can you hear me?'

'Huh?' Seb groaned.

An arm reached down. 'Come on, get up. Are you OK?'

'Y-Yeah.'

'Good. Go long. We can't let Tom and Demetrios score again.'

'Right. Cool.' Seb jogged back into play, his veins still throbbing. Maybe Tom would come to Shock Box on Saturday night. Maybe they'd end up kissing in that alleyway round the back, the tiny cobbled one where no one would see them.

He shook himself. For fuck's sake. Tom. Was. Not. Gay. And, anyway, Seb hadn't come out to any of his friends – nor did he intend to, not in this life – so how exactly was he meant to kiss anyone?

'Sebastian!' Jasper yelled in exasperation as the ball flew down the field. 'What are you doing? You call that playing?'

'Goaaal!' George Demetrios cried. Flexing his muscles, he jogged in a circle. 'Demon Demetrios is on fire! Take that, suckers.'

Jasper kicked the ground. He'd always hated losing. 'Shut the fuck up, George. You've got to be the most irritating opponent alive.'

George made a pouty face. 'Oooh, can't take a bit of psychology? No wonder Dylan Taylor dumped you.'

'I dumped her, actually,' Jasper snapped.

'Oh, of course. You dumped the girl with the best boobs in England. Sure.'

'Look, just stop it about Dylan's breasts,' Jasper said. 'If you can't say anything respectful about her, don't say anything at all.'

'Oh, OK, *Mum*.'

Jasper punted the football away, clenching his fists. If George made any more rude comments, he couldn't account for what he'd do. His phone beeped. He yanked it out of his pocket. It was a text from Alice.

Dylan says she's willing to talk. Meet her 10:35pm EXACTLY, Sat night, Shock Box, far left-hand side of the bar. DO NOT BE EARLY. Top secret. No contact till then or it's off.

Yes. Hope soared in Jasper's chest. Dylan was willing to talk – he'd known she would be – she was generous like that – generous and kind and funny and gorgeous . . . God, he missed her. Maybe, just maybe, he could win her back.

'Who was that?' George said, swiping at Jasper's hand. 'Your mum?'

'No, it was yours.' Sticking his phone in his pocket, Jasper clapped his hands. 'All right! Ready to get whipped?'

'What,' Tom Huntleigh laughed, 'like you're whipping us right now?'

'Time out!' George called. His phone was vibrating in his jeans pocket. He glanced at the screen – Alice. Excellent.

Talked to Dylan. She thinks you're well fit. Meet her 10:30pm EXACTLY, Sat night, Shock Box, far left-hand side of the bar. DO NOT BE LATE. Top secret. No further contact till then or it's off.

A grin spread over George's face. So, Dylan Taylor thought he was well fit? He'd always known she had good taste. He'd be shagging her by next week. *Jasper von Holstadt, eat your heart out, old buddy*, George smirked to himself. Nothing could stop him now.

Chapter 9

Dylan pressed her fingers to her ears, trying to block out the noise from the Dining Hall as she hunched over her French textbook. How the hell was she supposed to memorise a hundred vocab words in the next ten minutes? Impossible. Why hadn't she studied?

Suddenly, a tray clattered on to her table.

'Budge over,' someone said.

Frowning, Dylan glanced up.

'Oh! Hi,' she stuttered, catching sight of Alice Rochester. The queen of the Lower Sixth, trying to sit with her at breakfast? This was a first.

'So are you gonna move over or just sit there drooling?' Alice demanded. 'Tally and Sonia need space.'

Dylan's eyebrows arched, but she shoved her books aside. If Alice and the crew wanted to eat with her, she wasn't going to complain – even if she did have a French test first thing after breakfast. And even if her French grades had been abysmal so far this term.

'Morning,' Tally said, plonking herself at the table without looking up from her phone. There was a goofy grin on her face – a definite I'm-sending-cheesy-texts-to-my-boyfriend grin. Dylan sighed. Why did everyone in the world have a boyfriend except her? A figure hovered in her mind: a tall, sauntering boy with a handsome, haughty face – a face that radiated sunbeams when it smiled. She screwed her eyes shut. No, she had to stop thinking about Jasper von Holstadt. She'd lost her virginity to him exactly twenty-five days ago, and after that he'd dumped her. He was a bastard. And that was that.

Only . . . he hadn't seemed like a bastard. He'd been so sweet and funny and tender that weekend when they'd gone home together. He'd held her in his arms and kissed her hair and her nose and her forehead, and laughed at her jokes . . .

'Oh,' Alice said, 'your set's only on chapter twelve?'

'Huh?'

'In French.' Alice was scanning Dylan's vocab list. 'We're on chapter fifteen. Then again, I *am* in the top stream. I don't know why, since I'm always dossing off in French. I suppose it's all that practice I get, talking to the staff of our villa in St Tropez. They're constantly complimenting me on my accent.'

Tally chortled. 'Yeah, and I'm sure it's completely genuine. They're not angling for tips or anything.'

Alice balled up her napkin. 'You're just jealous,' she snapped, chucking it in Tally's face.

'So am I,' Dylan said. 'My accent sucks. I've never even been to the south of France.'

'Um, no offence,' Alice said, shoving a piece of bacon into her mouth, 'but I wouldn't spread that around, if

I were you. It's like saying you've never been skiing in the Alps or something.'

'I haven't.'

'What? Shut. Up. That is *ridiculous*.'

'Maybe. But it's true.'

'We go every year – the gang, I mean. This year we're all going to Jasper's chalet in Val d'Isère for New Year. Me, T, Tally, Rando, Seb, Jasper – Oh, shit!' Alice clapped her hand to her mouth. 'I totally shouldn't have mentioned Jas. I bet he's the last person you want to hear about.'

'No. It's fine.' Dylan put down her fork. She seemed to have lost her appetite.

'So, have you heard from him?'

'I . . .'

'Like, in the last week?'

'Well . . .'

'Or, you know, from any of the boys?'

'No. Why would I?'

'Hmm? No reason.' Alice tucked back into her bacon and eggs, trying to ignore the guilty feeling that was welling under her ribs. Fine – it wasn't exactly nice to rub Dylan's nose in her break-up. And it definitely wasn't nice to plot against her the way Alice was. But Dylan had no one to blame except herself. What did she expect, showing up at a new school, in a new country, and hogging all the lime-light? Her own personal St Cecilia's fan club?

Tally giggled. 'Aw, cuuute!'

'What?' Alice muttered.

'Oh, nothing.' Tally tittered again.

59

'*What?*'

'Nothing; just Rando. He's so darling.'

No one asked why. Alice smeared butter over a slice of toast.

'Sooo darling,' Tally repeated. 'Every morning I make up a silly new nickname for him and text it to him, and then he makes up one for me. This morning I said he was my Peachie Poochie Pie Man, and then he said I was his Sweetheart. Look. Isn't it *adorable?*'

Alice stuck two fingers in her mouth like she was going to vomit. Dylan didn't crack a smile. She was still staring somewhere past their table.

'I hate to break it to you, but "sweetheart" isn't exactly a made-up nickname,' Alice went on. 'It's like, if we're talking originality, Rando fails. He's clearly not trying very hard.'

'Of course he is!'

'OK, you tell yourself that.'

'Shut up, Al! Why do you even care?'

'Huh? Because . . . because . . .' Alice blinked, fumbling with her fork. 'I-I don't. Do you think it looked like I cared, Dill?'

'Well, I . . .'

'*Excusez-moi,*' snapped a familiar voice.

Dylan looked up. Sonia was hovering over her, balancing a low-calorie smoothie on her tray. Above her head, the Dining Hall's crooked old beams cut slashes across the white ceiling.

'Why is our table so crowded?' Sonia barked. Her eyes were narrowed in Dylan's direction.

60

'Shut up!' Dylan's plate jumped in the air as she slammed down her palm. 'If you don't think there's enough room for your fat arse, you can always go sit somewhere else!' As soon as she stopped shouting, the blood rushed to her cheeks. What the hell was she thinking, exploding at Alice's BFF like that?

'Bitch,' Sonia sputtered. 'C-can you believe she just said that?'

Dylan braced herself for the backlash. Suddenly, she heard a cackle to her left.

'Oh, Sone, your face!' Alice howled. 'It was just a joke, babe. Chill.'

Dylan gaped in astonishment.

'W-What?' Sonia squeaked.

'Come on, let it go. Sit down.' Alice patted the chair next to her, still shaking with laughter.

Sonia sniffed. Sticking her nose in the air, she placed her tray on the table as far from Dylan as possible.

'Look, I'm sorry,' Dylan said. Not that she wanted to apologise to Sonia, but she did have to share a dorm with the girl. And she could think of better things than being murdered in her sleep. 'I don't really think you're fat. You're like, really skinny. I just have kind of a sharp tongue sometimes.'

'Hmph.' Sonia folded her arms.

'No shit,' Tally said, lifting a spoonful of porridge smothered in brown sugar and cinnamon. 'You've got quite a temper.'

A sly look crept over Sonia's face. 'That is so true,' she

jumped in. 'Hey, Ali, remember when Dylan attacked you outside Tudor House and pushed you into the flower beds? That was so shocking. You were just standing there, and then – *wham!* Face down in the daisies.' She shot Dylan a smug look.

But Alice only snorted with laughter. 'Yes! That was ridiculous! Hey, Dill, remember how we got caught rolling round in the dirt?'

'I do!' Tally guffawed. 'Al, all that mud on your face? I've never seen you look so ridiculous. And those leaves sticking out of Dylan's hair – I think I'm gonna die laughing.' She rocked back and forth. 'Oh, rank; I think I just snorted porridge up my nose!'

'Ewww!' Alice squealed. 'It's dribbling down your chin.'

'Hey, Tally, you're really making a meal out of that oatmeal,' Dylan chimed in. 'Get it? Meal? Oatmeal? Get it?'

'Waaah!' Alice guffawed. 'You're doing a real poor job with that poor-ridge. Get it? Poorridge!'

She, Dylan and Tally dissolved into hysterics.

Across the table, Sonia shook her smoothie so hard it started to fizz. What the fuck was going on? First of all, those jokes were the un-funniest thing she'd ever heard. And second of all, Alice Rochester, her BFF, her oldest friend, the coolest girl in school, was taking Dylan's side against hers. Seriously? Maybe Alice had been drugged. Maybe she'd been replaced by some kind of nightmare alien. Either way, this was so not OK. Someone was going to pay.

Chapter 10

Collages lined the stairway up to the first floor of the Art Block. Dylan inhaled deeply. Oil paints, chalk, freshly dried clay – that sharp, dusty smell was one of her favourites in the whole school. She stopped to gaze at one collage, made of bottle tops and wood splinters and shards of broken glass – like some remnant of a vicious bar fight before heading up to Miss Baskin's classroom.

'Hey,' she said, taking her easel next to Farah Assadi's.

'You'll never guess what I did on the weekend,' Farah said. She wasn't one to waste time on polite greetings.

'Let me see . . . did you snog that bartender guy again?'

'What bartender?' Farah's big eyes, outlined in smoky black, looked momentarily baffled. 'Oh, Donny. No, that was just a one-night thing. No, this weekend I went to a boutique club night in Angel. There's this new venue behind the station, and you know I told you my cousin's friend's brother organises club nights? Turns out he is. So. Cute.' Farah ran a hand through her pixie cut and crossed her skinny legs. 'He's called Rostam and he goes to uni at London Met, so we went back to his halls afterwards and did pills and stayed up till nine a.m. He is such a good kisser.'

'And? Did you . . . do it?'

'Duh. Obviously. At this point in my life, I've decided if I like a guy enough to snog him, them I like him enough sleep with him.'

'Oh, yeah, I know what you mean.' Scooping up a pencil, Dylan graffitied a few shapes on her wooden easel. Now was probably not the best moment to confide to Farah that she'd only slept with one guy. Or that breakfast with Alice had got her all upset about Jasper. Farah treated her love life like a train station – if she missed out on one boy, she forgot about him and caught whoever came along next.

Miss Baskin swept into the classroom, wearing knee-high sheepskin boots with beaded tassels, and a smock dress that looked like it had been hand-sewn by drunk hippies.

'Just because she's an Art teacher, doesn't mean she has to dress like one,' Farah snorted.

Dylan didn't reply. She liked Miss Baskin. The Art teacher had been encouraging about her work, and the Art Studio had provided one of her only refuges when she'd first arrived at St Cecilia's. Hard to believe that was three whole months ago now.

'Morning, girls,' Miss Baskin said in her airy voice, perching on a corner of the tabletop. Miss Baskin never sat in chairs as long as there were other surfaces available. 'As promised, we'll be starting our end-of-term project today. What you produce over the next couple of weeks will be exhibited at the December Parents' Day and Carol Concert. So make it good.'

Too Cruel for School

Dylan kicked her foot against her chair leg. Parents' Day: no way would her mom be showing up at that event. She was probably too busy shagging Victor Dalgleish even to remember Christmas, never mind a carol concert.

'For this project, I want you to go deeper than you've gone before,' Miss Baskin continued. 'I want you to make a piece of art – in whatever medium you choose. The only requirement is that it has to be based on something you've never told *anyone*. Yes, Felicity?'

'You mean, like, a secret?' asked Felicity Foxton.

'Exactly. A secret you've never told anyone in the world.'

'What?' cried Gabby Bunter, looking terrified. 'But . . . But I can't.'

'You mean you have no secrets?' Miss Baskin replied.

'No, I mean . . . they're secrets. That's the whole point. I can't just tell everyone.'

'And we don't want to know.'

Dylan was sitting as straight as the ruler in her pencil case, her ears attuned to Miss Baskin's every word. This project sounded fascinating – something to sink your teeth into.

'Girls, I'd like to make one thing quite clear,' Miss Baskin said. 'I'm not asking you to give away your secrets. I'm asking you to explore your most intimate thoughts and experiences through your art. Think of the Expressionist artists – Jackson Pollock, Edvard Munch, Wassily Kandinsky. We don't necessarily know what their art portrays, but we know it means something. It has a strange power. I want you to try to achieve a similar power in your projects.

It's one thing to draw a flower that's sitting in front of you; it's another to draw an emotion that no one can see. That's what I want you to achieve.' Miss Baskin held up a stack of notebooks. 'I want you to take the rest of this lesson to think of what secret you might explore. Use these notebooks to write about it. And keep them safe.'

Farah cackled as a notebook landed on her lap. 'OMG – I've got the funniest idea ever,' she whispered, digging Dylan in the ribs. 'I'm totally doing my project based on an orgasm. All swirly colours and explosions. I *love* the thought of Granny and Granddad trying to make some-thing of that on Parents' Day. *Why Farah, how wonderfully creative. Is it a fairy land? We must hang it in the living room!*'

Dylan smiled politely, but she hadn't heard a word of what Farah said. She was staring at her notebook's orange cover, twisting her pencil round and round between her fingers. An irresistible image had lodged itself in her mind. What if she explored *that* secret . . .

She hadn't talked about it, hadn't even allowed herself to think about it, since she'd left New York. Dylan drew the orange notebook closer to her chest. Maybe it was time.

Chapter 11

Silence filled the dorm room. It was disturbed only by the rustle of exercise books, the click of computer keys and the *scratch-scratch* of pens. Lauren Taylor hunched over her desk, attempting to write an essay on *Brighton Rock* – which was pretty impossible considering the fact that her English class had been reading the novel all term and she'd never even heard of it before Monday afternoon. Behind her back, like a strange pressure, she could feel the presence of the other Year Ten girls in the room: Georgie Fortescue, Charlie Calthorpe de Vyle-Hanswicke, and Minky Coombes. They were sitting cross-legged in a row on Georgie's bed, like a line of crows.

Charlie groaned. 'Does Señora Valdez actually think it's possible to do this much prep in one night?' Sighing, she flipped a page of her Spanish textbook and grimaced at the diagram of a car, with vocab labels pointing to all the different parts. *Steering wheel. Brakes. Tyres. Hazard lights.* Charlie shook her head. Who the hell needed to know the Spanish word for 'hazard lights'? She was fourteen. She couldn't even fucking drive. There was no doubt about it: GCSE's were the brainchild of evil genius teachers whose sole aim was to torture their pupils into madness with stupid assignments like this.

'Ow,' Charlie whispered, as something poked her leg through her navy blue St Cecilia's trackie bottoms. 'What?'

'Shhh.' Georgie Fortescue grinned slyly and shot a look at Lauren Taylor's desk. As usual, Georgie was wearing heavy make-up: waterproof mascara, dramatic eyeliner encircling her eyes, and pink lip gloss. She'd coated her face with foundation to cover up the spots on her cheeks. 'Ewww,' she muttered loudly, and fanned her fingers in front of her nose. 'What the hell is that smell?'

Charlie giggled.

'*Eeewww*,' Georgie repeated. No response. She broke into a fake coughing fit.

'Are you OK?' Lauren asked, raising her head from her Mac.

'Rank!' Georgie cried as soon as Lauren opened her mouth. 'That stinks.'

Lauren sniffed the air. 'I don't smell anything.'

'Ugh!' Charlie pinched her nostrils together. 'I smell it, too.'

'*What?*' Lauren repeated.

Georgie, Charlie and Minky all gagged in synch.

'Gross! I guess someone forgot to floss this morning,' Georgie whispered, just loud enough for Lauren to hear. 'I didn't know halitosis could reach this far.'

'Do you have a spare gas mask?' Charlie whispered back. 'I left mine in my room.'

Georgie cracked up.

Lauren stared at her computer screen, her face burning, her jaw tight. *Ignore them. Ignore them. Eventually they'll get bored and shut up.* She tried to sit up straight – that would show them how little she cared – but her back felt like it had a big fat target painted on it. Her room-mates had been mimicking her and whispering about her ever since she'd arrived. Why did they hate her so much? Dylan hadn't had any trouble like this. But Dylan was probably too cool. People respected her.

'Pfff.' Georgie made a fart sound. The others tittered. Then Charlie blew a raspberry, which practically sent Minky and Georgie into convulsions.

Finally, the giggles died down and calm returned. The minutes ticked by. But Lauren continued to stare at her screen, unseeing, until her vision burned white. Tears pricked behind her eyes. If she moved as little as possible, the others might forget she was here.

'God, I'm bored of prep,' Georgie yawned, tossing down her book.

'Me too,' said Minky Coombes. 'Shit, I'm, like, so stressed out. This summer's going to be awful. Why do they have to put exams in summer? Why can't they have them in the winter, when no one wants to go outside? Can you imagine when it's gorgeous and sunny out and we're stuck in here, revising our heads off?'

Charlie grinned. 'Minks, it's only December and you're already a bundle of nerves. For once in your life, would you like to not worry about things six months in advance? It's like you feed off stress – if you don't have something to worry about, you have to *find* something. I mean, I'm more concerned about what we're doing at the weekend.'

'What *are* we doing on the weekend?' Georgie asked, examining her greasy blond hair for split ends.

'Well, Mimah told me a bunch of the Lower Sixth are going to Shock Box on Saturday. I reckon we should sneak out and go, too. I'm trying to spend more time with my sister at the moment; what she did for me – taking the blame for Mum's pills like that – it was so amazing.'

'Yeah, we get it,' Georgie snapped. 'Your sister cares about you. Congratulations.'

Charlie bit her lip. She should have known better than to mention family; Georgie didn't exactly have the best relationship with her own siblings – or parents, for that matter. Charlie had only been BFFs with Georgie since the end of last school year and, to tell the truth, she was still a little afraid of her. Georgie was the most bad-ass girl in their year. Charlie and her ex-group of goody-two-shoes friends had always stayed out of her way, but, ever since Charlie's dad had left, she'd been drawn to Georgie's give-a-shit lifestyle.

'Are any Hasted House Year Tens going to Shock Box?' Minky asked.

'Yeah. Felix is,' Charlie said. She'd been going out with Felix Hedley-Bunk for just over a month now. He had a cute, roguish face, and was good friends with Alice Rochester's younger brother, Hugo. 'We texted about it this morning. I said I'd meet him and Hugo there.'

Hugo. Across the room, Lauren's fingers froze above the

keyboard. *Hugo Rochester*. Were they talking about the adorable boy in the photo on Charlie's bulletin board? Maybe she could find out more about him – and how to meet him.

'Hey, Georgie,' Charlie said brightly, 'if we go to Shock Box it might help you reach your target.'

'What target?' Minky chirped.

'Georgie's trying to snog a hundred guys before her fifteenth birthday.'

At her desk, Lauren swallowed. *A hundred* guys?

'Yeah. No big deal.' Georgie jumped off the bed. 'I snogged twenty-seven at the Crystal Ball in September, and that got my total up to fifty.'

'But your birthday's in February,' Minky squeaked. 'How are you going to snog another fifty guys in, like, less than three months?'

'Um, hello? Ever hear of the Feathers Ball? It's only a couple of weeks away. And it's a total snogathon. I'm planning to kiss at least thirty more there.'

'You so will,' Charlie said. 'Mimah went to the Feathers when she was fourteen. Apparently guys actually queue up so they can stick their tongues down your throat. Can you imagine if your first snog was with some sweaty random you hadn't even spoken a word to?'

Georgie giggled. 'Mine *was* a bit like that, actually.'

'No way!'

'Way. When I was ten, I went to this Pony Club meet, and my cousin's friend jumped on me after the gymkhana. He was wearing a yellow riding hat with green polka dots.

71

I thought it was so cool.' She snorted, straightening the plaited hairband across her forehead. 'When was yours, Minks?'

'I was twelve.'

'And? Details!'

Minky blushed. 'OK, well, It was in Turkey, on holiday with my parents. My sister and I met these two beach boys at our hotel – you know, the ones who set up the beach chairs and stuff? They persuaded us to sneak round to the back kitchens with them and snog.' She grimaced. 'It was a bit disgusting – mine kept licking my teeth.'

'Rank!' Charlie shrieked.

'Um, excuse me,' Georgie cut in. 'Of course it was rank. I mean, you kissed a serving boy, for fuck's sake.' She rolled her eyes. 'Hotel staff aren't known for their sexpertise. How about you, Charl?'

Charlie shrugged her petite shoulders. 'I'm not saying. I was such a latecomer, it's way too embarrassing.'

'Oh no you don't! Spill.'

'Spill, spill, spill!' Minky echoed.

'OK, OK! Remember that Paloma Faith concert last winter at—'

'Hang on,' Georgie interrupted. 'Hang on. Please tell me I heard that wrong. Your first snog was *last winter*? That is *so* lame.'

'Shut up, you cow!' Charlie swatted her. 'I told you I was a latecomer. Anyway. It was at a concert. I was standing with Henry Hoggs-Barrell and the crowd was tossing us around so we got lost from everyone else. We were right at the front, and then Paloma started singing "*New York*", and suddenly I fell into him, and he just grabbed me and kissed me.'

Minky clasped her hands. 'That is so romantic! *Her name was New York . . .*' she sang. 'I love that tune.'

'Put a sock in it, Minks. Hmmm,' Georgie mused loudly, 'I wonder how many boys Lauren's kissed?'

Lauren stared at her computer screen.

'Lauren? Oh, Lauuuren?'

'*LaurenLaurenLauren!!!*' Charlie chanted.

Keeping her eyes fixed on *Brighton Rock*, Lauren tried to block them out. Not speaking couldn't be worse than speaking. Without fodder, they'd have to give up.

Then '*Lau*ren. *Lau*ren. *Lau*ren. *Lau*ren.' Georgie had joined in the chant.

Lauren's own name hit her like falling rocks. Her shoulders tensed against the avalanche.

'Hey Lauren, are you deaf?' Charlie yelled.

'Maybe we're too far away.' Lauren heard feet pounding the carpet behind her. Then Georgie was shouting in her ear. 'Lauren! Anybody there?'

'Maybe she hasn't kissed any boys,' Charlie mocked. 'Maybe she's a lezzer.'

'Yeah, maybe she's a muff-diver.' Minky poked Lauren in the back. 'Laaauren! Are you a lezzer? Are you a lezzzbian?'

'Maybe she can't hear you,' Georgie said. 'Maybe her hair's too long!'

'You're right!' Minky clapped her hands. 'I think she needs it cut.'

Darting to her desk, Georgie grabbed a pair of big metal scissors from the drawer. She snapped them open and shut. 'Mr Scissors is hungry.'

'Stop it!' Lauren cried.

'Come on, George,' Charlie laughed, 'that's enough, put them away. She knows we're not really gonna cut her hair.'

'Wanna bet?' Georgie cackled. 'Mr Scissors wants food. Yum yum yum yum.'

Lauren jumped up. 'Why are you doing this?' she screamed.

'It's not me, it's Mr Scissors,' Georgie guffawed, collapsing, hysterical, against the wall.

'Go away!' Grabbing her laptop and her copy of *Brighton Rock*, Lauren bolted for the door. Out in the corridor, she swayed one way, then the other, tears streaming down her face. She couldn't go the Common Room – that was the first place Georgie would look. She couldn't go find Dylan – Dylan would send her away. The toilets – they were the only safe place.

Running down the hallway, Lauren pushed through the swinging door and locked herself in the very last stall. She huddled on the loo seat, her knees to her chin, trying not to make a sound. But her sobs echoed off the clean white tiles.

Chapter 12

Five hundred metres across St Cecilia's manicured lawns, Sonia lay on her bed in Tudor House, home to the Lower Sixth. She crossed her arms over her chest in a peaceful meditation pose, and hit *play* on her iPhone.

'You are listening to "Lose the Weight, Get a Date",' came the soothing tones of Mickey Masterson, the world's most fabulous diet hypnotist. *'Together, you and I will realise your full potential. The great sculptor, Michelangelo, once said, "I can see the angel inside the marble, and I chip away to release it." Release the angel inside of you . . .'*

Sonia breathed slowly, in and out. In and out. Yes. Release the angel. Release the angel. Release the—

Crash!

Her eyes shot open. On the other side of the room, Dylan Taylor's desk was strewn with fallen textbooks. Stupid klutz. Trust Dylan to disturb her diet meditation with ridiculous accidents like that.

'Lie back. Relax. Think positive thoughts,' said Mickey Masterson.

Sonia screwed up her fists. How was she supposed to think positive fucking thoughts, when so far this had been the worst week ever? First, Bella Scott had gone all crazy on her just for spilling a cup of coffee. Then, this morning, Dylan had barged in on their gang's breakfast and completely ruined her delightful mood. By this afternoon, Sonia had been so worked up that she'd inhaled an entire jam doughnut. Fat, fat, fat. She pinched her tummy – it was definitely more wobbly than it had been a few hours ago. Disaster.

Sonia glared across the room. Dylan was now bent over some stupid orange sketchbook. She was doing a painting, and it was rubbish. It looked like a gravy stain.

Ooh, gravy . . . Sonia could practically feel the drool start to dribble down her chin. Gravy with chicken – roast chicken – and roast potatoes.

'Don't let your food control you!' Mickey Masterson ordered in her ear. *'You must control your food. You are a strong person. You are a beautiful person.'*

Sonia's eyes fluttered shut. Strong. Beautiful. Yes. She'd snogged Seb Ogilvy, hadn't she? And she could snog him again. In fact, that was exactly what she was going to do at Shock Box on Saturday night.

Then again, Seb hadn't asked her out on a date since they'd kissed, weeks and weeks ago in the wine cellar of his house in London. He hadn't ever texted her. Maybe he liked someone else. Maybe he liked *Dylan*. Dylan was busty. And blonde. Some people might even think she was pretty – after all, there were plenty of morons in the world with no taste.

Just then, someone burst through the door. Sonia jumped so hard that her back seized up.

'Hey, nosejob, having an afternoon nap, are we?' Mimah said from the doorway. 'Have you got that calculator I lent you last week? What are you listening to?'

'Nothing. Music.' Sonia sat bolt upright and shoved her iPod under her bum. Mimah and Tally and Alice teased her mercilessly about her diet tapes and diet pills and diet meals, and Mimah was the meanest of the bunch. She ate as much as she pleased, and managed to stay lean and muscly from playing all that sport. Lucky bitch. Not that Sonia would want man-shoulders like Mimah's, obviously.

'So, my calculator?' Mimah asked. 'Where'd you put it?'

'In the drawer.'

'Cool.' Mimah walked over to Sonia's desk, which was spotlessly clean, with pencils and notepads and textbooks lined up in rows. 'I reckon I'll need it for tutoring tomorrow – those stupid townies probably won't bring their own. Ugh, I can't believe I have to do this boring volunteering thing.'

Ping ping.

Mimah slid her phone from her pocket. 'Hey, wicked!'

'What?'

'My invitation to Lucian Scott's Christmas party – from Bella. OMG, have you seen the picture she sent with it? So cute.'

Sonia smoothed down her cashmere jumper. 'Hmm, yeah, well, my invite hasn't come through yet. My network must be slow.'

Ping ping.

'That must be it now!' She snatched her iPhone from

77

under her bum. But the screen was dark. She shook it; still nothing.

'Hey,' Dylan cried, picking up her phone, 'I got an invitation, too.'

'*What?*' Sonia whipped round, her eyes narrowing to the width of razor blades. 'That's impossible.'

'Oh, but it's not. See?'

Sonia turned pale. 'Well, Bella must be sending the invitations in alphabetical order. I mean, "Jemimah" and "Dylan" come before "Sonia", obviously.'

Dylan shrugged. 'Sure. Except that Mimah got her text before I got mine. And D comes way before J.'

'She's right,' Mimah grinned. 'Looks like you might be out in the cold, Sone. Oh, well. I've got prep to do. Toodle-oo.'

The bedroom door clicked shut. Sonia blinked. Then she flopped back down on her pillow and stuffed her headphones into her ears. She lay stone-still, every muscle in her body clenched.

'*Get rid of the food that taunts you,*' crooned Mickey Masterson. '*Search through your cupboards and hunt down every last unhealthy snack. Gather them up and throw them all away.*'

Yes. Hunt them down. Throw them away. Grinding her teeth, Sonia glowered at Dylan, who was fiddling with her paints again. Everyone could be destroyed. Everyone had secrets. All she had to do was ransack the cupboards and sniff out what Dylan's were.

Chapter 13

Hasted Community Centre was in the ugly part of town, squatting at the grimy end of the Common between a McDonald's and a paint-chipped bowling alley. Mimah pushed through its scratched glass doors and peered round the neon-lit foyer. The knot in her tummy tightened. Stupid St Cecilia's. What had Mr Vicks been thinking? She'd never tutored anyone in her life. She was completely unqualified. Plus, this place was a dump. There wasn't even a receptionist to tell her where she was supposed to go. Maybe she should just run next door, grab a Big Mac, and flee back to school once her two hours were up.

Just then, a small notice tacked to the foyer's huge bulletin board caught Mimah's eye.

MATHS TUTORING
TUES & THURS 6:30—8:30 PM
ROOM 117

There went her excuse. Pulling her hoodie over her eyes, Mimah dragged her feet along the linoleum corridor. She'd purposely dressed down for this evening's tutoring.

It would be weird to wear anything remotely fashionable while she was helping some little old lady learn long division in a manky classroom.

'You're the one that I want . . . !'

Mimah jumped as a tune from *Grease!* assaulted her ears. The music was belting out of a large room. Peeking inside, she glimpsed rows of pre-teens shouting tunelessly along to a piano, while a harried conductor tried to get them to shuffle back and forth in time to the music. One frizzy-haired girl, wearing pink leggings and an orange T-shirt, kept going the wrong way and bumping into the boys next to her. Mimah grinned. She peeped through the next doorway, into a much smaller room. Here, a group of women were chatting away round an avalanche of wool, thread and squares of colourful fabric. One plump, middle-aged woman threw back her head.

'So Jimmy was just sat there on the sofa like a great big walrus,' she cackled, 'and I thought to myself, "What do I need a husband for, when I could get a pet pig instead? God knows, it'd probably provide more interesting conversation. And eat less."'

The others howled with laughter.

Mimah chuckled, too. Actually, being sent out of school in the middle of the week was kind of cool. It was crazy to think that this vibrant, real world was just a mile or two away from the Victorian buildings and landscaped gardens of St Cecilia's.

She came to the end of the corridor. Voices were buzzing from an open doorway, where an elderly man sat holding a clipboard. He was wearing faded trousers, a blue shirt and a somewhat vague smile on his face. 'Name?'

'Jemimah Calthorpe de Vyle-Hanswicke.'

'Jemimah Whatty-what? Don't have any students with names like that on my list. Evening, Larry,' the man called, nodding at a greasy-haired geezer who was strolling past them into the room. He turned back to Mimah. 'Did you sign up?'

'Yes. I mean, no. I mean, I'm supposed to be a tutor.'

'A tutor? You can't be more than sixteen. What are you, a child prodigy? Ha!' He gave a rasping laugh. 'Bloody hell, that's from too many cigarettes, that is. Don't you ever start smoking, young lady.'

Mimah forced a smile. 'It's a bit late for that, I'm afraid.'

'Well, it's never too late to stop. Do it now, before you end up like me.' The man glanced back at his list. 'Ah, yes, here you are: Jemimah Cally Villy-Wicky, or whatever it says. Right, the powers that be have assigned you to one-on-one tutoring with one of our new students. Should be quite straightforward. Student's not here yet, though. Take a seat and wait – any desk you like.'

'Thanks.' Mimah headed towards the back corner of the room, slipping into a seat behind Larry. His pupil, a Pakistani woman, was holding her pencil so tight it was about to snap.

'No, no, Mrs Patel, you're overcomplicating things,' Larry was saying. 'Remember what we learned about the nine times table?'

Mimah slumped back in her chair. *Great,* she thought,

staring at the space heater as it blasted hot air into the room. Two hours of explaining Maths to amateurs – not exactly the most scintillating way to spend Thursday evening. If only she could be playing lacrosse instead. Yesterday afternoon, she'd strolled past the lax team as they practised for their end-of-term match against Purcell's Girls School, and her stomach had clenched so tight she thought she might be sick. Banning her from lacrosse was one of the meanest punishments Miss Colin could have devised, the disloyal, vindictive cow. Mimah had dedicated so much time and passion to the school team. She hit the end of her pencil against the desktop. Being alone in the world totally sucked.

'Are you Jemimah?'

'What?' Mimah snapped.

'I said, "Are you Jemimah?"'

Mimah raised her head. The boy on the other side of the table had a deep voice. He was tall and arrogant looking. But not arrogant like Jasper von Holstadt, who came from a line of haughty German emperors, arrogant in a hard way, with a scornful face and sardonic brown eyes – which, right now, were examining her.

'Bloody hell, how old are you?'

'Seventeen.' Mimah held his look. It felt like they were two boxers, facing each other across the ring. 'So?'

'Fan-fucking-tastic.' The boy dragged a hand through his thick brown hair. 'Just my luck – ending up with the dud. In the course-description they said they had ex-teachers and graduate students as tutors. I wasn't expecting a toddler.'

He rolled his eyes. 'I'll see you round, OK? No offence but I don't need to be wasting my time.'

The boy swung on his heel.

Mimah gaped after him. Talk about attitude. She'd met some rude pricks in her time, but they were nothing compared to this jerk. She watched as he argued with the clipboard man, flinging his arms around. '*Not qualified* . . .' '*Completely pointless* . . .' '*Younger than me* . . .' The phrases floated back to her over the heads of the other tutors and tutees. After a minute, the boy shrugged sullenly and stomped back to her desk.

'Looks like I'm stuck with you. Apparently there's "Nothing he or anyone else can do,"' he sneered, making air quotes and dropping into a chair. 'Useless bureaucratic fool. Anyway. I'm Aidan.'

'Wow, Aidan, it is such an honour to meet you.' Mimah smiled sweetly. 'I'm so glad you decided to stay. Now tell me, what brings you here this evening?'

'Wow, Jemimah, that's a great question.' Aidan smiled sweetly back. 'I've always thought it'd be really fun to learn how to carve ice sculptures. This *is* the ice sculpture club, right?'

Mimah shot a death-stare across the table. 'Look, *Adrian*, or whatever you're called – however little you want to be here, I guarantee you that I want to be here ten times less. So do me a favour, and either cut the bullshit or fuck off.'

Aidan shrugged. A crinkle appeared for a split second at the corner of his mouth, but disappeared before Mimah could even be sure she'd seen it.

'Fine.' He pulled off his threadbare sheepskin jacket and draped it over the back of his chair. 'I'm here because I failed my Maths GCSE and I need to pass it. Happy now?'

'How long ago did you fail?'

'Let's see, I was fifteen back then and I'm eighteen now . . . So . . . three years.'

'Excellent.' Mimah pretended to tick something off in her notebook. 'I can see we won't have to work on your basic adding and subtracting skills. That's a plus, at least. Pardon the pun.'

Aidan folded his arms. 'Are you always this charming to your students?'

'Only when they're as pleasant as you. Why do you want to retake Maths? You failed when you were fifteen – why do you give a shit about passing now?'

'Because.' Aidan stretched out his legs. His jeans looked like they'd been slept in for the past five years. 'Not that it's any of your business, but I want to train as an engineer. I need qualifications.'

'Engineer? Really?' Mimah smiled patronisingly. 'Isn't that a bit ambitious for someone who couldn't even pass an easy-peasy Maths GCSE?'

'Typical.' Aidan shook his head. 'That is so bloody typical.'

'What?'

'You. Your attitude.'

'I think you'll find *I'm* not the one with the attitude.'

'Oh, sure. Just because I failed an exam when I was fifteen years old, you think I should consider myself a failure for the rest of my life. Ever hear of second chances? Oh, no, of course not. People like you don't need second chances.'

'People like who? What the hell does that mean?'

'Like you need to ask. Posh princess. Lady of the manor. You've always had everything you wanted at the snap of your fingers. You've never had to deal with anything difficult in your life.'

'How dare you?' Mimah snapped.

'Kids!' said a woman at the next table. 'Quiet, please.'

Aidan shot her a *sorry-but-my-tutor's-a-maniac* look.

'Stop that!' Mimah whispered. 'How dare you?' She repeated. 'You know nothing about me.'

'Oh, yeah, of course I don't.' Aidan half grinned, half sneered, his wide mouth twisting. 'I don't know that you're a rich bitch who's always had everything she wants. I don't know that you've got second homes in Italy and the south of France, *dahling*. I bet you go skiing every Christmas and that all your friends call you "Jems". I bet you've never even met a bit of working-class rough like me.'

'That is . . . so not true!' Mimah sputtered. How dare this awful person think he'd got anything right about her? 'My life's been anything but easy.'

'Oh, yeah, things must be really tough at whatever posh school you go to.'

'You think you've got everything figured out, don't you?'

'No. Just you.'

'Well, for your information, I don't go to posh school. I . . . I go to state school. And no one ever gave me anything

85

in my life. I got where I am because I work hard and I'm clever.'

'Oh. Interesting. So how'd you end up with that accent, then? You sound like one of the Queen's corgies – if dogs could talk.'

'Oh, now you're saying I'm a dog?'

Aidan shrugged.

Mimah clenched her fists inside her hoodie. She'd teach him to be such a smug twat. She hunched her shoulders, assuming a forlorn face.

'Well, since you're being so nosey, I got my accent from my granny. See, my mum abandoned me when I was a baby, so Granny was the one who brought me up. She came from a wealthy family – well, before her parents cut her off without a penny.' Mimah timed a pause, then pushed her jet black fringe out of her eyes. 'Not that this is any of your business. We're both here for the same reason – so let's just work, OK? I take it you managed to bring the right textbooks? Or is that beyond your capabilities?'

'Oh. Here.' Aidan pulled a thick volume out of his backpack. Then he paused. 'Listen . . . Can we start over?'

'"Start over"? What is this, some kind of game to you?'

But Aidan was already speaking over her. 'I didn't mean to pry about your family, OK? I don't care what accent you've got or where you got it from. I need this tutoring – a lot. And it's going to be a waste of both our time if all we do is bicker.'

'So, are you apologising?' Mimah demanded, folding her arms.

'No!' Then, after a moment, with obvious effort, Aidan dropped his hunched shoulders. 'OK, fine, yes. Who gives a shit? All I want is to pass my GCSE in a few months, and that's it.'

'Great.' Mimah reached out her hand. 'Truce.'

'Truce.'

As Aidan took her fingers, she felt how coarse and calloused his palm was against her own, and for a second she wondered – was the rest of his life as rough as his skin? Her eye flickered upwards and caught his. They must have noticed at the same moment that they were still holding hands, because they both recoiled together.

'Uh, here's the book I've been using,' Aidan said, shaking himself off like a dog wringing off water. 'I've been going through the stuff a bit when I get home from work. My weakest subject's trigonometry. And quadratic equations. It's like, I've never been so shit at anything in my life.'

'Let me see.' Mimah rotated the book towards her. 'Yeah, I can help you with this,' she said, pointing the tip of her pencil at the first question. It was a difficult problem involving two right-angled triangles, and she launched into an explanation.

After a minute, Aidan stopped responding. When she looked up, his eyes were on her face. '*What?*'

'Nothing. Just . . . How did you get so good at Maths from going to one of the rubbish state schools round here? None of my teachers ever explained it like that.'

'Um, just naturally liked numbers, I guess. My parents

were always fighting when I was younger. So I used to escape into my room and work. Maths problems were something I could solve.' Mimah swallowed. That bit of her educational history was true, at least.

'Huh.' Aidan scrutinised her a moment longer before dropping his gaze to the page. 'So, if I work out the hypotenuse of Triangle A, then . . .'

'Mmhmm . . .' Mimah listened for a second, before her attention was distracted by the cuff of Aidan's jumper. It was frayed and worn, a light olive-green with a hole rubbed through the wool just below the thumb. His fingers lay curled on the desk. They were beautiful – long and sensitive-looking, each one at rest yet seeming to contain the energy of a coiled spring. Maybe being an engineer wasn't such a bad idea for someone with hands like that.

'Hey,' she blurted out, 'how come you dropped out of school? What kind of person does that? What have you been doing for the past three years, anyway?'

'None of your business, nosey.' Aidan tapped his textbook, crinkles forming at the corners of his eyes. 'Stop prying and help me with this.'

Mimah's mouth formed a petulant 'o'. Then, without answering, she shut it again, picked up her pencil, and lowered her head next to Aidan's, over the rows of numbers.

Chapter 14

'*Birds do it . . .*' sang Mrs Jenkins, fluttering her fingers like a bird. The Biology teacher was sitting cross-legged on the stage of the Little Theatre among a circle of Year Tens, her grey bowl-cut swishing in time to the beat. '*Bees do it . . .* Buzz, buzz, buzz.'

Lauren Taylor stared. This was her first PSHE group at St Cecilia's, and so far it was the stupidest experience of her life. PSHE, her housemistress, Mrs Gould, had informed her, stood for Personal, Social, Health and Economic education, and apparently it was where you talked about touchy-feely issues like why bullying was mean, why eating disorders were bad, and how to wash your face properly so you didn't get acne. Oh, and what sex was – which, since they were fourteen years old, they obviously didn't know already.

Lauren slid her gaze sideways. Two seats away, Georgie Fortescue leaned her head on Charlie Calthorpe de Vyle-Hanswicke's shoulder and convulsed with giggles. Georgie was wearing dark smoky eyeliner, too much foundation and laddered tights. Her dry blond hair straggled down her back and, as usual, looked like it had been styled by a crack addict.

'*Shhh!*' Charlie nudged George away, and grinned.

Lauren stared at her. When Charlie smiled, her pale, elfin face transformed. Her black eyes, usually distant and brooding, gleamed with an impish light. Her cheeks dimpled. Her delicate shoulders rocked forward with glee. No wonder Charlie had a boyfriend. She was always getting texts in lessons from that boy, Felix – the one who was friends with Hugo Rochester. The one who Charlie and Georgie had planned to meet tomorrow night. Lauren dropped her eyes. If only someone would invite her, too . . . She was about to sigh, then stopped herself. For the next forty-five minutes, she had to concentrate on not moving a muscle. Maybe if she kept completely still, Georgie and Charlie would forget she was there.

'Sex,' continued Mrs Jenkins. A triangle of hair at the front of the teacher's bowl-cut had gone white, which made her look a bit like a skunk. 'Sex is a beautiful and natural activity. Sex is a wonderful way to express your love for another human being.'

As Lauren watched, Georgie Fortescue smirked and whispered something to Charlie. Then she raised her hand, blinking angelically.

'Yes, dear?' the teacher smiled.

'Well, the thing is, Mrs Jenkins,' Georgie stammered, 'sex just sounds so . . . icky. What if something goes wrong? Like, what if the man goes to the loo inside you?'

Charlie's face contorted. She was obviously trying not to laugh. Mrs Jenkins nodded sympathetically.

'Georgina, dear, thank you for sharing your concerns

with the Circle of Trust. I know sexual intercourse can be a frightening prospect.' Clearing her throat, she repeated in a loud voice, 'Class, Georgina wants to know, "What if your partner goes to the loo inside you?" Well, rest easy my dears: it's impossible for a man to urinate when he is in a state of arousal! Isn't that good news? However, what you *do* need to worry about is your sexual health. Which is why, today, we're going to talk about Safe Sex.'

Just then, Lauren's pencil slipped off her lap. She held her breath, watching it roll across the floorboards, rumbling thunderously past Tabitha Fitzsimmons, Portia Mehew-Montefiore and Rosie Westmorland, before coming to a halt against one of Georgie's slouchy suede boots. Georgie raised her head. She glared at Lauren, her eyes cold and glittering like ice.

'Condoms!' Mrs Jenkins chirped. 'They are a very wise choice of contraception. Always make your man wear his mackintosh. Make him squeeze into that tight rubber suit. Don't let him in without a raincoat – no matter how hard he knocks.' She winked.

Lauren closed her eyes. Gross.

'Herpes,' said Mrs Jenkins. She'd now launched into a list of STDs. 'Gonorrhoea, chlamydia, genital warts.'

Lauren heard snickering. She glanced around. It felt like people were smirking at her. Suddenly, she saw why. Every time Mrs Jenkins named a disease, Georgie Fortescue made a face and jabbed her finger in Lauren's direction. Lauren's cheeks burned as if someone was shining the theatre's spotlight right in her face.

'OK, girls, I'm going to need you to be mature for a minute,' Mrs Jenkins said. Reaching behind her back, she produced a medium-sized courgette, which she weighed in her hand. 'I like to think of this as representative of the average size of the male penis.'

Portia Mehew-Montefiore let out a yelp of laughter.

'Not if they're well hung,' Georgie whispered loudly. Everyone snickered.

'Girls!' Mrs Jenkins frowned. 'There's nothing to giggle about. The penis is a beautiful part of the human anatomy. Right,' she said, dangling a condom packet from her fingers, 'watch carefully while I demonstrate how to put on a prophylactic for maximum safety during intercourse.'

Mrs Jenkins held up the small rubber cylinder, jiggled it about, and proceeded to unroll it up the courgette. Lauren recoiled. If St Cecilia's was trying to eliminate teen pregnancy among its pupils, mission accomplished: no one would ever want to have sex after this little demo. She pursed her lips. Not that there was any chance of her losing her virginity any time soon. Popular girls like Charlie Calthorpe de Vyle-Hanswicke and Georgie Fortescue got boyfriends. Friendless losers like her got squat.

Raucous laughter floated down the hallway from Locke House's Common Room after dinner that evening. The tendrils of sound seemed to wind around Lauren, mocking her as she nudged open a door at the far end of the chilly corridor and peered inside. Empty. Good.

She flicked on the overhead bulb. Immediately, the grey

windows of the Practice Room became black mirrors, reflecting her face back at her from the night outside. Her eyes were hollow. Her skin looked translucent, as if she might fade to nothingness at the slightest push. Turning away from her ghostly image, Lauren lowered herself on to the piano bench and balanced a baby-blue calfskin diary on the instrument's closed lid. She stared at the blank page. What now? This was exactly why she'd never kept a diary before – who wanted to pour their heart out to a load of white paper? Lauren had been touched when her History teacher in New York had given her this book as a leaving gift, but she'd immediately buried it at the bottom of her suitcase and thought she'd never dig it out. Then, for some reason, this afternoon she had.

Her pen hovered above the page. How was she supposed to start? 'Dear Diary?' No way. Some girl in a cheesy movie would do that. But it might help to feel like she was actually addressing someone. Anne Frank had named her diary 'Kitty'. Maybe she could pretend her diary was a friend, too. The problem was, she had no friends. She hadn't even met a single person who was friendly – or nice, or kind. Unless . . . Lauren clenched her pen tighter.

'Dear Hugo,' she wrote. The boy's soft smile in Georgie's photo shone in her mind's eye.

My first week at St Cecilia's is almost complete. These last few days have felt like a century. English boarding school is very different from how I expected it to be.

93

Lauren paused. She read over the neat, constrained sentences. Then she scribbled in a frenzy,

Why is everyone so MEAN to me?? I'm lonely. I hate it here. I HATE it. I have no one to talk to. You're the only person who's smiled at me all week, Hugo – and you're just a boy in a photo, smiling for ever, stuck to a wall. I wish I could meet you, Hugo. I think in real life you'd be kind. I think you'd be gorgeous and sensitive and caring. If only I could meet you, I know you'd like me. You'd think I was pretty. You'd want to kiss me. I know you would.

Lauren bit the end of her pen, then scrawled in the top margin,

PRIVATE!! Do Not Read. To anyone who reads this, you're the meanest most untrustworthy person in the world!!!

She sat back, drained – and for some reason, the image of Mrs Jenkins's courgette popped into her mind. *Not if he's well-hung!* Georgie Fortescue's voice echoed in her head. She picked up her pen.

How did all the girls in my class get so experienced? Everyone seems like they've done so much. Some people have even had <u>sex</u>. I've never told this to anyone in the world, Hugo (you have to <u>promise</u> not to tell anyone), but I've never even kissed a boy. Oh my god, I can't believe I just wrote that down.

94

What if someone reads it? IF ANYONE'S READING THIS, FUCK OFF.

I'm 14 years old and I'm still waiting for my first kiss. Does that mean I'm a loser beyond repair? I lie about it all the time because if anyone knew, they'd think I was a freak. I'm dying to kiss a boy, but it just seems so far away. I mean, how do you get from talking to kissing? Does one of you just shut up and lunge? What if I head-butt him? What if my teeth get in the way? Maybe I need to pout more. Maybe there's some kind of 'kiss me' code – a way of sending subliminal 'kiss me' messages to the guy you like. Does it help if you lick your lips?

I sort of want my first kiss to be special – with someone I really, really like. But then again, I don't even care – I just want to kiss someone and get it over with. I just want to kiss someone so I don't have to pretend anymore.

The door flung open. Lauren hugged her diary to her chest.

It was Minky Coombes and her BFF, Isabelle Bruin.

'Ohhh,' Isabelle drawled. 'I didn't know you played piaaahno.'

'Um, I don't.' Lauren cringed at how mousy her voice sounded. Why was it that as soon as people started treating you like a loser, you started acting like one?

'Ohhh,' drawled Isabelle again. She had a dopey-sounding voice, and seemed incapable of pronouncing more than one word every five seconds. 'You don't play piaaahno, but you're using the Practice Room. Uhhh, whyyy?'

Minky pushed into the room. 'Look, would you mind pissing off? We want to practise our duet.'

'Yahhh,' drawled Isabelle. 'Our duet. Exactly.'

'Oh. Sure.' Stumbling out of her seat, Lauren shuffled round the two girls and into the corridor. As she wandered up the stairs towards her dorm room, she heard Georgie Fortescue's voice float into the hallway, and stopped.

'I just think it's selfish,' Georgie was whining. 'I can't believe you expect me to stand there next to you and Felix all of tomorrow night, looking like a total lemon.'

'You won't be a lemon, I already told you,' Charlie protested. 'He said he was coming.'

'Really? Is he really? But what did he say, though? Like, "I might come along," or "I'm definitely coming and I can't wait to see Georgie"?'

'Hmmm . . .' Charlie paused. 'It was more enthusiastic than the first one. But . . . well . . . I'd say it was somewhere in between. I mean, he definitely knows you're coming . . . When I told him, he said "Oh, cool."'

'Eee!' Georgie was evidently skipping around. 'It's happening, it's happening!'

Lauren crept closer.

'He likes me!' Georgie chirped. 'He's totally into me. I knew it. Just imagine, Charl – you and Felix Hedley-Bunk, and me and Hugo Rochester – we'll go on the world's most perfect double dates!'

Lauren sank back against the wall. She knew Charlie must have replied, because hysterical giggles were bubbling out of the room, but the words passed her by. All she knew was this: Georgie was destined to get together with Hugo. Hugo Rochester. Her dream boy. The winter wind howled outside, and her baby-blue diary lay heavy in her hand.

Chapter 15

Sonia crouched on the frozen ground and eyed the fence
that separated St Cecilia's from the route to Hasted.
Glaring, she straightened the neon-yellow band that she
was wearing across her forehead. 'Um, excuse me, *Dylan*.
Could you please shove your fat arse out of my way?'

Sighing, Dylan kicked her way through a pile of brown
leaves and stuck her hands in her coat pockets. She couldn't
be bothered with any of the usual sharp retorts she stock-
piled for Sonia. In less than half an hour, she'd be at Shock
Box, forced to watch Jasper von Holstadt looking gorgeous,
ignoring her and hitting on other girls. The perfect Saturday
night . . . Why had she given in to Alice and Tally's wheedling?
Stupid question. It wasn't like an invitation from the two
most popular girls in the Lower Sixth was easy to turn down.
Dylan cast a glance at her outfit. Like the others, she was
wearing Day-Glo leggings and a neon headband that Alice
had insisted she borrow. Apparently, this look was *de rigueur*
for Shock Box. She looked back at the school lawns lying
dark, guarded and silent. It was too late to chicken out now.

Sonia was inching forward on her stomach under the
fence.

'Poooo,' she whined, as her Dolce & Gabbana leopard-print scarf snagged on the barbed wire. 'Stupid countryside. Stupid school rules. I don't understand why we have to sneak out when we're allowed to go home at weekends, anyway.'

Alice rolled her eyes. 'Sone, how long have you been at St Cecilia's? If we stay at school for the weekend, then the curfew is eleven o'clock. So, unless you want to officially sign out and then have to rush back before eleven, we need to do this under the radar.'

'Yeah, whatever,' Sonia grumbled. 'St Cecilia's should abolish curfews altogether. I mean, we're almost seventeen. We're mature enough to make our own decisions.'

'Wow, that is such a good point,' Mimah said. She shone her torch ahead of the gang as they struck off across the dark field. 'Why don't you suggest it to Mrs Traphorn? I'm sure she'd see the error of her ways and immediately change the school policy on underage clubbing.'

'No need to get sarcastic, *Jemimah*,' Sonia sniffed. She checked that her pert new nose hadn't been scratched by the hedge. 'By the way, are you sure you should be here? You're on probation, remember? If we get caught, you'll be thrown into the gutter with all the other boarding-school rejects, and it'll be embarrassing to know you.'

'Gee, thanks for your concern, Sone. I'm so touched that you care.'

'Shut up, you two,' Tally cut in, skipping down the road. 'It's always bitch, bitch, bitch. Let's talk about something interesting, Like who everyone's pulling tonight.

And, by "everyone", I obviously mean Sonia, Mimah and Dylan, since Al and I are totally loved up already.' She clapped her hands, which she'd moisturised with rose-scented lotion and manicured with pale blue nail polish. 'OMG! I can't wait to see Rando! I've been missing his kisses all week. He is *such* a good kisser. Gentle, yet passionate and strong . . .' She shut her eyes, swaying back and forth.

'Anyway,' Alice interrupted, 'projects for the night: Sone, I assume you'll be trying to snog Seb again?'

'What? No. Why would you say that? What makes you think I still like Seb?'

'Um, the fact that you've been going on about him for the past six months? I'm guessing that one kiss two weeks ago didn't satisfy your lust.'

Sonia pouted. 'You're making me sound like a rampant sex-stalker. Anyway, maybe I've decided to move on to new territory.'

'That would be a relief for all of us,' Mimah muttered.

'I'll believe it when I see it.' Alice turned to Dylan. 'How about you?'

'Oh . . .' Dylan shrugged. 'I'm not into anyone. I'll just . . . hang out.'

'No, you won't!' Tally declared. 'That's against the rules.'

'Rules?'

'Yeah,' Alice chimed in. 'When we go to Shock Box, everyone must pull. Or at least try to pull.'

'Oh. I don't think so.'

Sonia snorted. 'Spoil sport. I knew she would be. I know

who this is about: Jasper von Holstadt. Dylan's still super hung-up on him, and it's pathetic.'

Alice and Tally exchanged looks.

'Come on, Dill,' Alice cooed, putting on a sympathetic voice. 'There are plenty of eligible Hasted House boys. Like . . . Oh, I don't know . . . I've always thought George Demetrios was sexy. It can't hurt to flirt with him.'

'Yeah,' Tally added. 'Like, you know, let him buy you a drink, if you happen to run into him at the bar . . .'

Sonia narrowed her eyes and started yanking threads out of her fraying scarf. Why the hell were Alice and Tally trying to help Dylan hook up with people, when they hadn't even given a shit that she might be over Seb? The conversation had been about her for less than one second before Dylan had stolen the limelight.

'Trust us,' Alice was saying, 'there's nothing like flirting with a guy's friend to make him jealous. Isn't that right, Tals? Tally's like, the expert at this. If you chat up George Demetrios, you'll have Jasper eating out of your hand.'

Dylan nodded, but said nothing. Instead, she pulled her hat further down over her straw-coloured waves of hair and traipsed on ahead.

Alice watched her. Maybe this make-Dylan-look-like-a-slut plan wasn't the nicest thing she'd ever done. Dylan still seemed seriously cut up about Jasper. Maybe it would have been nicer just to leave things alone. Alice fiddled with some loose coins in her pocket. That had never been her way, though – leaving things alone.

'Girlies!' called a high-pitched voice from behind them.

Alice frowned.

'Wait for us,' called someone else. Flossy Norstrup-Fitzwilliam was wobbling across the field on her high heels, flanked by Bella Scott and Felicity Foxton.

'How the hell did *they* crash our party?' Alice fake-whispered to Mimah, who'd walked up next to her. Now that she had her invite to Lucian Scott's Christmas party, there was no need to suck up to Bella. 'I thought we were travelling light tonight – just the inner circle.'

'*I* asked them,' said Sonia. 'I thought that since Bella finally invited me to her dad's party, I should invite her to more things with us.'

Mimah snorted. 'You mean you invited her in exchange for an invitation to her dad's party. Admit it.'

Sonia threw her nose in the air. 'As if I'd be that common – bartering for invitations. I did nothing of the sort. Hi, Bella!' she chirped.

'Girls, wait up,' called Felicity Foxton, stumbling along in her furry platform boots. 'Do you think I should have put on more foundation? Can you still see the spot on my nose?'

'Gross,' Alice muttered.

'I mean, maybe I should squeeze it – has the tip of it gone white yet? Or maybe I should leave it. Or maybe I should wait till we get to Shock Box and pop it in the loos.'

'Or maybe,' Mimah said loudly, 'you should talk about it all night and we can have a vomiting party in the street.'

Alice burst into giggles. 'I'm so glad you didn't get expelled, babe,' she said, tucking her arm through Mimah's as the two of them strode ahead of the pack. 'What would I have done without you?'

Mimah giggled. 'Oh, I'm sure you'd have managed. Just think – you would have had so much more time to listen to Sonia's amazing conversation.'

'Oh, joy. Speaking of being expelled,' Alice said, 'I forgot to ask you – how's that stupid tutoring punishment going?'

'How do you think? It's lame.'

'I knew it. What are the people like? A bunch of dumb townies trying to pass their GCSEs?'

'How'd you guess? My student is this high-school dropout with bad clothes and a bad attitude. I can't wait till Mr Vicks says I can stop.' Mimah's torch shone on a stile up ahead. 'Here we are.'

Climbing over, the girls dropped into a narrow, cobbled street. The pub on the corner was bursting with punters and juke-box music ricocheted off the old Hasted bricks. Mimah pocketed her torch.

'OMG, only a week and a half of school left,' Alice gushed as they strolled past the pub. 'And that means only two weeks till Lucian Scott's Christmas party. What are you wearing? I feel like going seriously glam this year. I might wear this fur gilet thing that I bought at the . . .'

Suddenly, Mimah's heart gave a jolt. Alice's chatter faded from her ears. Instinctively, she retreated into the doorway of a shop. A little way down the street, a group of boys perched on a doorstep, swigging booze from a bottle. It was the shock of dark hair that had caught her eye – the tall figure, the slim, muscular shoulders. Aidan was leaning back against the wall, his eyes turned to the sky, his elbows resting on his knees. He was wearing a blue Adidas tracksuit top and the same jeans he'd had on the other day – faded, wrecked, frayed at the seams. One of his friends cracked a joke and he chuckled, locking his arm round the guy's neck. Laughter lines creased his profile.

'Oi.' Alice poked her. 'Are you listening to me, or are you too busy staring at those hideous home-made hats in the window?'

'Huh? I was listening.'

'Oh, god,' Alice sneered, noticing Aidan's gang. 'Check out that group of chavs. Pathetic. They think they're so hard.'

'How do you know they're chavs?' Mimah retorted. 'You don't know anything about them.'

'Oh, yeah, like I can't guess. They're townies. They probably have shitty jobs at Tesco's. Oh, and they're hanging round the streets on Saturday night 'cause they clearly can't afford to go anywhere else.'

Mimah didn't reply. Aidan was craning his neck to take a gulp from the bottle, and she could practically trace the liquid streaming down his throat.

Heels clip-clopped on the pavement behind her. It sounded like a herd of horses was trampling down the street.

'Maybe I'll go to my dermatologist and make him prescribe me something,' came Felicity Foxton's piercing voice. 'I've absolutely got to have flawless skin so I can look hot in all our holiday photos. Mummy and Daddy are taking me and Tubbs to Courchevel and it would be *too* embarrassing to be seen on the slopes with such an enormous spot. Can you imagine what Bozzy Bosworth would say?'

'Sone,' came Tally's voice, 'you owe me a drink, remember? I bought us that bottle of champagne at Kiki Club last weekend.'

'Yeah, babes, don't worry,' Sonia called. 'Daddy gave me some cash – I'll just buy a round using that. The drinks at Shock Box are so cheap it's a joke.'

Cowering in the doorway, Mimah prayed for Alice to stay silent – if she spoke, their hiding place was done for. She sneaked a glace at Aidan. He'd lowered his eyes from the sky and was smirking in her friends' direction, a big, caustic grin on his hard, chiselled face.

'Hey, let's go round the other way to Shock Box,' she whispered to Alice. 'I know it's longer, but – those townies. They're kind of freaking me out. They look rough. Remember when Rando got punched on Guy Fawkes' night? There are no boys here to protect us now.'

'Good point,' Alice whispered back. 'Come on, follow me.'

As they turned the corner away from Aidan, Mimah breathed a sigh of relief.

But her relief was tinged with a strange aftertaste. She'd never known how it felt, until now, to be embarrassed about who she was.

Chapter 16

'Welcome to Shock Box!' Tally cried, banging open the dingy basement door.

A wall of hot, beer-soaked air hit Dylan in the face. She felt an arm land around her neck.

'You'll either love it or you'll hate it,' Alice shouted in her ear. 'Since you're a Shock Box virgin, we're going to have to get you super wasted – just this once.'

'Oh, right, since usually none of us drink at all,' Dylan said, attempting to sound cheerful even though she was using every ounce of her willpower not to prowl the room for Jasper.

'Vodka shots for everyone!' Tally cried. 'Or, no, maybe tequila.'

'Or sambuca.'

'Oh, god, no, please not sambuca!' Dylan forced a giggle, covering her face with her hands. 'Last time I had that, I ended up deciding I'd been reincarnated as a dog and crawling all the way home.'

'Love it!' Alice cackled. 'Dill, you are so hilarious.'

Dylan caught Sonia glaring in her direction, but decided to ignore it. Actually, getting drunk sounded like a fucking awesome plan to her. It might take the edge off of seeing Jasper. And it might make this place look more like a club and less like, well, a shit-hole.

As if on cue, 'I Will Survive' blasted over the speakers.

'OMG, a Shock Box classic,' Tally shouted, throwing her arms in the air. She, Alice and Sonia immediately began gyrating like a trio of cool-girl clones. Their Day-Glo outfits shone like tropical fish under the club's ultra violet lights.

Dylan took stock of Shock Box while she went through the motions of dancing, too. The place was basically a low-ceilinged basement stuffed with underage boarding school teens, all wearing the Day-Glo uniform. It was like a giant American Apparel ad. There were crappy speakers, a plywood bar, rusty pipes criss-crossing the ceiling, and sticky stuff on the floor under Dylan's feet. Something plopped on to her hair. She looked up. Droplets of condensation were wobbling overhead, dripping every now and then on to the dance floor. A rain shower of collective sweat.

'Let's go find the boys and make them buy us drinks,' Tally said.

'This way,' Alice pointed. 'Tristan texted me to say they have a booth.'

The crew pushed their way through the dancing crowd, past a boy wearing neon-pink leggings and a shiny gold headband. He was grinding with a tall, pointy-nosed girl whose headband matched his. The couple jumped on each other.

'Ugh,' Sonia sniffed. 'Has anyone else had enough of Jamie Darlington and Yasmin de Fleury's snogfest? They haven't been able to keep their tongues out of each other's mouths ever since they got together at the Glamour Winter Fashion afterparty.'

Tally stared. 'It's like watching seals mating.'

'Yazz the Spazz.' Alice shook her head. 'Poor saddo. Jamie'll get bored of her eventually. Everyone does.'

'Why?' Dylan asked.

'Because—'

'Ali, watch out!' Sonia cried, throwing herself in front of her idol. Right in their path, a boy had jumped up and caught hold of one of the ceiling pipes. He was now improvising a dance that involved flailing his legs in the air, practically kicking bystanders in the face.

Alice gulped. 'Nice save, babe. That idiot could have broken my nose.'

'I know.' Sonia clutched her friend's arm. 'Not that a broken nose would have been so bad, Ali. We could have got matching nose jobs. Like twins.' She shot Dylan a triumphant look. If that New York fool thought she could steal Alice away by hijacking every single conversation, she was wrong. Sonia would always be there to protect her favourite person in the world from harm.

The boy on the pipes was now attempting to perform chin-ups in time to the music.

Mimah stared up at him. 'Freddie Frye, fucked off his head, as usual: check.'

'Didn't you almost snog Freddie Frye once?' Alice asked.

'Yeah. *Almost* being the operative word. He's rough.'

'He's not *that* bad. I was thinking – you didn't say who

108

you wanted to pull tonight. Maybe you could try him. Easy target . . .'

Mimah grimaced. 'No thanks. His teeth are bigger than my horse's.'

'So pick someone else then! Come on, Mime – who was the last person you snogged? It's been ages. You need some action.'

Mimah's eyes flicked off to the side. 'Hi, Charlie!' she called.

Dylan followed her gaze. Charlie Calthorpe de Vyle-Hanswicke and Georgie Fortescue had emerged from the crowd, trailed by two boys, one dark-haired and one blond. Something about the blond one seemed familiar.

'Hey, Mime!' Charlie kissed her sister on the cheek. 'You remember Felix, right?'

'How could I forget?'

Felix's cheeks turned pink. 'Hi, nice to meet you again, Jemimah. Um, thanks again for . . . umm . . . covering for us the other week. That was really generous.'

'*Generous?*' Mimah crossed her arms. 'I didn't do it for you.'

There was an awkward silence, luckily broken by a shriek from Alice.

'Hugo!' she called, catching sight of the blond boy. 'What a lovely surprise! Why didn't you tell me you were coming tonight?'

Hugo . . . Dylan shut her eyes. So that's where she'd seen him – he was Alice's younger brother, the blond boy in the photo in Lauren's dorm room. She watched as he squeezed his sister's shoulders. He was a few inches taller than Alice, even though Alice was one of the tallest girls in their year.

'Figured I'd see you here,' Hugo said. 'Anyway, I thought maybe if you knew I was sneaking out of school, you might try to stop me from aping your bad behaviour.'

'As if. You know T and I have been inducting you in the art of rule-breaking for the past fourteen years.'

'I'm *totally* not surprised to hear that,' cut in Georgie Fortescue. 'Hugo's the funnest person I've ever met. He's always up for sneaking out of school and doing completely mental things.' She tossed her hair and smiled seductively. 'Aren't you, Huggy?'

'I told you not to call me that!'

'Awww, you know you love it,' Georgie said, ruffling his hair.

Dylan thought she noticed Hugo recoil slightly, but it was hard to tell – the dance floor was packed, and everyone was being pushed to and fro. Alice had been grabbed by Sonia and was now jumping up and down to 'YMCA'. The DJ clearly loved his cheesy seventies hits.

'Hey, is my sister here?' she asked, turning back to the Year Tens.

'Who's your sister?' Georgie demanded.

'Um, Lauren Taylor? Your new dorm-mate?'

Hugo raised his eyebrows. 'I didn't know you had a new dorm-mate.'

'Yeah, we do. So?' Georgie pursed her lips. 'She's not here. Why would she be?'

'Oh, I just thought – you know, you might have brought her.'

'No. Oh, well. Sorry.'

'But – is she settling in OK? I haven't—'

'Sorry, can't hear you! Loud music,' Georgie bellowed, flashing a fake smile and slipping her arm through Hugo's. 'Coming, Charlie?'

'Yeah.' Charlie watched the others dance away, then looked at Dylan. 'What were you saying?'

'Oh, thanks for staying. I just want to check Lauren's OK. This whole boarding-school thing is totally new to her.'

'Yeah.'

'And our mom kind of just dumped her here so she could go off with her new boyfriend, and we never get see our dad anymore. Our lives have totally changed within the space of, like, three months. And . . . I just want her to be doing fine.' Dylan knew she should shut up. Pouring out your worries to a virtual stranger wasn't exactly the British custom. But Charlie seemed to be listening. 'Anyway, I'm sure Lauren's OK. I'm probably just being a paranoid big sister. Well, have a good night.'

'Yeah,' Charlie repeated. Her eyes seemed to be contemplating something in the middle distance.

'Um, OK, bye,' Dylan repeated. She started off in search of Alice. Someone trampled over her foot.

'Oops. Sorry,' Georgie Fortescue threw over her shoulder. 'Charl, darling! There you are – I thought you were behind me.' She jerked her thumb towards Dylan. 'What did *she* want?'

Charlie shrugged, her habitual give-a-shit sneer descending over her pale, elfin features. 'Nothing important.'

'Shocker. Here – I got you a rum and Coke. Double. We are gonna get waaasted!' Throwing back her head, Georgie downed her drink in one, her blond, bird's-nest hair flying out behind her. 'Watch this,' she slurred, shimmying towards Hugo, nestling her skinny hips against him.

Charlie did watch. She watched Georgie stumble over Hugo's feet in her too-high heels, wobbling like a newborn colt on her too-skinny legs. She watched Georgie's microscopic tutu skirt bounce up and down, up and down over her hips, flashing views of her skimpy pants. And she watched the lewd grins that Hugo and Felix exchanged over Georgie's head. She was glad that Georgie couldn't see them, too.

Chapter 17

'One, two, three, down!' shouted Sonia, and knocked back her fourth tequila shot, even though it was only quarter past ten. Sticking her arms out like aeroplane wings, she span round and round on the dance floor. 'Wheee!'

'Stop it!' Alice cried. 'You're making me dizzy.' She brushed Tristan's arm. The DJ, in one of his rare non-cheesy moments, was playing Florence + The Machine and T was dancing in his usual way, his chestnut eyes downcast, his lips arranged in a kissable pout, his hips rocking to the beat. 'Careful of your shoulder, babe. Isn't dancing against the doctor's orders?'

'Since when do I follow orders?' T said. With a slow, sexy smile, he tugged her close and kissed her. 'I wish I could tear your clothes off right here.'

'You'd never manage it,' Alice teased. 'Not with that sling on.'

'Oh, you'd be surprised.' T kissed her again and Alice snuggled closer, feeling the envious stares from the surrounding crowd. Everyone fancied Tristan Murray-Middleton – he attracted girls like flowers attracted bees – and it gave her a thrill to know what a high-profile couple

they were. Having a coveted boyfriend was half the satis-
faction of having a boyfriend at all.

The opening bars of 'Billie Jean' blared through the
speakers.

'Tune!' Alice cried, rocking her hips against T's.

'God, no,' he groaned. 'Michael Jackson is so main-
stream. Why can't they ever play alternative electro, or
something?'

'Because it's Shock Box – not Fabric.'

'Yeah. And it sucks.'

Alice rolled her eyes. 'Someone's being a downer.'

'No, I'm just saying – doesn't it strike you as ridiculous
that everyone's dancing to this shit music and pretending
it's good?'

'Or maybe,' Alice snapped, 'people are just enjoying
themselves and not worrying about being cool.'

'Oh, look who's talking,' T retorted. 'The Queen of
Cool, herself.' He turned away. 'You were right – my
shoulder is hurting. See you at our booth. Tally should be
back there by now with the drinks.'

'Fine.'

Frowning, Alice threw herself back into the circle with
Sonia, Rando and Seb. The floor was packed. She could
hardly move without hitting someone. Suddenly she was
thrown right up against Rando.

'Cosy, isn't this?' he said.

Alice giggled. 'What are you talking about? I've got
plenty of room.'

'By the way, have you seen my amazing Jacko move?'

114

Clearing a space around himself, Rando spun a pirouette on the tip of one foot.

'Nice! Been working on that at home, have you?'

'Maybe. Or maybe I was a rock star in a former life.'

'Or a ballerina.'

'Hey! Watch it.'

'Guys!' Sonia shrieked in Alice's ear, clearly wasted. 'Isn't this amaaazing? I love dancing!'

'Too bad you're rubbish at it,' Alice said.

'I feel like kissing someone!' Sonia screeched. Shooting out her arm, she hooked Seb's collar, dragged him towards her and planted her mouth on his. Seb's eyes bulged. Sonia tightened her grip.

'Help,' Alice groaned. 'I can't watch this.'

'Quick, over here,' Rando laughed, pulling her deeper into the crowd. 'Turn around. Don't look.'

'Ugh. Is there anything worse than the sight of two of your friends snogging?'

'I know! It's like, where are you supposed to look? Are you supposed to smile indulgently, like "Aww, isn't that sweet"'? Or ignore it – like you haven't noticed the people you were just talking to are suddenly saliva buddies?'

'Maybe you're supposed to blindfold yourself, like this,' Alice said, clapping her hand over Rando's eyes.

He smiled. Warmth blossomed in Alice's cheeks as she watched his dimples deepen. Her heartbeat quickened. She drew her hand away.

Rando looked down at her and, suddenly, his eyes grew serious, their laughter fading.

'There you guys are!'

It was Tally. She bounced over to them, her white-blond hair gorgeously tousled by the crowd. 'I've been carrying our drinks round forever. OMG, is that *Sonia and Seb*?'

When no one replied, she swivelled her gaze from her boyfriend to her best friend and back. 'Hello? You two! What have you guys been talking about? My Christmas present, I hope. I keep trying to drop subtle hints to Rando, but I don't think he's even paying attention. Are you, babe?'

'Huh?'

'To my Christmas pressie hints!'

'Oh, shit.' Rando grinned. 'You've been dropping hints?'

Alice watched as Tally swatted her boyfriend, gazing up into his eyes, flashing her radiant smile: the smile that sent all the guys crazy; the smile that irradiated her porcelain face and made her eyes sparkle like morning seas under the sun.

Alice cleared her throat as loudly as she could. 'Well, I could always help Rando out with your present.' She paused. 'And maybe Rando can help me choose something for T?'

'Oh, yeah.' Rando nodded. 'Sure.'

'I love it!' Tally clapped her hands. 'My BFF and my boyfriend shopping for my pressies together. Eee!' Standing on tiptoe, she brushed her lips against Rando's. He hooked an index finger into the waistband of her miniskirt.

116

Alice tore her eyes away. Her chest felt full, like she'd swallowed a balloon. What the hell was wrong with her?

'Hey!' Dylan tapped her on the shoulder. 'There you are. I lost you.'

'What? Oh. Yeah. Hey.' Glancing at her watch, Alice jumped to attention. 'Shit!'

'What's wrong? What time is it?'

'It's . . . It's time for you to buy us drinks! Shock Box virgins buy the first round.'

'Since when?'

'Since always. I'm sure I told you.'

'But you already have a drink.'

'Irrelevant! Since when do you make the rules? Hurry up – the bar's that way.'

'OK, booze-hound, I'm going.'

'Good. Oh, and Dylan!'

'What?'

'Make sure you go to the far left-hand side of the bar – it's emptier. Far left!'

Alice gazed after her for a few seconds, biting her lip. Then, shaking herself, she nudged Tally. 'I hate to interrupt, lovebirds, but Tally and I have to do something.' She tapped her watch. 'Tals? Coming?'

The loved-up gaze on Tally's face gave way to a sly smile as she saw the time: 10:28pm. 'Coming,' she grinned.

Rando raised an eyebrow. 'Where?'

'Don't you worry. We'll be back soon. Everything's under control.'

*

Dylan stood on tiptoe, attempting to catch the bartender's eye. The bar was a no-man's-land of sticky patches and beer spills, and she was determined not to touch it with any part of her body.

'Hello,' she waved. 'Excuse me? Hellooo?'

'Hellooo yourself,' breathed a voice in her ear. Dylan jumped. A set of hairy knuckles appeared on her arm.

'It's only me,' grinned George Demetrios. He flashed her a conspiratorial wink – which, combined with the fluorescent orange face-paint daubed across his cheeks, made him look insane.

'George! You shouldn't sneak up on people like that. Nice to see you, though.'

'Yeah. Fancy meeting you here. Heh, heh, heh.'

'Yeah. Ha, ha.' Dylan nodded and smiled, even though she had no clue what George's significant laugh was about. Maybe he was trying to share some kind of in-joke that she couldn't remember. She'd been drunk with Alice and the Hasted House boys a few too many times lately to recall all the ridiculous conversations she must have had. 'So, are you having fun?'

'Fun? Baby, my night didn't start till now.' Slicking back his hair, George leaned on the bar. He smelled like a cologne factory and was wearing enough hair gel to drown a small animal. 'What are you drinking? My treat.'

'Oh, thanks, that's sweet. But I'm supposed to get drinks for the girls. Maybe next round?'

'Forget about the girls. I'm sure they can wait. Our time

118

is here. Our time –' George wiggled his monobrow up and down – 'is *now.*'

Dylan suppressed the urge to giggle as she studied George's expression. Actually, Alice was right – he was kind of sexy. In a caveman-chic sort of way. And Tally was right about flirting with other guys – trying to make your ex jealous was one of the most basic rules of dating. Not that Jasper seemed to be anywhere in the vicinity. But maybe if she hung out with George Demetrios, she'd stop *thinking* about him so much.

'OK,' she conceded. 'Let's have a drink.'

'Excellent! What can I get you?'

'Vodka-cranberry juice, please.'

George gestured for the bartender. So far, so good. Dylan was looking fit. And, after all, he hadn't expected to snog her straight away. She needed some warming up – all babes did. Surreptitiously, he stroked his stubbly chin. It had been six hours since his last shave, which meant his face was already the consistency of sandpaper. His mum constantly assured him that hairiness was a sign of manliness – but, as far as he was concerned, it was a sign of not being able to pull girls. Having a prickly face definitely put chicks off snogging him on nights out. It was one of the banes of his existence. Hopefully, Dylan wouldn't mind. Maybe they could make a deal: if she promised not to mind about his stubble, he'd promise not to mind about her absurdly huge breasts. Girls got insecure about being large up top. He could probably use it as leverage. 'Chin-chin,' he said, raising his glass.

'Cheers. So, orange. Interesting . . .' Dylan was pointing at his top. 'Hard colour to pull off. I mean, it suits you.'

'Why, thank you. It suits me even more in the summer when I'm tanned. Did I tell you I spend most summers in Greece?'

'No.'

'Well, I do. My granny's got gorgeous olive groves that sweep all the way down to the sea. She makes the best stuffed vine leaves. You should come and stay this summer. Granny would love you.' George gulped down more of his drink. Talking about olive groves and sea: good. Talking about his granny: bad. Very bad. What the hell was wrong with him? Was Dylan making him nervous? He never got nervous around girls. Then again, he was usually pretty drunk whenever he talked to them.

'So, is that true? Is that really how they make it?' Dylan was asking. She'd obviously been rabbiting on about something. George assumed an attentive frown. It was never a good idea to let a chick know you weren't listening to a word she was saying.

'Yes, I believe it is,' he nodded sagely.

'Cool. I love olive oil. I've always wanted to go to Greece. I bet you'd be a really good tour guide.'

'Believe me,' George said, taking a step towards her, 'I am.'

In a far corner of the club, Tally squeezed Alice's arm. 'Scandalous!' she giggled. The girls were standing on a table, peering over the heads on the dance floor. 'He's practically feeling her up.'

120

'He's stroking her arm!'

'They'll totally be snogging in a second.'

'Too late. Look who's coming – right on time.'

Over by the bar, Dylan leaned closer to George Demetrios.

'You have nice hair,' he was saying, touching a strand. His fingers were gentle. And he was looking at her face instead of at her boobs, which made a change.

George let his hand drop to her waist. Dylan let her eyes meet his.

Then, suddenly, he staggered backwards. 'Owww!'

'What the fuck do you think you're doing?' Jasper von Holstadt yelled, yanking George round to face him. His cheeks burned with fury.

'What do you mean?' George grimaced.

'Trying to get off with my ex? Classy.'

'What do you care? You dumped her. She's fair game.'

Dylan opened her mouth to protest – but before she could, Jasper shoved George's shoulders. 'How dare you? Keep your hands off her! She's mine. And she wants to talk to *me*.'

'Doesn't look that way,' George jeered, shoving Jasper back.

Regaining his footing, Jasper drove a fist into George's stomach. George doubled over, then ran in for a head-butt.

'Stop it!' Dylan screamed. She skittered out of the way as the boys lurched towards the bar.

Crash! A glass capsized. Blood-coloured wine dripped over the fighters.

On top of their table, Alice clutched Tally. 'Shit! They weren't supposed to get violent. They were just supposed to think Dylan's a manipulative cow for leading them both on.'

'Don't worry, maybe they'll still think – Oooh!'

'Ow!'

Jasper had George's head in a lock. George stamped on his foot, then sprang up as soon as Jasper's grip eased off. His orange face-paint gleamed like war-paint.

'Aaargh!' he grunted, catapulting Jasper into a cluster of onlookers.

Tally clapped her hands to her mouth. 'Shiiit!'

Alice crossed her arms. 'It's not *fair*.'

'What?'

'Why don't boys ever fight like that over *me*?'

'Oh. My. God,' Tally guffawed. 'You planned this whole thing just to prove that you were the boss with the guys – and now it's making you jealous?'

'Shut up.'

'Lads!' the bartender was yelling. He'd finally noticed the fight amidst the general noise and chaos of the club. 'Knock it off. Right. Now!'

Panting, the boys fell back. George dabbed at his face. 'My cheek's bleeding, you dickhead,' he snarled at Jasper, stumbling towards the loos.

'Any more fighting and you're out of here!' the bartender called after him.

'We're out of here, anyway,' Jasper panted. He grasped Dylan's elbow and pulled her with him. 'Come on, now we can talk.'

Dylan, who'd been watching the violence in shock, suddenly snapped out of it, tearing her arm free. 'How dare you touch me!' she shrieked. 'How dare you act like you own me?'

Jasper recoiled. Finally he seemed to register Dylan's expression – her pale face, her eyes like burning coals on snow. His own eyes widened in alarm. 'Wait, I didn't mean—'

'Get away from me!'

'But . . . I thought . . . I was just trying . . . You said you wanted to talk.'

'Are you hallucinating? I never said that.'

'But, you did! I got a text. From Alice.'

Dylan's jaw dropped. But, quickly, she waved the confusion away. 'Whatever. Alice was probably just trying to help. She knows our break-up sucked. That doesn't mean you can treat me like a *thing* – a possession to fight over. I'm a human being!'

Jasper glared down at his fists without saying anything. The tip of his Converse trainer was torn. He stared at it, for some reason unable to focus on anything else.

'Well!? Are you just going to stand there like an idiot?'

'Excuse me?' Jasper snapped his head up. Women never yelled at him like this. His own mother didn't even yell at him. No way should he be putting up with it. 'Actually, no, I'm leaving now. I can't be bothered with this. I thought

I was doing you a favour, but obviously not. Have a nice life.' He wheeled on his heel.

Her heart swelling, Dylan watched the crowd close in around him. What had she just done?

She'd blown her one and only chance to get back together with the boy she loved.

Chapter 18

Charlie swept into the Dining Hall on a trail of frosty December air. The smell of woodsmoke in her nostrils was immediately replaced by the smell of sizzling bacon and frying mushrooms, and she smiled. Sundays at St Cecilia's were the best. The weekend newspapers were laid out on tables at the back of the hall. Coffee and tea were brewing in huge metal urns. And the cooks would be serving up eggs, sausages, baked beans, toast, waffles, and plenty of other brunch specialities well into the afternoon.

'But why not?' Georgie Fortescue was frowning into her phone. Her forehead creased as she listened. 'I wanted to see them, too, though. Oh. But I thought the whole family was – But, Mummy, it's a special occasion! You promised I could— Oh. OK. Yeah. Bye.'

'How's your mum?' Charlie asked.

Georgie shrugged.

'So . . . are you going home for her birthday next weekend, then?'

'No.' Georgie pursed her lips. There was a silence. She slid a cheese croissant off the pastry rack, inspected it, crinkled her nose and slid it back.

'Oh. Why not?'

'Because.' Georgie crossed her arms. Then she uncrossed them again. 'Hattie and Lavinia are both home from Bristol next weekend and Mummy wants to spend "quality time" with them. Alone. On her birthday.' She blinked rapidly, and it looked like her lower lip was quivering. 'We were all supposed to go out for this great family lunch. I spent ages picking out Mummy's present, and she doesn't even care. You should see my parents when my sisters are around – they start salivating like a couple of Great Danes. "Ooh, Hattie, we just knew you'd get the lead in the university musical. You clever thing. Ooh, Livs, your new boyfriend is so gorgeous and *so* well-connected. Exactly what you deserve, of course. You two are the best daughters in the world." They never say that stuff to me.'

Charlie squeezed her BFF's arm. 'Parents are so dumb.'

'At least *your* parents know you exist. Fine, they're fucked up. But did they pack you off to boarding school all by yourself at age six – just you and your suitcase in a car with the chauffeur? No. I swear, Mummy and Daddy don't even want me home during the holidays. If they could pay St Cecilia's to keep me here, they would. I don't know why they bothered having me at all.'

Charlie flicked her hair back. 'Well, maybe you were a mistake! You're seven years younger than Hattie and eight years younger than Lavinia. Mummy probably forgot to take her pill one day.' She grinned, then immediately regretted it as Georgie's face tightened, like a rubber band about to snap.

126

'Fuck off! You think that's funny?'

'N-no.' Charlie felt the blood rush to her cheeks.

'Oh, really? So why did you say it, then?'

'I don't know. I was just being an idiot. I'm sorry.'

'You should be. Does it make you feel good to be a bitch about other people's families, just 'cause your own is so fucked up?'

'Come on, George – don't be like that. I was only joking. I never would have said it if I thought it was true.'

'Yeah, well, next time, think before you speak,' Georgie said, glaring across the hall. A sly smile crept over her face. 'Ha, look who's eating all by herself.'

'Wait, where are you going?' Frowning, Charlie watched her friend stride off towards Lauren Taylor, who was sitting at an otherwise-empty table. She started after Georgie, then shrugged. It wasn't up to her to protect Lauren, no matter what Lauren's big sister said. And it definitely wasn't a good to idea to contradict Georgie Fortescue when she was in as foul a mood as this. The last thing Charlie wanted was more of her friend's bile directed at her.

'Oi! What are you writing?' Georgie said loudly. She slammed her tray into Lauren's. Tea sloshed everywhere. 'Oopsie. Accident.'

Lauren kept her eyes fixed on the table. But she snatched up the baby-blue book she'd been scribbling in and slid it on to her lap.

'Hoping I'll go looking for it under there, you lezzer?' Georgie cackled. 'You want me to go burrowing in your crotch for your dumb diary? You *wish* I wanted to read it.'

She moved her tray further down the table to where Charlie was sitting. 'Loser,' she smirked. 'Why are there so many uncool people in the world?'

'How's your hangover?' Charlie asked, trying to change the subject. 'Mine sucks. I've got the worst headache of all time.'

'Lightweight.' Georgie sipped her coffee. 'Did Felix give you any info?'

'About what?'

'About if Hugo likes me, obviously.'

'Oh. Not really.'

Georgie frowned.

'But, hon, guys don't really talk about that stuff. They're not like girls. Felix would probably think it was weird if Hugo, like, confided in him.'

'I thought you said Felix was sensitive.'

'Yeah – with me. But he and Hugo probably just talk about sports and stuff.' Charlie cleared her throat. 'Here's what I think: if Hugo likes you, and I mean really likes you and doesn't just want to sleep with you, then he probably wouldn't tell anyone. Trust me. It's a guy thing.'

'What, just 'cause you've had a boyfriend for, like, four weeks, you're suddenly the guy expert?' Georgie poked her chips and baked beans round her plate.

Charlie sighed. She clearly couldn't say anything right today – which sucked because, even though Georgie had her faults, she was Charlie's best friend. Only friend, in fact, since Charlie had dumped her old, goody-two-shoes group at the end of last year.

Suddenly, Georgie giggled.

'What?'

'Watch this.' Picking a baked bean off her plate, Georgie positioned it on her thumb and flicked it. *Plop*. It landed right on Lauren's ponytail. Lauren didn't notice.

'Genius!' Georgie doubled over with laughter. She flicked another baked bean, then another and another. 'Help me.'

Charlie blinked and watched as her friend smeared half a french-fry with ketchup and chucked it down the table.

'Come on, wuss!' Georgie prodded.

But before she could throw anything else, Lauren shoved back her chair and bolted for the Dining Hall doors. Charlie sighed and stared thoughtfully after her, picking out the globs of sauce and ketchup all over Lauren's cream cashmere jumper. She barely noticed the wolfish look Georgie cast at the baby-blue diary tucked under Lauren's arm.

Chapter 19

'Whose job was it to remember the cushions?' Tristan complained in a stoned voice, lying back on the cracked wooden bench. The old boat sheds, which he and Seb had adopted as their weed-smoking hangout, were strictly off-limits according to Hasted House school rules. They'd been replaced by shiny new sheds last year, leaving these models choked by pondweed and rotted with damp.

'Ouch. There are nails sticking out everywhere.'

'Careful, man,' Seb droned. 'That plank looks like it's gonna crack in two any—'

'Fuuuck!' T yelped, as he landed on the floor, the bench in pieces around him.

Seb burst into a high-pitched giggle.

Lolling his head to the side, T kicked his legs in glee. 'We should s-s-sue!' he gasped.

Seb adopted a lawyerly tone. '*We, the undersigned, testify that Hasted House school provided us with a dangerous, butt-ugly and altogether shit environment in which to smoke marijuana, thereby seriously endangering our health. Yours sincerely, Tristan Murray-Middleton and Sebastian Winston Patrick Ogilvy.*'

'Owww,' T half-laughed, half-groaned, 'the pain. I think I re-broke my collar bone.'

'Here, have another toke.'

'Thanks. I reckon we go to supper early, dash off our prep, then re-watch a bunch of episodes of *Mad Men*. I need to chill. I'm still hungover from last night.'

'I'm up for that.'

Hauling himself upright, T leant back against the dusty wall. 'I've gotta say, it's afternoons like this when I'm glad there are no girls at school with us. How nice is it to just chill and plan our own thing?'

'Agreed.'

'Speaking of girls – you and Sonia, Saturday night – what the hell happened?'

Seb rolled his eyes. 'She jumped on me.'

'Well, you want my advice, dude? Stay away from that chick. She's crazy.'

Seb's eyes bulged. '*That's* your advice? You've been trying to get me to snog Sonia for months and now you think I should stay away from her?'

T shrugged. 'The girl follows Alice round like a lapdog.'

'Oh, *really*? Your observational skills astound me.'

'Shut up, man. I believe in giving people chances, OK? But she's getting psychopathic. Last night, every time Al and I found somewhere private to hook up, Sonia hunted us out. She's like some kind of freak sniffer dog. Al and I barely got to second base. I touched her boobs for a total of five seconds.'

'Oh, great. I'm so glad you feel you can tell me all the graphic details of your sex life.'

Tristan giggled. 'Sorry, mate. But, seriously, if it wasn't for Sonia's crazy obsession with *you*, I might think she was a lesbian – desperate for a bit of Alice. Not that there's anything wrong with lesbians. If Sonia's one, she should just come out and say it. Loud and proud.'

'Yeah,' Seb murmured. He shut his eyes and dragged deeply on the joint, smiling as a mist wrapped itself round his brain.

T's voice floated out of the dusk. 'Why are girls so weird?'

'Yeah,' Seb mumbled happily.

So, Sonia could be a lesbian and T wouldn't care . . . Interesting . . . It felt to Seb like his thoughts were swaddled in safe, warm cotton wool. Out here in the old boathouse, in the semi-gloaming of the late afternoon, it would be so easy to tell T everything – T, his oldest friend. The words bobbed up and down like little boats on the sea of his thoughts. *Hey, man, you know how you just said girls are weird? Yeah, well, I sort of prefer boys. Like, you know when I kissed Tom Huntleigh at Rando's party? That was cool.*

Oh, you're gay. Awesome, man, fictional T nodded in his brain. *Glad you told me. I'm happy for you. Come on, let's get some dinner. I think it's spaghetti bolognese tonight . . .*

Seb rubbed his eyes.

'Hey, man,' he croaked. It felt like he hadn't used his voice in a while. He cleared his throat. 'You know how you just said—'

Ring ring. Ring ring.

132

'Shit!' Seb groaned, holding his head. 'What was that?'

'I think it's my phone.'

'Hang up on them. So, anyway, you know how you—'

Ring ring.

'Dude, dude, just a sec,' drawled Tristan, fumbling for his mobile. 'Uhhh . . . Hello?'

'Hi. It's me,' said the voice on the other end.

T giggled. '*It's Alice,*' he whispered loudly, his mouth still on the receiver. 'Whoa, baby, you sound like you're inside a rabbit hole. Say something else.'

'T? Are you OK?'

'Hahahaha!' Tristan cackled. 'You're, like, right in my ear, but you're, like, so far away. Awesome.'

'Tristan.' Alice sounded annoyed. 'Are you stoned?'

'No! I mean, yeah. So?'

'So, it's a Sunday – the teachers have nothing better to do than patrol the grounds. Be careful.'

'Hey, chill, baby girl. I never get caught.'

'"Chill, baby girl"? Ugh, I hate it when you talk to me like that.'

'Like what?'

'Like some random *babe* you think you can impress by being stoned. *I* know you care about your school record. So don't try to pretend you don't – not to me.'

Tristan blinked and sat up straighter. 'Hang on, I'm not pretending anything.'

But Alice was in full flow. 'You already missed a week of school because of your collar bone. What'll your dad say if you get suspended and have that on your record?

He's been going on about your "bright future" for your whole life. And, anyway, don't you want to go to New College, Oxford with me? How do you think that's gonna happen if—'

'Whoa, whoa, whoa.' Tristan stood up and rubbed his eyes. 'How did this become about Oxford and my dad? Did you call me just to pick a fight?'

'Of course not! I was just calling to say hi. Can't a girlfriend do that?'

'Um, obviously, but—'

'No, obviously not. Look, I'll talk to you soon. Enjoy your little stoning session. Bye.' Alice hung up.

T stared at the phone. 'What the fuck?'

'What?' Seb said.

'Alice. I don't get it. She just went off at me about nothing. What makes her think that's cool?' Tristan started pacing the tiny shed. '*And* we had a bit of a spat last night. God, at least with mates you know where you stand. You'd never go all mental on me like that, would you?'

Seb said nothing. The mist in his head had thinned a little and he shuddered, thinking of the confession he'd been about to make. It felt like stumbling back from a cliff's edge, peering down at the spot where you'd been about to jump.

'You'd think it'd be easy going out with your supposed "best friend",' T was ranting. 'Let me tell you, it's the opposite. It's always so fucking intense. Like, she knows everything about me and she isn't afraid to use it against me.'

'Yeah,' Seb nodded. 'Sounds tough.'

'It is!'

'OK. So why do you bother, then?'

'Huh?'

'Let me put it this way: are you happy?'

T shrugged. 'Yeah. I guess so. Of course.'

'Great. So, I'm curious – what's good about your relationship? And don't say "sex".'

T grinned. 'I wasn't gonna. OK . . . For example, the conversation we just had – it was annoying, but in the great scheme of things, it doesn't matter – because it's Alice. That's the good thing about going out with your best friend: the little things don't matter.'

Seb cocked his head. 'Uh, dude, I'm no relationship expert – but aren't the little things exactly what *do* matter?'

'What do you mean? The fact that we just had a bad conversation means we're not right for each other?'

'No. I'm just saying – the little things are what make life worth living – all the little moments. Think about it: how many seconds do you spend talking to Alice and smiling? And how many do you spend feeling pissed off inside? A puddle is just millions of drops of rain. Know what I mean?'

'I dunno . . .' Tristan scrutinised the stained, sagging floorboards of the boat shed. Then, grinning, he shook his head. 'Why are you grilling me all of a sudden?'

'You brought it up.'

'I did? Well, it's getting a bit deep for a Sunday night,

mate. No point in creating problems where there aren't any. Right?'

Seb shrugged.

'Enough of this deep philosophising shit,' T yawned. 'Let's go get some dinner. It's spaghetti bolognese tonight.'

Chapter 20

A few miles across the frosty fields, Sonia peered at Dylan from behind the Biology textbook she was pretending to read. Her shiny, glossed lips curved into a smirk. Dylan clearly thought she was being subtle by angling her computer towards the wall; she obviously hadn't noticed the fact that her entire screen was reflected in the mirror behind her. Unbelievable moron. Sonia watched as Dylan clicked through Jasper von Holstadt's photos on Facebook, a pathetic puppy-dog look in her eyes. *Click. Click. Click. Click.* It was like having a front-row seat at a stalker convention.

There was a tap at the door.

'Come in!' called both girls in unison.

'Hey.' Farah Assadi stuck her head inside, complete with cropped haircut and overly-smoky eye make-up. Sonia gave a quiet snort. The riff-raff that Dylan attracted to their dorm room was a constant drain on her tolerance levels.

'Farah!' Dylan said. 'I didn't know you were back from London yet. How was your weekend?'

Farah flashed a white-toothed grin. 'OMG. Scandalous. You know that club night I told you about at Whisky Mist? Ree-diculous. Then Rostam, that guy I'm seeing, took us to a private party on top of Centre Point. The views? Ree-diculous!'

'Ahem,' Sonia interrupted, staring pointedly at her book.

'Sore throat?' Farah asked. 'Anyway, Dill, I think I'm gonna go work on my Art project for Miss Baskin. Want to come with me? I hate being in the studio all by myself.'

'Really? I kind of like it.' Dylan shut her laptop. 'Sure, let's go. How's your idea shaping up?'

'It's all right.'

'*All right?*' Sonia cackled loudly. 'Are you sure? Don't you mean *ree-diculous?*'

'Ugh.' Farah rolled her eyes. 'How about your project, Dill? Have you decided yet what secret you're gonna explore?'

'*Secret* . . . Behind her book, Sonia's ears pricked up. She sat very still, like a highly trained international spy.

'Yeah. I have decided, actually,' Dylan said.

'Well?'

'It's a secret!'

'God, you don't have to take everything so literally,' Farah objected. 'It's a stupid Art project.'

'Yeah, well, my concept's kind of private.'

'*My concept's kind of private?* Do you know what you sound like? Well, mine isn't. I'm still doing the orgasm thing. And I don't give a toss who knows about it.'

'That's lucky, since you've told half the year,' Dylan laughed, leading the way out of the room.

Sonia jumped up as soon as the door shut behind them. So, Dylan had something she wanted to hide – meaning it was just a matter of finding out what. Best place to start? Her computer. Sonia opened the MacBook and her neatly made-up eyes narrowed as she saw that Dylan had logged out. Obstacle number one: maybe the bitch wasn't as dumb as she looked. Fine. She'd start with Dylan's clothes, instead.

Sliding open the top drawer of her room-mate's dresser, Sonia wrinkled her nose. Her own underwear collection was arranged into subsections of colour and type, folded into adorable woven boxes that she'd made her mother buy from the Conran Shop. Dylan's underwear drawer was a horror show. Super-sized bras were tangled up with lacy hot-pants, woolly tights and fuzzy socks. Gross. Using the tips of her fingers, she extracted a double-D-cup monstrosity printed with teeny red blossoms. It looked like a genetic underwear mutant.

'What are you doing?' Alice asked.

Sonia staggered backwards. Her idol was standing in the doorway. 'What? Nothing. Why?'

'Oh, no reason. Just that you're holding up a bra that's about fifty sizes too big for those little pea-sized things you call your boobs. And I'm pretty sure that's Dylan's dresser and not yours.'

'No. It's mine.'

'Oh, really?' Alice pointed. 'Remind me, when was the last time you wore that particular pair of American-flag pants?'

'OK, fine, it's Dylan's. I lent her a . . . a pair of cashmere socks and I wanted them back. Brrr. Yeah, my feet are so cold.'

Alice folded her arms. '*You* lent *Dylan* some socks? You – the most anal person about foot fungus in the world? Yeah. Right. And, by the way, the only thing you'd ever lend Dylan is a knife to cut her throat.'

'I resent that! I'm a kind and generous room-mate. By the way, Al, how do you think Dylan got caught in the middle of that stag fight at Shock Box? Do you think it's 'cause she's a complete slapper?'

'I don't know.' Alice plopped down on the bed. 'I don't care. I don't give a shit about Dylan Taylor!' Suddenly heaving a teary sigh, she covered her eyes with her hands. 'Oh my god, why can't I find Tally and Mimah when I need them?'

Sonia immediately dropped Dylan's hideous bra and raced over to her BFF. 'Darling! What's wrong? What do you need Tally and Mimah for when you've got me?'

'I just had the most fucking annoying fight with T on the phone.'

'Ohhh, babe, why? What happened? Did you guys break up? If you did, it's OK, we can both be single girlies together. We can drink red wine and smoke ciggies and watch—'

'Of course we didn't break up,' Alice huffed.

'Oh. What happened, then?'

'Just . . . I don't know. T was stoned.'

'He's always stoned.'

'I know. It's not that. For some reason he was pissing me off. He's constantly pissing me off at the moment. I don't know how to stop it.'

'Babe, you've obviously got PMS.'

'Oh, shut up – you sound just like a boy. Boys always blame everything on fucking PMS. And, by the way, no.'

'OK, well, maybe you need to rekindle your romance! Invite him round for a romantic dinner. Create some private time just for the two of you. Light candles. Get out the aromatherapy oils. Slip into your sexiest lingerie. And try to communicate how special he—'

Alice gave a strangled scream. 'WTF?' she gurgled. 'Am I having aural hallucinations, or did you just turn into the blandest possible *Cosmo* advice column? Do you seriously expect me to do any of that shit?'

Sonia pouted. 'I don't know. I was only trying to help. I thought that article was good. I read it when I was still thinking about seducing Seb – which, by the way, I've now got out of my system. I don't think he's a very sexy kisser. Is T a good kisser? Or is he a bit too forceful and, well, un-passionate?'

'Argh!' Alice sprang to her feet. 'That is so not a helpful question to ask right now, Sonia. I knew I shouldn't have bothered talking to you about this. Look, I'll see you at supper, OK?'

She fled the room, clenching and unclenching her fists. Sonia clearly didn't understand – no one would. And the only thing she herself understood was this: she'd better get over her confusion pretty soon, or her life would come tumbling down, brick by brick by brick.

Chapter 21

'No, this should be minus fifteen, not plus fifteen, see?' Mimah said in a hushed voice, pointing at Aidan's Maths textbook. It was Thursday afternoon in the crowded classroom at the Community Centre and Mimah had decided to spend their second tutoring session working on quadratic equations. It had been a long, arduous slog. 'I get the feeling you're not paying attention.'

Aidan rubbed his eyes. 'Shit, yeah. I need coffee. I'm gonna take a vending-machine break. I mean,' he smiled wryly, 'if teacher doesn't mind.'

'Fine.' Mimah looked at her watch. 'Actually, it's already eight – shall we just skip the last half hour?'

Aidan cocked an eyebrow. His long legs barely fit under the desk. 'Trying to cheat me of my money's worth, eh?'

'Yeah, obviously, considering this is totally *free*. I'm a volunteer, remember? A community hero.'

'Oh, sure.' Aidan studied her. 'Well, community hero, why don't we split to Starbucks and finish off our session over some bourgeois caffeine sludge?'

'Uh . . .' Mimah blinked. Why was Aidan asking her out for coffee? And even more bizarre, why was she tempted to go? She calculated in her head: half an hour at Starbucks, plus a five-minute walk to the bus stop – she could still get back to school in time for her Thursday night sign-in with the Ho . . .

'Oi, what's the hesitation?' Aidan stood up and hooked his jacket off the back of his chair. 'It's not like I'm asking you on a date. But, yes – don't worry – I'm buying. I'm the one with a job.'

'OK. Thanks. The thing is, money's a bit tight for me right now,' Mimah said, trying to match Aidan's long strides as they headed down the corridor towards the foyer. 'Mum lost one of her night-jobs, so we can't afford many luxuries.' She sucked her face into her best impression of an 'I'm-poor' look – the kind of look you sometimes saw on people who shopped at tacky places like Primark – and shrugged apologetically. This townie façade was a piece of cake.

Aidan was looking at her quizzically. 'Your mum lost one of her jobs?'

'Yeah.'

'But I thought you said your mum abandoned you when you were a baby?'

Shit. Mimah rubbed her nose, trying to buy some time. 'Oh, yes, she did. I was talking about my granny just now. See, I call my granny "Mum" – she's always been like a mother to me.'

'Your grandmother works multiple night jobs?'

Mimah cleared her throat. 'Um, yeah. She's the age of most people's mums, anyway. It gets quite confusing. Sorry.'

Aidan shook his head. 'That's OK. Families are the craziest things, aren't they? I reckon you'd be hard-pressed to find someone who didn't have an interesting family background.'

'Agreed.'

He cast a glance at Mimah as they exited into the cold night. 'You're looking quite tarted up, by the way. More than last week, anyway.'

Mimah glared at him, struggling not to blush. It felt like this was the first time Aidan had looked at her all evening. And OK, maybe she had made something of an effort – wedged knee-high boots, tight jeans, a cool green parka – but obviously not for him. 'I'll take that as a compliment,' she said, flicking her fringe.

Starbucks was just a few doors down from the Community Centre on the street that ran along the edge of Hasted Common.

'You get a table,' Aidan said, striding inside and practically letting the door shut in Mimah's face. 'I'll get the coffees.'

'Oh, yes, sir. I just love taking orders. And, by the way, I'd like a hot chocolate – no whipped cream – thanks for asking.' Mimah slid into a deep leather easy chair and furrowed her forehead. Aidan's back was turned to her as he waited for their drinks, and she took the leisure of studying him – the ironic slant of his shoulders, the messiness of his hair, the muscles carved into his arms. Four hours – that was how long she'd known him now, and he was still the same terse, arrogant townie who'd stormed away from her desk last week. So what the hell was she doing here – in a dingy Starbucks on a Thursday night in the grimiest part of Hasted?

'You know,' Aidan said, sinking into the adjacent chair and sliding over her hot chocolate, 'I can't work you out.'

Mimah inhaled the delicious steam. 'I was just thinking the same thing about you.'

'Me first.'

'Don't you mean *ladies* first?'

'No, that would disqualify both of us.' Aidan grinned.

Mimah blinked. This was the first genuine smile she'd seen from him, and it gripped her by the shoulders and shook her, hard. His sardonic face became a canvas of light. Little creases appeared round his eyes and at the corners of his mouth. She swallowed her drink too quickly, scalding her throat.

'All right?' Aidan asked. 'Not used to drinking things in public?'

'Shut up.'

'Good comeback. So, here's my problem: you and your volunteering. I just don't get the impression you're the kind of girl who'd volunteer out of the goodness of her heart. It doesn't make sense.'

'Gee, thanks. What gave you that completely mistaken impression?'

'Well, first of all, what you said about not wanting to be here last week – that was a clue. A subtle one, but I'm good with subtlety.' Aidan grinned again. 'Honestly, I reckon you're too cynical for the whole "giving back" thing.'

'Thanks – again.'

'You're welcome. I think there's a different reason behind your tutoring hobby, and I'm going to find out what it is.'

'You do that,' Mimah said, kicking her feet on to the coffee table. 'And let me know when you have your answer, because I'll be interested to know what absurd fiction you've come up with.'

Aidan yawned.

'Bored, are you?'

'No. You're better company than you look. I had a late night last night.'

'What were you doing?'

'Just hanging out with some mates. Did a bit of studying. But I didn't finish work at the garage till almost nine.'

'You work at a garage?'

Aidan shrugged. 'I work lots of places – none of them matter. Like I told you, my goal is to be an engineer.'

'So, how come you dropped out of school, then? What happened to taking A-levels when you were still on track?'

'I was never on track.'

'What does that mean?'

Aidan stared into his black coffee. 'I was a troubled kid, OK? My dad – well, I don't want to talk about him. Let's just say I'm glad he's not in my life. A bit like your mum, I suppose.'

Mimah dropped her eyes.

'Anyway, I had a few discipline problems. I got kicked

out of some schools. Doesn't mean I was stupid, though, all right?'

'I never said you were stupid.'

Aidan bit his lip. 'No. You didn't. Sorry. So!' he said brightly. 'Your turn. Go on – impress me with your ambitions,'

Mimah hesitated. 'Haven't really thought about it,' she said, examining her fingernails. There was no question of telling Aidan about Cambridge – it would blow her cover wide open. 'Something to do with Physics, probably. It's my favourite subject – the problem-solving, the potential for new discoveries. I honestly love it.' Mimah didn't bother to stop herself; surely talking about Physics wouldn't give her away? 'I probably sound like a weirdo. I mean, being passionate about numbers and formulae and stuff – it's not really normal, is it?'

Aidan was watching her intently. 'No, I guess not. But who ever said you were normal? And *that* you don't even have to *take* as a compliment – I'm giving it to you as one.'

Mimah said nothing. She could feel his eyes on her, and for some reason she felt compelled to look anywhere but at him. Her glance fell on her watch. 'Oh, shit!' she gasped.

'What?'

'It's so late. I've missed my bus back to sch – I mean, back home.'

'That's OK. Just call your granny. It's not like you're five years old.'

Mimah jumped up and pulled on her coat. 'No! It doesn't

work that way. She . . . She worries. Fuck, I'm in such trouble. I've got to run.'

'Where do you live? Maybe I'm walking that way, too.'

'No. You aren't.' Slowing down, trying to be calm, she shot him a smile. 'I'm not the kind of girl who gives out her address to strangers. But see you next week. Same time, same place.'

Throwing the words over her shoulder, Mimah hurried out of the café and bolted across the Common to the taxi rank.

'St Cecilia's school, please,' she panted to the driver, scrambling into the seat, slumping back against the headrest. Eventually, she smiled a slow, dry smile. Thank goodness Aidan couldn't see her now.

Chapter 22

Tally inched her hand sideways and dropped a note on to Alice's desk.

Laying down her pen, Alice pinched the paper between her fingertips and unfolded it as stealthily as possible. Mrs Hoare had a gift for spotting shady activity in her English lessons, even though her eyes were as small and squinty as a rodent's.

Can't wait for our double date tomorrow night!! What you wearing?

Alice slipped the note under her file without replying.

'Conflicting interests,' Mrs Hoare declared. The teacher was weaving her copy of Shakespeare's *Julius Caesar* in the air. 'This play is full of them. For example, the conflict between public and private.'

Conflicting interests. Play full. Public. Private. Alice did her best to scribble down every key word that escaped the Ho's mouth. And any word that might prove to be a key word on closer examination. Then she highlighted each one with a different coloured pen. Examining boards loved it when you worked key words into your essays. They ate them up, like dogs gobbling doggie treats.

149

Another note landed on her desk.

Bella Scott says the martinis at the Wolseley are deelish!! I'm gonna surprise Rando with my new La Perlas!!! He loves the feel of silky undies. What OUTFIT you gonna wear???

Alice crumpled this bit of paper, and shot Tally a smile that probably came out more constipated than enthusiastic. She didn't quite understand why her best mate was getting so excited about the whole double-date-in-London plan. For some reason, it had been Tally's pet project all week. 'Babe, did it ever occur to you how cool it is that we're both in couples now?' she'd gushed after Shock Box last Saturday. 'This simultaneous boyfriend thing – it's never happened before. We should make the most of it.'

The Ho was now pacing between the rows of desks. 'Pay particular attention to how the characters divide their lives into public and private. There's the self they choose to show the world. And then there's the self they choose to keep behind closed doors.'

Divide lives. Choose. Closed doors, Alice wrote, trying to ignore Tally's chipper mood.

'And this,' said the Ho, folding her arms across her flat chest and smiling sourly at her pupils, 'brings me to your assignment for the weekend. Quiiiet,' she growled, as a collective groan rose from the class. She pointed to some essay questions on the whiteboard, raising her voice over the end-of-lessons bell. 'On Monday, I expect a thousand words from each of you exploring one of these topics. No excuses. Detention for anyone who thinks they can slip one past me.'

'What a bitch,' Alice mumbled, clapping her file shut. 'How the hell did we end up with her as our English teacher *and* our Housemistress? Let's get out of here.'

'Tally,' Mrs Hoare called, 'will you stay behind, please?'

Tally cast a nervous look at the teacher.

'Don't worry. I want to discuss your essay on *Portrait of a Lady*. It was quite an impressive piece of work.'

'Oh, sure, Mrs Hoare. Thanks very much.'

Alice slammed her bag on to the desktop. Tally was always being praised in English. It was a new development as of this school year, and it was annoying.

'See you outside,' she whispered. 'I thought we could sneak into Hasted and have a glass of wine at the pub. I'm fed up with Friday nights at school. We'll leave as soon as you're done with the monster.'

'Oh, sweetie, I'd love to,' Tally said, 'but I can't. I want to finish reading *Julius Caesar*.'

'Wow. I mean, thrilling as that sounds, I thought you wanted to look round the shops for presents for Rando.'

'Yeah, I do, but we'll be in London tomorrow, anyway. I can shop there.'

'Oh. Right.'

'Tally!' called Mrs Hoare. 'We haven't got all night.'

'Sure, run along.' Alice swung her bag over her shoulder. 'Enjoy your suck-up chat.'

Outside, the evening was beautiful – the last strains of pinkish afternoon light tinting the Great Lawn, a mist of woodsmoke drifting over the fields – and Alice inhaled a cold, sharp lungful. School was feeling smaller and smaller as term dragged on – the barbed gates caging everyone in; the regimented hours, day after day after day. She was so ready for the holidays and a fresh scene.

Turning towards Tudor House to drop off her school books, Alice paused. Maybe she should go to Hasted by herself. Tristan had Latin last thing on Fridays. His Latin lessons took place at an eccentric old teacher's house in town and, if she ran, she could surprise him on his way out. Maybe they'd get to spend some quality time alone before tomorrow's date – before they were thrust on stage in front of Tally and Rando as a supposedly model couple.

A change of clothes, a touch of make-up and a jog across the fields later, Alice found herself in Hasted. The windows of Estelle's Café, famous at St Cecilia's for its decadent hot chocolate, were garlanded with Christmas lights and piled with homemade mince pies. A few doors down, the White Hart pub was advertising 'Mulled Wine to Warm Your Cockles'. Alice's feet came to a standstill. A vision had popped into her head: her and Tally at this time last year, walking down this exact street. They'd been shopping for dresses for Lucian Scott's party and gossiping about Alice's huge new crush on a Glendale's boy called Gerald Coombes. The crush had burned out within two weeks, once she realised Gerald was a party boy on a mission, more into himself and his *awesome* dancing skills than any girls – but the memory had hit her like a flood.

Alice shut her eyes. That was the funny thing about holidays like Christmas: they acted as anchors among all the other nameless, drifting days of the year, giving you specific moments to take stock of your life. This time last year, she'd never even thought of T as a boyfriend. He was just her oldest, closest friend, to confide in and ask advice. This time last year, she hadn't even known Rando existed. He was just Jasper's cousin, far away at school in Scotland, a name without a face.

Alice paced ahead. Why the hell was she thinking about Rando? She was looking for Tristan – which was lucky, since that crazy Latin teacher's house was just round the corner.

'Hey!' A head popped out of the shop she was passing. 'Alice! What are you doing here?'

'Rando!' Alice halted in surprise. 'I was just thinking about you. I-I mean . . . What are *you* doing here?'

'I'm buying new drumsticks. Rivell's is the best music shop in town and mine are a bit worn out. The Paper Bandits have been practising loads lately – Tristan's a slave-driver. So, what are you up to?'

'I was looking for T, actually. I wanted to surprise him after his Latin lesson. Do you know if they got out yet?'

Rando nodded. 'Lessons let out fifteen minutes ago. But T's not in town – I just bumped into him on my way out of school – he and Tom Huntleigh were off to the Common Room to watch some Argentinian football match on Sky.'

'Oh. Football.' Alice gave an exaggerated eye-roll. 'Wouldn't want to interrupt football. Guess I'll just head back to school.'

'You could do that. It'd be a waste of an opportunity, though, wouldn't it?'

Alice eyed him keenly. 'What do you mean?'

'Nothing. Just, you're here now – why not let me buy you a drink instead? I'm sure T would be livid if he found out I'd seen you and let you wander home alone.'

'Oh, I . . .' Alice floundered. Then she looked at Rando's smiling face, his dimpled cheeks, his nose lightly peppered with freckles. 'OK,' she said. 'I suppose one drink couldn't hurt.'

Chapter 23

By the time Rando had led Alice into the back streets of Hasted, zigzagging through lanes and alleyways, the weather was beginning to turn. Not a sudden change, but a subtle one – a darkening of the sky, a gathering of vapours, a heightened tension in the breeze – like the first shadings of a frown on someone's face. Alice shivered in her short leather jacket.

'Hey, I didn't even know Hasted had all these weird little roads. Where are you taking me? We're right by the river, aren't we?'

'Yep.' Rando's blue-green eyes sparkled. 'And it's a surprise. A place I discovered a couple of weeks ago when I was wandering round town taking arty photos.'

'Oh, great,' Alice giggled. 'Why didn't you warn me you were a pretentious loser?'

Rando grinned. 'Because I knew you wouldn't come for a drink. Anyway, taking arty close-ups of cobblestones is not pretentious. You've obviously never noticed the profound nuances of the pavements.' Turning another corner into a cul-de-sac, he stopped. 'Found it!'

'Cool,' Alice said. They were standing in front of a tiny

old pub with a whitewashed exterior, diamond-paned Tudor-style windows, and a weathered wooden sign over the door. Its painted letters read 'The Crow's Nest'. 'Looks gorgeous.'

'I know. I'm glad I ran into you – I've been waiting ages for someone to show it to.'

'How about Tally?'

Rando tugged at the collar of his navy coat. 'Well . . . yeah . . . I'm not sure it's Tally's kind of place. It's a bit *country*, if you know what I mean. She's more into trendy cocktail bars. She's got that whole "I-grew-up-in-Moscow" thing going on – which is great and everything. I just thought she might not *get* this place.'

Alice nodded, biting her lip, trying to ignore the pit of unease in her stomach. Maybe she should tell Rando that Tally probably would like this place. Or that he should at least let Tally decide for herself. But, no, why should she? It was none of her business. She stepped inside, and stopped short.

'Looks like you weren't the first person to discover this place after all!' she yelled into Rando's ear as a whirlwind of noise and warmth boiled around them. 'It's rammed.'

'I can't believe it!' Rando bundled up the paper bag containing his new drumsticks and stuck it in the back pocket of his jeans. 'Whenever I think I've found some hidden gem that's totally off the radar, someone else gets there first. Maybe we should go somewhere else.'

'No way. This place is awesome. I love all the crazy low beams and stuff.'

'It is cool, isn't it? How about those old cast-iron pots hanging from the ceiling? I tried to take pictures of them when I first came here, but it was too dark.'

'You could always come back with a tripod. Look.' Alice pointed to the big old fireplace, which had a broad ledge running round it, covered in cushions. 'I bet we could squeeze in over there. Shall we splurge on a bottle of shitty pub wine?'

'A bottle?' Grinning, Rando raised his eyebrows. 'Controversial. Trying to get me drunk?'

'Yeah, right.' Alice poked him in the ribs. 'You're my best mate's boyfriend.'

'And you're my best band-mate's girlfriend,' Rando said, flashing his cheeky grin. 'So I suppose we're safe.'

Alice fumbled with her scarf. Somehow, it seemed to have caught her neck like a noose. 'Yeah, whatever; I doubt we'll drink it all,' she said, her cheeks flushed with the effort of disentangling herself. 'We've both got Saturday-morning lessons tomorrow.'

Five minutes later, they were perched near the crackling fire with their drinks. Rando tucked one of his legs underneath him and held up his glass. 'Cheers,' he said.

'Cheers.' Alice picked a thread out of her cushion. Suddenly, everything felt awkward. This was the first time she and Rando had been alone together since they'd met back in September, and it was weird. What if they had nothing to say to each other? What if the silence stretched and yawned into an earth-swallowing chasm?

'So!' she burst out, just to make a noise. 'What's it like

having Jasper as a cousin? Were you guys close growing up?'

Rando shrugged. 'Pretty close, back when we were kids. But the past ten years, before I came to Hasted House, we'd hardly seen each other at all.' Leaning back against the stone chimney, he swirled his wine. Dimples creased his cheeks. 'We used to spend every holiday together – at his family's place in Germany, or my family's place in Scotland. He's six months older, so he used to love lording it over me.'

'I can imagine. So, I take it he was always as arrogant as he is now?'

Rando's dimples deepened into a full-on grin. 'Oh, you noticed the old von Holstadt ice-king demeanour? Yeah, Jas has always had kind of a regal thing going on.' He chuckled. 'To be honest, this term's been good for our friendship. I feel like I've really got to know him.'

'And?'

'I think he's changed.'

'How?'

'He's so much less arrogant, for a start. I reckon that's Dylan's influence.'

'Dylan's influence?' Alice sputtered.

'Yeah. Jasper was used to getting exactly what he wanted until she came along. She challenges him, I think.'

'Excuse me,' Alice snapped, 'but did you not see Jasper attack George at Shock Box the other night? That was *"Dylan's influence"* for you.'

'That had nothing to do with Dylan. It's not her fault if two guys like her.'

'Of course it's her fault!' Alice glared into her wine. How could Dylan possibly have survived the Shock Box plot with her reputation intact? 'She craves male attention. She's never happy unless she's leading men on and stealing everyone else's limelight. I mean, it's kind of slutty, don't you think? Personally, I don't get what guys see in her.'

'Whoa,' Rando said. 'Someone has a grudge. What did Dylan ever do to you?'

'Nothing,' Alice grumbled. There was a silence. She tore a corner off the wine label and chucked it in the fire. Maybe she should give up on trying to sabotage Dylan. It clearly never worked. And, anyway, Tally was right – she did quite like Dylan now.

Rando chuckled.

'What's so funny?' Alice said.

'Nothing. Just, I never knew you had such an argumentative side. It's nice to get to chat properly – especially before the Big Double Date tomorrow night.'

'Oh, yeah.' Alice finished her wine. 'You looking forward to that?'

'Honestly?'

'Of course, honestly. You think I want you to lie?'

'Fine.' Rando poured another round from the bottle. 'Then, no.'

'You grouch!' Alice giggled, poking him.

'You asked! You've gotta understand, I've had terrible experiences of double dates. Last time I went on one, the other couple had a huge fight and broke up at the table.'

'Seriously? Over what?'

'Steak tartare.'

Alice guffawed. 'How can you break up over steak tartare?'

'Oh, very easily, apparently. The girlfriend didn't want her boyfriend to order it – she was terrified he'd get some horrific raw-meat parasite and then transfer it to her while they were having sex – which is obviously impossible. He ordered it, anyway, so she threw her fork at him, told him he was dumped and stormed out.'

'No way! And did he get a horrific parasite?'

Rando laughed. 'I have no idea, you weirdo. I hadn't even thought about it.'

'So what's the moral of your story? Double dates are just excuses for couples to air their dirty laundry in front of each other?'

'Exactly. But Tally's got her heart set on tomorrow night . . .'

'. . . and Tally can be very persuasive, so . . .'

'Aha!' Rando grinned. 'I can see I'm talking to the expert. Tally's got a huge determined streak, hasn't she?'

'Yep.' Alice draped a curtain of her shiny, chocolate-brown hair over her shoulder and held out her glass for more. '"Determined" runs in the family. Her mum's a ruthless Moscow socialite who works in TV and has no time for Tals whatsoever. And her dad's a City cokehead who lives in London with his pushy new wife. She doesn't exactly come from a line of shrinking violets.' Taking a sip of wine, Alice ran her tongue over her teeth to make sure she wasn't getting red-mouthed-monster syndrome. 'It's why we love her, though, right?'

'Yeah.' Rando stared into the fire. 'Poor Tals. Her family life sounds awful. She refuses to talk about it, though.'

'I know. She prefers her whole *I'm-a-glamorous-perfect-person-with-no-baggage-whatsoever* façade. Basically, Tally's problem is simple: she has no role model. It's just *sooo* Freudian. That's why the whole thing with Mr Logan got so out of hand.'

Rando frowned. 'What thing with Mr Logan?'

'Oh . . .' Alice's stomach lurched. Maybe she should ease up on the vino. Maybe she should stop running her mouth off. She should definitely not have mentioned Mr Logan, their hot young ex-English teacher who Tally had kissed earlier in the term. That would be a scandal she couldn't control.

'What thing?' Rando repeated.

'Oh, nothing. There wasn't a thing.'

'But you just said there was.'

'No, I just meant . . . only that Tally can be kind of wild.' Rando twisted his wine glass by the stem.

'But, like we said, it's all part of her charm. Right?'

Rando nodded. But he didn't look convinced. He looked faraway. He was staring at the floor, at some point beyond his black-and-white check Vans. Then, suddenly, he raised his eyes. 'You're a good friend to Tally, you know that?'

Alice started to shake her head.

'No, really. I've seen the way you are with her. I've seen the way you look out for her and protect her. I don't think you realise how important you are in her life. I'm not even sure she realises. But you're . . . you're . . .' Rando's blue-green gaze burned into her hazel one.

'What?' she whispered.

Rando swallowed. 'Ignore me. I'm talking crap. Shall we have another?' he murmured, grasping their empty bottle.

Alice could only nod. Her heart was pounding so hard it felt like her ribs might crack. She screwed her eyes shut, watching the firelight dance inside her lids all the while that Rando was at the bar.

'It's funny,' she said when he came back. 'I was just thinking, this is the first time the two of us have been alone. I mean, for longer than five seconds.'

'I know.' Rando ran a hand through his hair. 'I'm glad. I mean, that we're finally getting to talk.'

'Really?'

'It's so weird,' he went on. 'It's like, you see people at parties and you get drunk and dance and joke around, and you think of them as friends. But you hardly know them. I hate that. I never feel like someone's really my friend unless I've actually *talked* to them.'

'What, like, had a conversation?'

'Yeah, but I mean a genuine conversation. Not just chatting shit or gossiping. I want to know things about people – real things, that surprise me or give me an insight into their lives.'

'Wow.' Alice swung her leg against the ledge. 'I think that would eliminate half the people I call my friends.

We've always hung round in groups, ever since we've been at school. Take George Demetrios – I don't think I've ever met up with him by himself, but I've been to his house in Greece. I know his family. He's one of my so-called "good friends".'

'I have friends like that, too. I guess it's all part of being at school. Sometimes I think the only way we'll know who our real friends are is who we still ring in five years' time.'

Alice looked at Rando's profile. His skin was pale, almost translucent – so different from Tristan's tanned complexion.

'You think about these things a lot, don't you?' she said.

'I guess I do. I don't know why. My mum says I take after my dad – always over-thinking everything. Romanticising people. Expecting too much from my friendships. You know, my dad's a historian? He writes books that other historians read and then rave about. He spends hours and hours alone in his study, interpreting and reinterpreting relationships that happened centuries ago. So, I guess it's no wonder I do the same for ones that are happening today.'

Rando's profile was still turned to Alice. She was still watching it. 'Does it ever make you feel insecure, having such a clever dad?'

'A little.' Rando shrugged and took a gulp of wine. 'Not really. Mostly it makes me feel proud. And ambitious. Like, maybe if I work as hard as him, I can do great things, too.'

'God, you're lucky,' Alice sighed. 'My family has the opposite effect. They make me feel this huge, impossible pressure to be perfect. Actually, no, not even perfect – just worthwhile.' She clenched her toes inside her soft leather boots. She didn't know why she was saying this; she'd never said it to anyone before – not even T. But she realised as the words left her mouth how true they were.

'My brother, Dom – he's the oldest. He's gorgeous and cool and charming. He could charm his way into Buckingham Palace, even if he was wearing a balaclava and brandishing a gun.'

Rando laughed.

'Then there's Hugo – the baby – the sweet, angelic one. He's Mummy's favourite. And then there's me: the middle child *and* the only girl – two black marks against me in the book of family life. Mummy's desperate for me to grow up and get out with as little fuss as possible. Daddy's desperate for me go to Oxford. He wants me to save the family name after Dom failed to get in. He'll probably disown me when they don't even let me past the door.'

Rando raised his eyebrows. 'Have you ever talked to him about it?'

'Oh, that just proves you've never met my dad. No one ever talks about anything in our family.'

'I bet if you talked they'd listen. You're a hard person to ignore.'

'Yeah, right. I'm easy to ignore. Just ask my mum.'

'I don't need to ask anyone. I can see for myself.' Rando leaned forward, his elbows on his knees. 'How could anyone ignore you? You're one of the coolest girls I've ever met. You're clever and funny and genuine and vulnerable and . . . and beautiful—' He cut himself off. 'And you have a boyfriend who deserves you.'

Alice hardly heard this last sentence. Rando thought she was beautiful? But Rando was going out with Tally, the most beautiful person on the planet. Did he really mean it? She caught her breath and, raising her eyes, found he was staring at her. The flames played on his face. Questions glimmered in his blue-green eyes. His lips were soft and raspberry red. She could feel his breath on her own lips, drawing her in.

'I-I should go,' he whispered.

'Me too.' Alice's cheeks were burning. Grabbing her coat, she stood on shaky legs.

'I'll walk you to a cab,' he said, following her out the door.

They emerged into the blind alley, where a rush of cold air hit Alice in the face. She turned to Rando with a smile. Now that there were several paces between them, the whole thing seemed so stupid. Of course Rando hadn't been about to kiss her. Of course she hadn't been about to kiss him.

'Hot in there,' she remarked.

'And way too crowded.' Rando stuck his hands in his pockets.

'Nice pub, though.'

'Yeah.'

They threaded their way back through the narrow alleys, their aimless remarks bouncing off the buildings. Under their feet, the cobbled streets were wet. A rain was falling – a rain that soaked everything, so fine you could hardly see it.

Chapter 24

Dylan scanned the rows of oil paints at Green & Stone, the cool old art shop she'd stumbled across on King's Road. Behind her, every so often, the door swished open and shut again, as someone detached themselves from the flood of Saturday London shoppers and sought out the quiet, dusky interior of the shop.

Dylan hummed to herself. For her art project, she needed oranges and scarlets and yellows and purples – colours she could set on fire, paints she could sink her fingers into and scrape round the canvas. Tucking her orange notebook under one arm, she picked out two reds to compare.

'Dylan?' said an incredulous voice behind her.

She wheeled round.

'Jasper?' she cried, stumbling backwards into the shelves. Tubes of oils tumbled round her, along with a can full of paintbrushes and the orange notebook Miss Baskin had given her. She struggled to stand up.

'Are you OK? Let me help,' Jasper said, reaching for the book.

'Get off!' Dylan shrieked.

His eyes widened in shock. 'Whoa. Fine,' he muttered, throwing his hands in the air. 'Sorry I bothered.'

As he turned on his heel, Dylan stared at the notebook. She bit her lip.

'Jasper, wait!' she called. But he was gone. Panic fluttered in her chest. Flinging her bag over her shoulder, she trampled over the paints she'd scattered, knocking down more as she ran through the shop.

'Oi! Young lady,' called the man behind the counter. 'Who do you think's gotta clean that up?'

'Sorry,' Dylan cried, legging it out the door on to King's Road. No sign of Jasper. On a whim, she stumbled round the next corner – and saw him. 'Wait!'

'What?' He stopped, only half-turning round.

'I— I'm sorry,' she panted. 'I didn't mean to be a bitch back there. It's just . . . My notebook . . .'

'Yeah, I get it, it's private. Why didn't you just say so?' Jasper was wearing a beige cap and a grey cashmere scarf, which threw his ice-blue eyes into relief. He was regarding her coldly, his mouth a thin line. 'Just because we broke up doesn't mean you have to be rude.'

'Broke up?' Dylan's face darkened. 'Are you on crack? We never broke up – you just started ignoring me with no explanation! After we had sex! And now *I'm* being rude?' Her lower lip started trembling. *Fuck.* She shut her eyes, trying to control it.

'God, don't cry.' Jasper glanced up and down the street. They were on one of the roads leading off Chelsea Embankment and the houses were all gorgeous: wide, pristine façades, sparkling windows, gardens at the front and back. 'Come on.' His voice softened. 'Let's not fight out here.'

Dylan folded her arms.

'My house is right over there – look – with the green door. Why don't you come in? We can talk.'

'I don't know. I'm not sure I want to be in your house.'

'Come on, it's freezing.' As if on cue, an icy gust of wind blew from the direction of the Thames. 'I'll make you some tea.'

Shivering, Dylan allowed Jasper to lead her along the tree-lined pavement, and waited while he unlocked his front door. She'd never been to the von Holstadts' before and, despite herself, she looked round curiously as they walked through the front hall, their feet echoing on the antique parquet floors. The house smelled of fresh flowers and perfumed candles. Through open doorways on the way to the kitchen, she caught sight of elegant furniture, stone sculptures and window nooks draped in vivid silks, with views of an extensive lawn stretching out beyond.

'What sort of tea would you like?' Jasper said. They were in the massive, gleaming kitchen and he'd slid open a soundless cupboard to reveal rows upon rows of exotic teas and tea leaves.

'Wow,' Dylan muttered.

'Yeah, my mum regularly stocks up from Le Palais des Thés in Paris. She even has a special water-heater to make sure the water's at exactly the right temperature. Apparently, it has a big effect on the flavour of your specific selection.' Jasper had put on a pretentiously nasal voice. He looked at Dylan and smiled tentatively.

She gave him a pinched smile back, then turned away. 'I don't mind. You choose.'

'Hmm . . .' He flourished his fingers along the rows. 'How about *Grand Jasmin Mao Feng*? Or *Thé des Sables*?'

'Fine. Either. I mean, it's *tea*.'

Jasper's bravado seemed to deflate. The sound of bubbling water filled the room, followed by the steam and click of the kettle. He poured two mugs and carried them to the counter. 'Have a seat.'

'So what were you doing in Green & Stone, anyway?' Dylan asked, as the tea's delicate aroma curled around her. 'I mean, no offence, but you're not exactly arty.'

'All right, no need to rub it in. I was trying to buy stuff to make a sign for the Paper Bandits. We're playing at the Hasted House end-of-term talent show.'

Something thumped in the hallway. Dylan started. The last thing she wanted was to meet the extended von Holstadt family.

'Don't worry,' Jasper said, as if reading her mind. 'There's no one home; my parents are in Germany. That was probably just one of the cats. Aww, yes, look who it is,' he added in a soppy voice, as a Persian grey with bright blue eyes sloped through the kitchen door. It leapt on to the worktop and Jasper scooped it in his arms, petting it and whispering in its ear. 'Hey Dr Faustus, how are the mice today? Aren't you a cute little thing? Aren't you a good boy?'

Dylan's heart gathered speed. The sight of men stroking small animals was always irresistible. But the sight of Jasper von Holstadt – the coolest guy she knew, not to mention the only boy she'd ever had sex with – going gooey over his cat was too much. She kneaded her hands, still a bit red from the cold. If only Jasper wasn't so out of reach. If only he hadn't dumped her by flirting with another girl right in front of her face.

'Question,' he said suddenly, letting Dr Faustus down.

'OK. What?'

'Why did you go mental on me in that shop?'

'Oh.' Dylan curled her hands round her mug. 'I guess, that book you touched – it's really private and I didn't want you to read it – even by mistake.'

'What is it? Your diary or something?'

'It's notes. For this art project I'm doing.'

Jasper rolled his eyes. 'Oh. *Schoolwork*. Wow, sounds super personal.'

'It is. Look, you wouldn't understand.'

'Try me.' Jasper's voice was gentler now.

Dylan was silent for several seconds, but finally she shook her head. 'I can't. The stuff in that book – it's stuff I've never told anyone.'

'Now I'm really intrigued.'

'Don't be. We all have secrets, right? All I'm asking is for you to respect mine.'

'Do I have a choice? Unless I steal the book out of your bag . . .' Jasper grinned mischievously.

Dylan swatted him. 'You wouldn't dare!'

170

'Wouldn't I?' He lunged towards her, grabbing at her handbag on the kitchen workshop.

'Stop!' she squealed, pushing him off.

'Make me.'

'No!' she giggled, as he started tickling her with one hand and groping for the bag with the other. 'You're not getting it! Over my dead body!' Then, all of a sudden, she stopped laughing and jumped off the stool, her face furious and pained. 'Just *don't*, OK?'

Jasper recoiled. 'Are you all right?'

'No! I don't – I don't understand . . .' Dylan could feel her lower lip start trembling again. 'Why did you just stop talking to me?'

'What are you—?'

'If you didn't want to go out with me, why couldn't you just say so? Why did you have to ignore me like that?'

'Oh. Shit.' Jasper put his head in his hands. 'I don't know. I think I panicked. The thing is . . .' He rubbed the back of his neck. 'I really liked you.'

'I really liked you, too. I've never felt that way about anyone before and . . . and it was just so . . .' Dylan's voice caught in a sob.

'Please,' Jasper whispered. 'Please don't cry. I wish I could go back and change how I acted. I never meant to be such a bastard. I'm so, so sorry.'

'When you ignored me, it just made me feel so . . . upset . . . and rejected . . .' Dylan tried to wipe the tears away, but there were too many. They fell down her cheeks as if there were an ocean behind her eyes.

'Hey,' Jasper murmured. 'I'm sorry. Baby, come here.' He drew her towards him. Lifting her hand from her face, he replaced it with his lips and kissed away a tear. Then he kissed away another. And another. The salty droplets melted on the tip of his tongue.

Suddenly, he was kissing Dylan's soft, amazing mouth. Letting out a little moan, she grabbed him and kissed him back. He ripped off her skirt and they tumbled to the floor, struggling with his jeans, fumbling in his wallet for a condom. Their breathing turned ragged as they thrust against each other.

It was over very fast.

'I'm sorry,' Jasper whispered into Dylan's hair when they were done. 'I couldn't control myself. Was it any good for you?'

She turned to face him, her eyes shining like two flowers after dewfall, and nodded. 'It was better than good.'

'I missed you,' he said.

'I missed you, too.'

He kissed her still-wet eyelashes. He kissed her nose, and her cheeks, and her lips, and they did everything again, slowly and gently this time, their lingering movements reflected in the polished kitchen floor.

Chapter 25

'Right this way, ladies,' said the maître d' of the Wolseley, leading Alice and Tally to a table in the very centre of the buzzing restaurant. Alice held her chin at a bored, nonchalant angle and swung her hips sexily as they walked past tables of trendy Londoners grazing from shellfish platters. She'd been to the Wolseley several times before. Black and white marble floors gleamed under her feet. Domed ceilings and cascading chandeliers gleamed over her head. The whole restaurant emanated 1920s-style London glamour. Sucking in her cheeks as she passed an immense mirror, Alice smiled smugly. Her shimmery make-up and scraped-back hairstyle looked flawless, despite the fact that she and Tally had got ready on the train from Hasted and rushed straight here. The boys hadn't arrived yet, even though it was five past nine. Alice's shoulders loosened in relief.

'Hey.' Tally kicked her as the maitre d' glided away. 'Look – two o'clock. Am I hallucinating, or is that Michael Cera?'

'*Ohmygod*, it is! It's totally him. Grey Goose martini with an olive please,' she added to the waiter. 'I knew we'd see someone famous. I see celebrities every time I come here.'

'Michael Cera's a good one. I get ten points for him.'

'No, you don't! You get zero points. We weren't even playing.'

'Yes, we were. We always play Spot the Celeb.'

Alice narrowed her eyes. 'No. We weren't. If we'd been playing. I would have been looking harder.'

'What, instead of checking yourself out in the mirror?'

'Shut up!'

'OMG, OMG, he's looking at you!'

'Where?' Alice almost shrieked, whipping round. 'You bitch!' She jabbed at Tally with her fork. 'He is not.'

Tally was slumped in her chair, laughing hysterically. 'S-sorry, I couldn't resist.'

'You total cow.' Alice grinned despite herself. 'OK. I admit, that was sort of funny. But only sort of! You're in a good mood tonight.'

'I know.' Composing herself, Tally leaned conspiratorially across the table. 'I'm really excited to see Rando. I can't explain it. It's like, I miss him whenever we're not together. I . . . I think I might be falling in love with him, Al.'

'Whoa. Really?' As calmly as possible, Alice took a sip of the water the waiter had just poured. 'Have you said "I love you" yet?'

'No. But I think I'm going to, this weekend. I just can't believe it's all happening so fast! I never thought I'd feel this way again. After Mr Logan, I thought my heart was dead.'

Alice swallowed. 'So maybe you should be careful – I

174

mean, "I love you" is a big deal. Maybe you're not ready. I mean . . .' she bit her lip, 'do you think Rando feels the same way?'

'Yes.' Tally's eyes were shining. 'I don't believe the connection I feel could possibly be one-sided. I don't believe love is really love unless the other person feels it, too.'

'But what about unrequited love – the kind all the poets write about? You were in love with Mr Logan, and he didn't feel it back.'

Tally's mouth seemed to tighten a little. 'That wasn't really love. It was infatuation – maybe even obsession. I realise that now. I've grown up a lot this term. Cheers.' She held out her cosmo.

Alice clinked her glass, trying to ignore the heavy feeling in her chest.

'But enough about me and my new-found happiness,' said Tally, shaking a frond of white-blond hair over her shoulder. A cloud of her flowery perfume wafted across the table. 'How are things with you?'

'Oh, fine.'

'Are you sure?' Tally's sea-grey eyes clouded. 'Because you and T didn't seem to spend much time together at Shock Box last weekend. Are you still having doubts?'

Alice blinked. She hadn't realised her BFF was paying attention to anything other than herself and her all-consuming passion for Rando. That was one of the things about Tally: one minute she'd seem totally and utterly self-absorbed, the next, she'd say something so perceptive that she might as well be a shrink. Alice straightened her menu so that its edge was perfectly aligned with the table. It was moments like this that reminded her why she and Tals were best friends in the first place.

'Did you end up seeing him in Hasted last night?' Tally asked.

'Actually, no.' Alice cleared her throat. 'I've been meaning to say, I bumped into—'

'There they are!' came Tristan's voice.

'Boys!' Tally cried. 'Finally.'

The conversation was suspended as the guys descended on the table, with everyone exchanging kisses and shuffling their chairs.

'You look pretty,' T said, resting his hand on Alice's leg.

'Thanks,' Alice said. She was watching Rando out of the corner of her eye. He looked scrubbed and handsome, his wavy hair tamer than usual, his blue-green eyes offset by his green V-neck jumper. He murmured something in Tally's ear and she giggled, her perfect teeth gleaming in her perfect, symmetrical face. She clapped her hands.

'Hey, everyone, I have an idea. Tonight's a celebration, right? The first time the four of us have gone out together!'

'True,' T said.

'So let's do a round of Russian toasts! I always miss Moscow at this time of year.'

Rando kissed her cheek. 'Really? You never talk about Moscow.'

'I'm talking about it now, aren't I, silly?'

'Yeah, but I mean, your family and stuff . . .'

'Oh, boring. Who wants to know about them? So, come on, who's up for it?'

'Me!' Tristan cried. Alice and Rando nodded.

'Eight shots of Stoli!' Tally called to the waiter. 'We'll start with two per person,' she said, dishing out the drinks when they appeared. 'I'll go first.' She lifted one of her shots between two fingers and blurted out a stream of words in Russian.

'Whoa, what does that mean?' Rando asked.

Alice peeked at him. He was staring at his girlfriend, obviously rapt by her incredible beauty and exotic foreign charm.

Tally beamed. 'I said, "To the luck that brought us all together – tonight, tomorrow, and in life!"'

'Cheers,' Rando said, drinking and entwining Tally's fingers with his.

Alice banged her glass on the table. Shoving it away, she snuggled into Tristan's shoulder and ran her foot up his leg.

'You all right?' he asked.

'I'm great,' Alice purred, giving him a smouldering look.

'Are you sure?' T winked. 'Because I hear a couple of us met up for a few too many drinks last night.'

Tally raised her eyebrows. 'What? Which couple of us met up for drinks?'

'Here's a clue,' T said. 'It wasn't me and it wasn't you. Who's left?'

Alice felt her face getting hot.

'Babe?' Tally turned to Rando. 'Ali? You didn't tell me you guys met up.'

177

'Oh, no, that's because we didn't meet up,' Alice blathered. 'I bumped into Rando in town and there was no one else around so we decided, you know, to get a drink.'

'Exactly.' Rando kissed Tally's neck. 'Like I told Alice, T would never have forgiven me if I'd let her wander back to school on a Friday night without any refreshment. Wish you'd been there, too.'

Alice stared at the menu. OK. Rando had obviously spent last night humouring her while thinking about Tally. And he'd spent today laughing about his hangover with T. Well, fine. That was fine. Rando loved Tally and she loved Tristan. And now they were on a double date. So why the hell was she so hot and bothered?

A movement caught her eye on the other side of the table. Tally and Rando were snogging.

'Bread?' she said loudly, shoving the basket in between them. 'You guys have the rest. Tristan doesn't like bread in restaurants.'

'No, I do,' Tristan said. 'I just never eat it.'

'Same thing.'

'It's not the same thing. I like bread – I just don't want to get full before my food comes. I want to enjoy the meal I've actually ordered.'

Alice gave a mental eye-roll. Since when had T become the most boring, pedantic person on the planet? He was making their relationship look bad.

He grinned. 'Anyway, it's better than some of your weird compulsions, Al.'

'Excuse me?'

178

'There are plenty of things you're weird about, too. Remember when I tried to take you horse riding in Hyde Park as a surprise, and you refused to sit on the saddle because you said too many other arses had been there first?'

Rando guffawed.

'Al!' Tally shrieked. 'I can't believe it – I'd never do that, my sweetheart. That's no way to behave when your boyfriend takes you out for a treat.'

'Yeah, I know,' Alice snapped. 'Which is why it's not what happened. Because what Tristan forgot to mention is that we were both twelve years old at the time. So what if I was having a few cleanliness issues? All twelve-year-olds get OCD once in a while.' She gave a loud, contented-sounding sigh. 'That's the thing about me and T – we have so many wonderful memories – you know, such a lot of history together. We're not, like, some new couple scrabbling to build up experiences, clutching at every little thing we've got in common.' Alice slicked on some lip gloss and tried to curb her irritation. Luckily, Tally and Rando were now too busy making moon-eyes at each other to notice their relationship had just been insulted.

'So, who's doing the next toast?' Tally hiccuped, draining the dregs of her cosmo and grabbing her second vodka. 'We can't let these get warm.'

'I'll do it,' Alice said, lunging for her glass, even though she had no idea what she was going to say. The sooner this little Russian charade was over, the better. 'Uh . . . To the food!'

179

Tally threw her head into her hands in mock despair. 'No, no, no.'

'"To the food"?' Rando repeated. 'What kind of weird toast is that? We haven't even ordered yet. Anyway, aren't Russian toasts supposed to be all philosophical and shit?'

'Oh, food is a philosophy to Alice,' Tristan chuckled. 'You obviously have no idea how much she loves it. It's a running joke in my family. One time, when we were with my parents at this restaurant in the south of France, she ordered three chocolate soufflés for dessert – all in one sitting – and devoured every crumb.'

'Shut up!' Alice turned red. 'Rando's gonna think I'm some kind of pig.'

'Exactly. I'm just trying to help him get to know you.'

The table burst out laughing. Alice forced herself to laugh as she stabbed the butter mound with her knife. Why was T being such an unromantic jerk? Why was he suddenly dredging up these stupid stories from their past?

'Oooh,' Tally cooed out of the blue, as she stared boozily at the flower arrangement in the centre of the table. 'Isn't this vase just so cute? I think I'm gonna steal it.'

Alice rolled her eyes. 'Tals, what are you talking about?'

'The vase, dummy. I want it.'

'No, you don't. It's just a stupid bit of glass. You'll get bored with it as soon as you get it home.'

'Al!' Tally swatted her. 'How many times do I have to tell you, that is so not the point.'

'Then what is the point?' Rando cut in. He was staring at Tally, his forehead slightly furrowed.

'To have fun!' she cried, poking him in the chest. 'It's a challenge. It's subversive. Don't be such a loser. OK, so the way to do this is to get the waiter used to seeing the table without the vase. It's a technique I've developed based on psychology.'

'Sounds sophisticated,' Alice snorted.

'Watch and learn, cynics. I'll hide it under my chair,' Tally chirped, slipping the vase off the table and lowering it to the floor, 'and if the waiter asks where it is, I'll just pretend we put it down there to make more room.' She straightened up. '*Et voilà!* Who's a genius?'

Alice glanced at Rando. There was a slightly baffled expression on his face, mixed with concern. 'Hey, are you sure you should drink so fast?' he said to Tally. 'Those vodka shots are pretty lethal. And all you've eaten is a bit of bread.'

'Aw, you're such a cutie for looking out for me,' Tally gushed, ruffling his hair. 'But you're forgetting my Russian heritage. I could drink a bottle and still be fine. It's like water to me! I'm going to the loo.'

As she pushed her chair back, there was a smash and a tinkling.

'Shit!' she squawked, jumping a foot in the air.

'What was that?' Alice cried.

'Um, I think it was the vase,' Rando said, peering under the table.

'Oh, fuck!' Tally squealed, giggling uncontrollably.

Their waiter materialised. 'May I help? Is there a problem?'

'Why y-yes,' Tally snorted between giggles. 'This vase appears to have sm-sm-smashed!' She was red in the face from laughing so much. 'It can't have been very good quality. Would you mind clearing it up before I cut myself?'

'Of course, madam,' the waiter said with a slight bow. 'I'm very sorry about that.'

'Yes, well, I suppose it's all right,' Tally replied. Once the waiter had made his escape, she flung her arms round Rando's shoulders. 'Aren't I an amazing actress, baby?'

He smiled. 'I thought you needed the loo.'

'Good point.' Tally stumbled as she reached for her handbag.

'Are you OK?' Rando asked, catching her round the waist. 'Do you need me to come with you?'

'Uh uh,' Tally tittered, wagging her head from side to side. 'You can't come into the ladies', silly!'

'I'll go,' Alice said, scraping back her chair.

'Thanks,' Rando said quietly, glancing up at her. His eyes seemed to reach into her own, hooking on to something deep in her soul. Alice caught her breath. *Stop. For goodness' sake, stop imagining things.* Rando was the perfect boyfriend. He was grateful to her for helping his girlfriend out – nothing more.

Turning away, she linked arms with Tally. Her only job right now was to help her drunk, infuriatingly gorgeous best friend down the stairs.

Chapter 26

'I cannot believe they didn't invite us,' Sonia whined. She was perching next to Mimah in the Four Horsemen, one of their crew's regular Hasted pubs, glaring into her gin and tonic. Next to them, Seb and George Demetrios were shooting pool, the overhead lamps turning their faces into planes of shadow and light.

'Let me get this straight,' Mimah said. 'You can't believe that Alice and Tally didn't invite you to London, with their boyfriends, on their romantic double date?'

'Exactly. It's so rude.'

Mimah rolled her eyes. 'Wow. You are really special, you know that?'

'What's that supposed to mean?'

'Nothing. Nothing.' Mimah widened her eyes and rattled the ice in her vodka and cranberry juice.

'Girls, want to play?' Seb asked.

'What, doubles?' Mimah stood up and stretched. She was wearing a short red sweater-dress, grey wedge ankle boots and a cluster of long necklaces. She'd also, for a change, swept her hair into a glossy updo. Not that she need have bothered – there was no one here to impress. 'Sure. Come on, Sone. Some exercise'll do you good.'

'Exercise?' Sonia screeched. 'You call prancing about with a long polished stick "exercise"? Besides,' she sniffed, 'I can't play pool. I don't know how. I'll look stupid.'

'You never look stupid,' George Demetrios leered. 'You're too fit.'

'Oh, shut up, George.'

'Fine. Just play with us.'

'Give me one good reason why I should.'

'Here's one,' Mimah grinned. 'If you play, you might actually get good. And everyone knows men love a woman who's good with a cue. It's the sexiest skill there is.'

'Oh, really?' Sonia huffed. But there was a gleam in her eyes. 'Well, I suppose I could try. I like to do my friends favours, and you do need a fourth player. But I hope you realise this is against my will.'

'Excellent.' George Demetrios rubbed his hands together. 'You can be my partner, since I'm the best and you're the worst.'

'Yeah, right, you're the best,' Seb muttered under his breath.

'Got a problem, Sebbie? Oh, deary me!' George slapped his hand over his mouth. 'How rude of me – perhaps you two want to be on the same team so you can snog again?'

'No!' Sonia and Seb said in unison. Sonia stuck her nose in the air, while Seb stared into his pint glass and blushed.

'Awww, isn't that sweet. Fine, so it's me and Sone versus Seb and Mime. Oh, and you two can go first,' George added, casting a conceited smile in Sonia's direction. 'Since I won the last game and all.'

'Great.' Putting down her drink, Mimah broke the rack and potted two red balls.

'Oh, no!' cried Sonia, tugging on George's jumper. 'They're already winning. I told you I was bad at this.'

'What are you on about? We haven't even had a go yet. They're not winning.'

'Um, yes they are. They're ahead. And ahead equals winning. Haven't you ever played a game before?' Snatching a cue from the rack, Sonia dangled the narrow end between her manicured fingers. 'Now what?'

'OK, try going for that yellow ball, there.'

'Like this?' Sonia trotted towards the table on her four-inch heels and squatted down until her nose was in line with the green baize.

'Uh, not exactly,' George smirked. 'Unless you're about to do a poo. Stand up straight. Good. Now, bend over the table—'

'OMG, you sleaze!' Sonia slapped his arm. 'You only want me to play so you can check out my arse.'

George chuckled. 'Not just your arse.'

'How dare you!' Sonia screeched. 'I refuse to stand for this sexist anti-feminism. Just because I have a hot body and like to wear tight clothes doesn't mean you're allowed to drool on me! You should keep your eyes on the floor – or in the gutter, where they belong. Humph.' Tossing her glossy black hair, she stuck her bum out, aimed for a yellow ball, lunged, and stabbed the table. 'Stupid game. I can't do it.'

'Don't worry,' George said soothingly. 'Have another try. The others don't mind.'

'Mind?' Seb said. 'Oh, no, why should we mind? It's only your first go and you're already cheating – but of course we don't *mind.*' Flopping into a chair, he dragged his fingers through his quiffy blond hair.

'Competitive, isn't he?' George breathed into Sonia's ear. 'Now, let me show you.' Setting down his pint, he cradled an arm round her back and curled his hands around hers on the cue. 'Feel that position?'

'Yeah.' Sonia had never been this close to George before. Somehow, it wasn't as repulsive as she'd thought.

'Slide the cue between your thumb and first finger, like this,' George was saying. 'Start slowly. Don't get over-excited. Feel it glide against your hand . . .'

'Oh, god, that's it,' Seb cried, leaping up. He turned to Mimah. 'Are we playing, or are we watching some kind of fucked-up version of a nature documentary – George the bull trying to hump Sonia the peacock?'

Mimah burst out laughing.

'What are we even doing here?' Seb grinned. 'Isn't there someone you'd prefer to spend Saturday night with? Someone you have a crush on, or something?'

Mimah fidgeted. 'No. You?'

Without answering, Seb stood up. 'I'm getting a drink. Want one?'

'No thanks – I'm gonna buy some cigarettes. See you in a minute.'

Grabbing her coat, Mimah left the pub and crossed the

street towards the corner shop. She pulled her scarf closer as an icy wind hit her in the face. Seb was right – what on earth was she doing here? She was seventeen, for fuck's sake, not seventy. Old men sat around in pubs watching their mates play pool – young girls like her should be out having fun. Sometimes it felt like Hasted and school and work and planning for the future were sucking away her life.

'Every time I see you, you look more and more tarted up,' said a voice.

Every muscle in Mimah's body tensed.

'And every time I see you, you look worse and worse,' she retorted, turning to Aidan.

She realised with a jolt that her statement wasn't true. In fact, it was the opposite of true. Aidan was leaning nonchalantly against a doorway, his hands thrust into the pockets of his beat-up leather jacket. His sardonic brown eyes were gleaming at her from underneath a trapper hat. 'Out here all alone?'

'I'm with—' Mimah stopped herself. 'Yeah. I'm on a cigarette mission.'

'Dressed like that?'

'I was with some people earlier. They've gone home.'

'Drove them away, did you?'

'Maybe. If only I could have the same effect on you.'

Aidan gave her a sidelong smile. 'Walk with me?'

'Didn't you hear what I just said?'

'Sure. But I figured that was just your way of flirting.'

'Oh my god.' Mimah's mouth dropped open. 'You're

187

so egotistical! I'd never flirt with you. First of all, you're my student.'

'Uh huh.' Aidan grinned.

'And second of all, you're the most irritating person I've ever met!'

'Duly noted. Now will you walk with me?'

Mimah folded her arms and stuck her chin in the air. 'Well, I suppose I might as well take a stroll. I felt like stretching my legs, anyway.'

'That's convenient.'

'Oh, please shut up. Why don't you tell me what *you're* doing out here?'

'Just chilling. Sometimes I like to go for walks by myself. Clears the head.'

'Well, I hope I'm not ruining the effect.'

'No. I reckon you're a pretty head-clearing influence, actually.'

'Oh.' Mimah glanced quickly at Aidan. His profile was impossible to read. They walked in silence. She fiddled nervously with the loose change in her pockets as he whistled a disjointed tune, seemingly oblivious to the weirdness of them spending Saturday night together out of choice.

Mimah couldn't tell if it was five minutes or twenty before Aidan came to a halt. 'Here we are.'

'Where?' she asked, looking round.

'My favourite place in Hasted.'

'Oh.' They were standing in front of a low-rise 1960s housing block – all blank brick walls and cement walkways. 'It's ugly.' Mimah said.

'Please, say what you really mean,' Aidan scoffed. 'I never said it was pretty. I said it was my favourite place.'

'What's so good about it?'

'Look. Right there.'

He gestured to a basement window. Its floral curtains were drawn back, revealing, inside, a stooped, elderly man in corduroys and braces. He was sitting at a small round table. A circle of lamplight shone over him and he was sipping tea. As Mimah and Aidan watched, the man stood. He shuffled over to a vast bulletin board full of old, faded postcards and, untacking one, stared at the back. He seemed to read something there. Then he switched it with another postcard. He repeated this ritual five or six times.

'Who is he?' Mimah whispered. 'Your grandfather?'

'No. I have no idea. I walk past here all the time just to watch him. Whatever he's doing – cooking or listening to the radio or sewing a button on to a cardigan – he'll always get up eventually and go through those postcards.' Aidan glanced at her. 'I have this idea that he's some sort of World War II hero. Maybe the cards are letters from his sweetheart. She died in France or something, and that's his shrine to her.' The corners of his lips crinkled. 'Or maybe I'm just turning into a stupid sentimental git at the ripe old age of eighteen.'

'Or maybe,' Mimah said, ignoring this, 'all the postcards were written by him.'

'What do you mean?'

'I don't know. Maybe they're letters to his daughter. Maybe they had a fight a long time ago, and she won't speak to him now, and she returns every letter he sends. Now those bits of paper are the only family he has.'

Aidan looked at her. 'His daughter, huh? Why his daughter?'

'No reason. Sometimes kids don't forgive their parents for things.' Mimah's teeth were chattering.

'Are you cold?'

'N-no. A little. I didn't think I'd be outside for this long.'

'You should be wearing gloves,' Aidan said. He took her hand.

'What are you doing?'

'Calm down.' He raised her fingers to his mouth and blew into his cupped hand. The feel of his warm breath made Mimah go very still.

'Better?'

'Better.'

For a minute, neither spoke.

'I-I should go,' Mimah said, her voice barely a whisper. 'My friends'll be wondering where I am.'

'I thought you said your friends went home.'

'Oh. Yeah.' Mimah shook her head, confused. Her cheeks felt feverish in the icy air. 'Gotta go.'

'See you Thursday, then.'

She paused. 'No, I realised after I left last week – that was our last tutoring session before the holidays. I finish term next Wednesday. So I guess I'll see you . . . in January.' For some reason, the words made her throat tighten.

'You think that's a good excuse?' Aidan teased. 'I need more tutoring before January. Come on Thursday, anyway.'

'I can't.'

'Why? Where will you be?'

'Nowhere. With Granny. It's . . . her birthday.'

'We can't disturb Granny's birthday, now, can we? How about Tuesday night, then? I'm not working.'

Mimah hesitated for a split second. 'OK,' she said. 'Tuesday. Six o'clock. On the corner where I bumped into you.'

'Good.' Aidan raised a hand in farewell. 'See you then.'

As she hurried back towards the pub, Mimah half expected her feet to sprout wings. She stripped off her coat, hoping the cold air would slap some sense into her brain. Because how could it be that wandering the streets of a crappy town, spying into basements with a moody, sarcastic boy, made her feel more exhilarated, more vital, than she'd felt in her whole entire life?

Chapter 27

Tally woke up the next day to a blur of watery winter light and the sound of pages turning. Rolling over, she reached across the bed. Her hand found nothing but rumpled sheets.

'Rando?' she croaked.

'Over here.'

Tally rubbed her eyes. Rando was sitting in her armchair, boxers and T-shirt on, looking through a photo album that she usually kept crammed at the bottom of her wardrobe along with all the useless crap her stepmother foisted on her for birthdays and Christmas. 'What are you doing, baby?'

'You never told me you had a grandfather in Moscow,' Rando said, not looking up from the page.

'Huh?'

'Your granddad. Are you guys close?'

'Yeah, I guess. Ugh, it's early. Come back to bed. How'd you find that thing, anyway?'

Rando didn't seem to hear. 'Who's this?'

'I can't see.'

Uncurling himself from the chair, he carried the album to the bed. 'This couple, here.'

'Oh,' Tally said, hugging her knees to her chest. 'That's my dad and my stepmum.'

'Really? See, I wouldn't have recognised them if I'd bumped into them in their own house – even though I've stayed here loads of times.'

'Well, duh. They're never here when we're here. They go away practically every weekend.'

'What are they like?'

'Dunno.' Tally yawned. 'They're OK.'

'Do you get on?'

'Sort of. Not really. Who cares?'

'I care, silly. It must have been hard – your dad marrying someone else, having to treat a total stranger like family.'

Tally shrugged. 'I guess.'

'Is that it?' Rando sighed. 'Is that all I'm gonna get out of you?'

'What else do you want me to say?' she laughed.

'I don't know.' He stared into her radiant face as he might stare into a dark pond, searching for the shimmering gold-fish and tangled reeds in its depths. 'Anything! Anything else you think – or feel. You never tell me that stuff.'

'Of course I do.' Tally nuzzled his neck. 'Gorgeous boy. Like right now, I *think* you should kiss me. I *feel* like getting naked.' Shoving the photo album to the floor, she wriggled free from the duvet and peeled off his T-shirt, pressing her warm body against his.

'Wait . . . I . . .' Rando's voice faded. He could never think properly at times like this. He relaxed into Tally's kiss. His hands slipped down her waist.

193

'I love the way you touch me,' she breathed in his ear.

Rando rolled away to get a condom. As he turned on his side, the sprawled leaves of the photo album caught his eye – and something he saw there made him pause.

'Babe, come on,' Tally murmured, nestling into his back. 'I'm waiiitiiing.'

Rando rubbed his forehead. 'Hang on . . . I . . .'

'Hellooo? Does someone need some help?' She reached round and stroked his chest, giggling.

'No, wait. Don't.'

'Hmmm? Don't what?'

Rando grabbed her hand. 'Just stop!'

'Oh.' Tally shrank from the sharpness in his voice.

'Sorry. It's just . . .' Rando heaved a sigh. He closed his eyes. 'We need to talk.'

'Oh,' Tally whispered. The world seemed to fade out of focus. She swallowed. 'About what?'

'About us.' Rando sat up. He hunched forward, staring at his toes.

Tally stared at him.

'I-I don't think this is working,' he blurted out. 'I think we should just be friends.'

Tally's breath left her body. It felt like a lightning bolt was stabbing through her chest.

'No!' she cried. 'You can't do this. I love you!' The words came out before she could stop them. She covered her mouth with her hands – this wasn't how it was supposed to happen.

Rando was gaping at her. 'Oh my god. Tals . . . I don't

know what to say. I don't understand. How can you love me when you refuse to talk to me about anything?'

'What do you mean? I talk!'

'No. That's what I thought when I first met you. I thought you were this vivacious, trusting, vulnerable girl. But give me one instance when you've ever told me anything that I couldn't have found out from your Facebook page.'

Tally's face creased. 'Don't be horrible. I tell you things all the time.'

'Like what?'

'Like last night, in the restaurant, with Alice . . .' Her eyes widened. 'Shit. I know what this is about.'

Rando gripped the sheets, his knuckles turning white. 'What?'

'Oh, my god, how could I not realise?'

'*What?*'

'Last night – you must think I'm such an idiot. I didn't mean to embarrass you. I didn't mean to break the vase – it's never happened before. I'll never try to steal stuff again. Please believe me.'

'Oh, the *vase*.' Rando unclenched his hands. 'Tals, it has nothing to do with the vase – that was an accident.' He gave a small smile. 'Shit, I'd forgotten about that – it was actually kind of funny.'

Tally tried to smile, too, but tears were running down her face. 'No, stay,' she pleaded, as Rando reached for his jeans.

'I can't. There's no point. It won't make any difference.'

'Please don't do this. I'll talk more about stuff, I promise.'

'Oh, Tals, that's not the point,' Rando said. 'You can't force it like that. We're too different.'

'I'll change!'

'Don't say that.'

'I will, though. I want to. Spend the day here and you'll see – maybe you'll change your mind. Please!'

Rando looked back at her from the doorway, his face taut and pained. 'It's no good. I have to go.'

Grabbing his overnight bag, he disappeared, his footsteps receding down the hall.

As soon as the front door slammed, Tally crumpled like a wounded bird. Her empty room, her big empty house, suddenly seemed desolate and cruel. Glancing at the floor, she saw the photo album, open to a page full of pictures of her and Alice. She fumbled for her phone. At least there was one person in the world she could always call.

Chapter 28

Alice froze, open-mouthed, in the middle of Victoria station, clutching the copy of *Grazia* she'd just bought for the train ride back to Hasted.

'He *what?*' she demanded.

'He d-d-d-dumped me!' repeated Tally's sobbing voice through the phone.

'That's what I thought you said. I can't believe it.'

'Me n-n-neither. I'm so miserable!'

'Oh, poor honey, I'm so sorry. Did he say why?'

'Yeah. He said I didn't t-talk about myself enough. He said he didn't really know who I w-w-was.'

'What on earth does that mean?'

'I don't kn-know.' Tally caught her breath in between sniffles. 'As if any boy would want to hear me go on about myself all day. What a bullshit excuse.' There was a fresh volley of sobs. 'Will you come over?'

'Aw, babe, I'd love to . . .' Alice glanced across the station at the ticket barrier and shifted from one foot to the other. 'But . . . I can't. I'm already on the train back to Hasted.' She widened her eyes as if to make herself look believable,

197

even though Tally couldn't see her face. 'It's literally pulling out of the station.'

'Oh. But it's only two o'clock. I thought we'd go together this evening.'

'I would have waited, but T had a family lunch and I had nothing to do. I thought you were busy.'

'Can't you get off?'

'I wish I could, sweetie, but the doors are locked. Are you coming back to school soon, though?'

'I guess. I don't want to stay here by myself, staring at the walls. Plus, there's no food in the house. Dad and the bitch never leave anything for me.'

'Poor you, sweetie. We'll make this better – I promise. We've only got three more days before the holidays, anyway.'

'Yeah,' Tally sobbed, 'and then we're going to Jasper's for New Year, and I'll have to see him there. Maybe I'll cancel my ticket.'

'Babe, we'll work it out. Just don't do anything rash. OK?'

'OK.'

'Love you. Bye.' Alice hung up.

The loud station sounds – screeching brakes, echoing announcements, shouting weekenders – faded from her ears as she crossed through the barriers, boarded the train and glided through the carriages. What kind of monster lied to their best friend at a time like this? She shut her eyes. The kind of monster who, next to the sympathy she felt for Tally, also felt something else, something forbidden: a strange, muffled elation.

Rando saw her at the same time she saw him.

He was sitting alone in a two-person row, leaning against the headrest, wearing the same jeans and V-neck jumper he'd had on last night – and he was looking at her, his eyes tentative yet piercing.

She stopped short. 'Oh. I didn't know you were on this train.'

'Hello to you, too.'

'Is that seat free?'

'Yeah. Do you want me to move over?'

'No.' Alice slid past him, into the window seat.

Rando pulled his backpack out from under her feet. 'I guess you've heard?'

'About you and Tally? Yeah.'

'Is she OK?'

Alice shrugged, suddenly wondering why the hell she'd sat next to her best friend's brand new ex. At the very least, she should be ranting at him for his behaviour. 'Kind of sudden, wasn't it?' she blurted out. 'Don't you think Tally deserved some kind of warning? Don't you think you acted like a bit of a bastard?'

'Maybe.' Rando stared at his lap. 'I guess.'

'Yeah, well, I *know*. One minute you're all lovey-dovey at dinner, the next minute you're dumping her?'

He sighed. 'I know – I know how it looks. But there's no nice way to break up with someone. And I've been thinking about it for a while, I promise. I wish I could have made it work but, once you start having doubts, there's no going back. Doubts poison a relationship – don't you think?'

'I-I don't know. I've never thought about it.'

Suddenly, Alice felt cold. She reached for her scarf. It was her favourite one – electric blue with black leopard spots. T had helped her choose it last year. She shut her eyes, crumpling the scarf in her lap. Why had she never realised before how little room they gave you on these stupid trains? The back of the seats in front seemed to loom up like a wall, closing her in. She gazed out the window. Shabby houses were rushing past them, their windows so close you could practically reach in and pluck the cheap-looking ornaments off the sills.

'Can you believe people actually live in places like that?' Rando said.

Alice turned her head. He was looking out the window, too, his face right next to hers.

'I know,' she said, darting her eyes away. 'I mean, I get it that some people are poor, but, hello? A house on a train track? Get some taste. Go live in a field or something instead.'

'Exactly.'

Silence descended. Alice could practically hear her watch ticking off the seconds. She leafed through *Grazia* – not that she gave a shit who Cheryl Cole was dating, or what tacky designer rip-offs you could buy on the high street for a tenth of the price. Sitting here had obviously been a mistake. They were only five minutes into the hour-long ride to Hasted and the conversation had already stalled – which wasn't surprising. Rando was practically a stranger. They'd spent a total of one evening together, and they'd been drunk. Suddenly, she had an idea.

'Hey, I know what you need after your stressful day.' Alice dug into her Anya Hindmarch overnight bag, and slipped out a silver flask. 'Here.'

'What is it?'

'Whisky.'

'You carry a supply around?'

She rolled her eyes. 'No! Don't worry, I'm not an alcoholic. I just nicked this from my parents this morning. They have really good stuff and Tals and I like to –' She cut herself off. 'Oh. Sorry.'

'That's OK. Yeah, give me some.' Unscrewing the lid, Rando took a sip. 'Wow. It is good.'

He swigged again and Alice watched as he drew away, a drop of alcohol glistening on his lips. She drank, too, feeling the whisky burn and slide its way down her throat. Outside, the sun was low in the sky. It beamed through the window, angling across their seats, its winter rays warming Alice's face.

'Mmm,' she murmured, leaning back, 'I wish we didn't have to go back to school. What's the point, anyway? We've only got three days left.'

'Thank god,' Rando said. 'I always get edgy towards the end of term. Do you ever find that boarding school starts to feel like a police state – everyone always telling you where to go?'

'And what to wear and what to do.' Alice nodded. 'Totally.'

'And it's not just teachers – it's my friends, as well. If I disappear off by myself even for half an afternoon, they go mental and demand to know where I've been.'

'Boys do that, too?'

'Big time. It's the pack mentality.' Rando grinned, nudging her. 'But you know all about that.'

'What's that supposed to mean?'

'Come on, everyone knows you're the leader of the pack at St Cecilia's.'

'I am not!' Alice protested, but she was smiling. So, Rando had noticed she was the queen of the social scene. Interesting. She hadn't realised he was paying attention.

'There's no point denying it,' he was saying. 'Take Sonia, for example – she follows you round like a piece of toilet paper stuck to your shoe.'

'That's mean!' Alice giggled.

'It's funny 'cause it's true.'

Alice swigged some more whisky. 'Anyway, even if I am the leader of the pack, that doesn't mean I'm in control.' She chewed her thumbnail. Maybe it was the alcohol, or the closeness of the train, or the fact that the sun was sinking lower and lower outside, but for some reason she felt compelled to confide in Rando. 'The pack still controls you, even if you're the leader. *Especially* if you're the leader. I feel like everyone's always watching me and expecting things from me.'

Rando was regarding her intently. Suddenly, he laughed.

'Poor princess! Soon you won't be able to do anything you want to do at all. You'll be too busy looking after your minions.'

Alice gave him a shove.

'I'm being serious!' Rando protested. 'Leading the pack is a big job. It's like being royalty. Take Elizabeth I – she was so busy leading England that she never married anyone. Her love life was a complete failure.'

Alice lolled her head back. 'How helpful. I'm so glad I'm confiding my problems to you. Are there any other completely irrelevant historical figures you'd like to bring up?'

They were both giggling.

'Shit, I'm tired,' Rando said. 'Even I don't know what I'm babbling about anymore. Give me some more of that booze.'

He slipped the flask from Alice's hands, his fingers brushing over hers.

'Maybe we should just stay on this train to the end of the line and see where it takes us,' he said, glancing out the window. 'Maybe it'll take us to the sea. We could end up in Cornwall and forget about school and eat oysters on the beach. We could sit on the sand and taste the spray of the waves.'

'Mmmm.' Alice smiled lazily. The whisky was making her head heavy and soft. 'I love oysters. They're an aphrodisiac, you know.'

'I do indeed. I've tried force-feeding them to girls I like, but it's never worked out.'

Alice chuckled. Her eyes fluttered shut and then open.

'Sleepy,' she murmured, laying her head on Rando's shoulder. This was OK – this didn't count as flirting. She was too tired to flirt. And, anyway, Rando wasn't Tally's boyfriend anymore . . .

Alice must have fallen asleep, because when she opened her eyes, the familiar fringes of Hasted were slipping past outside. She blinked, raising her head. Above the low brick buildings, the sun was setting in a crescendo of clouds – navy on purple on pink on orange on yellow. That's when she saw him looking at her. No, looking was the wrong word. Rando's eyes were burning into hers, warming her, like the whisky had warmed her throat. The train was rocking like a lullaby. She let it rock her towards him, slowly, slowly, closing her eyes as he came nearer, nearer. She tilted her mouth up. She felt the warmth of his skin. And then her lips touched his. Whisky swam in her head. Suddenly, she was kissing him. He was pressing into her. His hands were on her body.

The train jolted to a stop. They were thrown apart.

Alice's eyes shot open. 'Oh my god,' she whispered.

'I'm so sorry,' Rando murmured. He seemed frozen to the spot. 'That was a mistake.'

'Oh my god,' Alice repeated, as if these were the only three words she'd ever learned. 'I have to go.' Grabbing her bag, scarf and coat, which she didn't even stop to put on, she stumbled down the carriage and out into the evening.

*

Too Cruel for School

Several seconds earlier, unseen by Alice, a girl's figure had slipped out of a nearby seat and through the same train door. Now she hurried down the platform, swaddled in a cape. Furtively, she glanced back. Then she pulled her hood over her head and melted into the winter twilight.

Chapter 29

'Hurry, girls, stay with the group!' chirped Mrs Gould, the ridiculously cheery Year Ten Housemistress, as she bounced along Hasted High Street. It was Monday morning of the last week of term and the teacher was leading her annual mission into town to choose the cakes and decorations for the Locke House Christmas party.

'Lauren, dear, are you all right?' she asked brushing her gloved hand over the top of Lauren Taylor's hair.

'Yes, thanks, Mrs Gould.'

'I'm afraid you look rather cold. Our winters may not be like New York ones, but they're still pretty nippy. Here, wear this for a while.' She plucked her pink knit pompom hat off her own head and plopped it on Lauren's instead.

Lauren's cheeks burned. Great. Borrowing the teacher's ugly home-made accessories – just what she needed in order to raise her street cred. As soon as Mrs Gould's back was turned, she tore off the hat and stuffed it in her jacket pocket. But it was too late.

'Psst! Lauren!' Georgie Fortescue whispered from behind. 'Oi. Pompom freak.'

'*What?*' Lauren demanded, whipping round.

'Oooh, PMS much?' giggled Charlie Calthorpe de Vyle-Hanswicke.

'Georgie smirked. 'We were just wondering why you're refusing to wear Mrs Gould's gift. Not very grateful of you, is it?'

Lauren's eyes darted to and fro. They'd reached the party supply shop and the group had come to a halt. Georgie and Charlie were between her and the pavement. She couldn't get away.

'What's the matter?' Charlie snickered. 'Embarrassed, cause you're the teacher's pet?'

'Teacher's pet, teacher's pet! I bet the teacher makes you pet *her* when you're alone. Does she?' Georgie crept her fingers round Lauren's waist. 'Don't worry, you can tell us.'

'We saw how she stroked your hair,' Charlie whispered in her ear.

'No need to be embarrassed, little lezzer. Doing favours for your teacher is perfectly—'

'Stop!' Lauren cried in a strangled voice so Mrs Gould wouldn't hear, and elbowed Georgie away.

'Bitch!' Georgie muttered, nursing her ribs. 'I'll get you. You just wait and see. I'll—'

'Georgie!' Charlie whispered. 'Shhh. Look who it is.'

Georgie straightened up. Lauren followed her roommate's gaze – and froze. There, across the street, was Hugo Rochester – the boy she'd been daydreaming about for weeks.

Suddenly, Georgie was reduced to a drivelling wreck. 'OMG, where the hell is my lipstick?' she burbled, tapping

Charlie's shoulder. 'How's my hair? Hey, hey, can you see my spot?'

'No!' Charlie groaned. 'How many times do I have to tell you, you don't have a spot!'

'Hugo, darling!' Georgie trilled in a totally different voice to any Lauren had ever heard her use. 'Hellooo!'

Hugo turned round and, catching sight of Georgie's fluttering fingers, waved.

'Wait right there,' Georgie mouthed. She and Charlie detached themselves from the rest of the Year Tens and sneaked across the street, their movements attracting envious stares and whispers from the other girls. Lauren sighed. It was clearly the same here as at her old girls' school in New York: knowing boys was currency. Knowing cute boys was gold.

On the opposite pavement, Georgie tossed her straggly blond hair and kissed Hugo's cheek. 'What a nice surprise, darling! Ugh, I wish I could have a cigarette right now. Can you believe we're out here with a bunch of losers, choosing tinsel for an all-girls, booze-free soirée? Like anyone gives a shit. Our House party's compulsory, or I wouldn't go.'

Hugo grinned. 'That's school for you. They just love to infantilise everyone.'

'Yeah. Exactly.' Georgie folded her arms. Only Hugo could get away with using four-syllable words and not sounding like a pretentious tosser.

'Who's the blonde girl?' he asked. 'The one you were just talking to.'

'Why?'

'No reason. Just . . . I've never seen her before.'

'Well, I'm sure that was a huge loss to your life,' Georgie sneered.

'She's Georgie's room-mate,' Charlie interrupted. 'Lauren Taylor. She's American. New.'

'Ohhh . . .' Hugo nodded. 'That was her sister who came up to you at Shock Box, right?'

'Right,' Charlie said. She felt a twinge of guilt, remembering her conversation with Dylan that night – but she quickly suppressed it. She had better things to do than babysit some new girl, no matter how much family drama was happening in both their lives.

Hugo was still watching Lauren. Charlie laughed. 'Hey, nosey boy, shut your mouth before the bugs fly in.'

'What are you gawking at, anyway?' Georgie grumbled.

'Nothing. Just, she's interesting looking.'

'*Interesting*?' Charlie teased. 'Don't you mean "pretty"?'

'No.' Hugo turned pink and shoved his hands in his pockets.

'Of course that's not why he's looking at her,' Georgie cut in, switching on her most charming smile. 'Hugo knows more than enough pretty girls already. Right, sweetie?'

'Not sure where you got that idea,' Hugo grinned. 'You can never know enough pretty girls.'

Georgie's grin faded. So, Hugo Rochester thought that knowing her wasn't enough? She'd prove him wrong. And if she could get rid of the Lauren Taylor circus sideshow while she was doing it, so much the better.

Chapter 30

'How's this for eye-catching?' Jasper demanded, barging through the Practice Room door at lunchtime on Monday. He was holding up a shiny Paper Bandits banner, decorated with cut-outs of fireworks and stars. 'Dylan and I spent most of yesterday making it, so you'd better be impressed.'

'Not bad,' Tristan said. 'I refuse to believe that you had anything to do with the artistic elements, but whatever. You're turning out to be a pretty good band manager, after all.'

'And musician,' Jasper added, shaking his cowbell. 'Don't forget, I contribute to the Paper Bandits' sound, as well.'

'Yeah. Right.' Tristan shot Seb a smirk across the room. Jasper was the latest member of the Paper Bandits and the only one who couldn't play a tune for shit. But they'd let him in, anyway; their agent had decided his brooding good looks were a necessary ingredient in their popular appeal.

'Now, if only we could get some real gigs, instead of playing lame end-of-term talent shows,' Tristan said. He strummed a few chords on his guitar, tuning it. 'This kind of thing is so not good for our street cred. And you know what else isn't good for us? The fact that we were supposed to start rehearsal ten minutes ago.'

Just then, the door swung open.

'Sorry I'm late,' Rando said. His face was pinched and pale. Without meeting anyone's eye, he crossed the room and sat behind his drum kit.

'Mate!' T exclaimed. 'Are you OK?'

'Yeah, thanks, I'm fine,' Rando said, examining his drums for dust.

'You look like shit, cuz,' Jasper remarked.

'Where have you been?' T asked, putting down his guitar. 'I've barely caught a glimpse of you since Saturday night. I heard about you and Tals – that's rough.'

Rando nodded. 'Thanks.'

'No offence, but I was shocked when Alice told me. I thought you were totally into her.'

'We all did,' Jasper said.

'What happened?' Seb asked.

'Was it because of the vase?'

Rando rubbed his forehead. 'Guys, I'd rather not talk about it, actually.' Glancing up, he finally met Tristan's eye. 'But thanks for asking.'

'No problem, mate. I'm here if you want to chat. Right!' T clapped his hands. 'Practice time! I've written this new song about—'

Ring ring. Ring ring.

'Ugh,' Seb moaned. 'Your bloody phone is always interrupting us. If it's Alice, could you please not pick up?'

Something clattered to the floor on the other side of the room. 'Sorry,' Rando mumbled, retrieving his drumstick.

Tristan pulled his mobile out of his pocket. 'Weird.'

'What?' Seb said.

'It's Bella.'

'Bella Scott? What on earth does she want?'

'Probably to retract T's invitation to her dad's Christmas party,' Jasper grinned.

'Or maybe she wants me to tactfully disinvite *you*,' Tristan shot back. 'Hello? Hey. Bella . . . Yeah . . .'

Everyone watched him curiously.

'Yeah, good thanks. You? . . . Yep, should be fun . . . *Are you fucking serious*?!' T's eyes almost popped out of his head.

The others exchanged looks.

'What? What?' Seb and Jasper whispered. T waved them away.

'Of course! Are you sure?' He started pacing back and forth. 'Wow, thanks, Bella, that's so thoughtful . . . OK, sure . . . See you then . . . And hey – thanks again. Bye.'

'What happened?' Jasper practically shouted once T had hung up.

'Hmm?' Tristan stuck his hands in his pockets. 'Oh, nothing. Just . . . Guess who's playing at Lucian Scott's Christmas party this weekend?' There was a pause. 'Us!'

'What?' Jasper leapt into the air.

'No way!' Seb cried.

'Way! Apparently one of the bands Lucian booked dropped out last minute, and Bella suggested us. She

212

thought we were really good at the Young Leaders' Ball last month and she wanted to do us a favour.'

'Unbelievable,' Seb said. 'I never knew Bella was so cool.'

'Yeah.' T raised his eyebrows. 'Huh. Me neither.'

'Guys,' Jasper said, 'can we just take a second for how amazing this is? The place will be packed with film stars. Fame, here we come!'

'Hurrah!' Seb bellowed.

Seizing Rando's drumsticks, Jasper banged out a cacophony on the drum kit. 'C'mon, cuz – aren't you excited?'

'Yeah, totally.' Rando gave a wan smile.

'So, get into it then!' Jasper cried, beating the bass drum. ''Cause this is awesome!'

The Practice Room door swung open again.

'Guys,' George Demetrios yelled, 'what's up with the racket? I could hear it all the way in the Common Room.'

'We're celebrating because we're incredible musicians who are playing at Lucian Scott's party next Saturday!' T cried, dancing round with his guitar.

'Wait, seriously? Oh,' George frowned, backing up. He'd caught sight of Jasper behind the drum kit. The only things he and Jasper had exchanged since their fight at Shock Box were glares and insults. He'd even cancelled his ticket to Val d'Isère for New Year; he was going to visit his granny in Greece instead. 'See you guys later. I'd better go.'

'Hang on,' Jasper called. 'George! Come back, man. Please?'

'Why?'

'Look, how about we put our . . . disagreement behind us?' Jasper stuck out his hand. 'What do you reckon?'

George chewed his lip. 'Well, I guess it's about time. It's stupid to fight this close to the holidays, isn't it? Christmas cheer, and all that.' He took Jasper's hand. 'Plus, I hear you're back with Dylan now.'

Jasper looked slightly embarrassed. 'Oh. Yeah. But that's not why I'm trying to make up.'

'I know. But still, congrats.'

'Really? You're not pissed off?'

George shrugged. 'No. I mean, she's fit, I'd totally do her, but you were there first. On to other conquests.'

'Thanks, mate. I appreciate it.'

'My, my, my.' A fake sniffling sound came from Seb's corner of the room. 'Isn't this a beautiful moment?'

'It is indeed,' Tristan fake-sobbed. 'In honour of this touching occasion, here's the song I've been working on: it's all about friendship. Rando, in all seriousness, mate, it might cheer you up, too. I'm calling it "Bros Before Hos".'

'Right on,' George chuckled, leaning against a chair-back to listen.

When I'm feeling down,
When the romance ends,
When the music fades,
You'll be there, my friend.

When my girl walks out,
When the night turns black,

Too Cruel for School

When love turns sour,
I know you've got my back.

Girls come and go.
Love's season flies.
Flowers wilt, leaves fall,
But friendship never dies.'

As T sang, the others swayed back and forth, grinning. Only Rando didn't join in. He was staring at the drumsticks lying in his hand. They were his new ones – the ones he'd bought at Rivell's on Friday evening just before bumping into Alice. He twisted them between his fingers, round and round.

Chapter 31

Sniffle. Sniff. Sniff. Sniffle.

The muffled noise assailed Alice's ears across the dorm room. Alice stared fixedly at her History textbook. Finally, unable to stand it any longer, she looked across at the armchair where Tally was slumped.

'Feeling any better, sweetie?'

'Of course not!' Tally moaned. 'I'll never feel any better. My life's ruined. Ruined!' She punched one of the cushions on her lap to emphasise this point.

Alice sighed. Tally's eyes were red, her skin was blotchy, her lips were puffy and her white-blond hair was sticking out like splinters of lightning. But, still, she looked beautiful. She looked like some pre-Raphaelite painter's impression of heartbreak.

'Aw, babe, your life isn't ruined. Things'll get better. He obviously wasn't the right guy for you.' Alice almost slapped her own face as she was saying this. As if lame clichés were going to help anyone. 'I really don't think Rando understood you.'

'Don't say his name,' Tally wept. 'I can't bear to hear it. I can't bear to see him. I'm cancelling my ski trip tickets.'

'No, you aren't,' Alice said. 'Don't do anything rash. I'm sure you'll feel better in a few days.'

Tally kicked a slippered foot against her chair. 'I won't! You only think that because *you'd* feel better in a few days. You're always proper and restrained. But I feel things deeply. I'm a very passionate person.'

'Excuse me?' Alice's eyes were narrowed, but Tally didn't notice.

'It's true. You're so sensible, but I'm romantic and sensitive.'

'Don't you mean "a drama queen"?' Alice snapped her book shut and stood up. 'I'll have you know that I feel things deeply, too! Just because I don't go on about myself the whole time and broadcast every tiny beat of my heart doesn't mean I don't feel things.'

Tally looked at her miserably. 'Don't yell at me. I'm already upset.'

'Yeah, and I'm sorry, but the whole world doesn't revolve around you. I'm going to work in the Library.'

Alice strode across the Great Lawn in her beige wedge ankle boots, biting her lip as she pictured the silent, shadowy Library. Sitting at a desk for hours, pretending to revise Tudor History while she was actually brooding about her own very-recent history, sounded too much like torture. If only she had someone to talk to. All of a sudden, her feet seemed to switch direction of their own accord.

The Art Block was buzzing, even though it was 8pm and the holidays started in two days. Alice pushed along the top-floor corridor. Reaching the entrance to the Lower Sixth studio, she stopped. Farah Assadi's husky voice was spilling through the doorway.

'We were going out for dinner with his friends, and he asked me to wear my most padded push-up bra,' Farah was saying. 'He was desperate for all his mates to think I had huge boobs. I told him to fuck off!'

She and Dylan laughed.

'So did you dump him?' Dylan asked.

'Of course. But I'm expecting him to ring and try to get me back. I know he thinks I'm really good in bed.'

The two girls giggled again. They were sitting at their easels, drinking from chipped mugs of tea and making the occasional dab with their paintbrushes. It all looked very cosy. Alice sighed. It must be nice to work and socialise at the same time. Shame she was awful at Art. She could barely draw a triangle.

'Alice!' Farah said suddenly. 'What are you doing here?'

Dylan looked up.

'What are *you* guys doing here?' Alice retorted. 'You and Dill are always hanging out up here – it's like some weird little club.'

'We're finishing our end-of-term projects,' Farah said. 'They're going on show for the parents on Wednesday, when everyone comes for the Carol Concert.'

'Everyone except my mom, that is,' Dylan said.

'Oh, don't worry, loads of people's parents don't come,' Alice said, walking round so she could see their paintings. 'My parents probably won't – they get so bored with all the school events. Whoa . . .' She was scrutinising Dylan's canvas, and shivered. 'There's something insane about this. What's it supposed to be?'

'That's the point – you're not supposed to know. We're meant to be exploring a secret emotional experience and making the viewer feel something.'

'Mine's an orgasm,' Farah butted in.

Alice cackled.

'What?' Farah demanded.

'Nothing. Just, your orgasm looks kind of like the eye of Jupiter.'

'Yeah – it's a celestial experience. What's your point?'

Alice smirked. 'Oh, no point whatsoever. What's yours, Dill?'

'I told you, it's a secret.'

'You'll never get it out of her,' Farah snorted. 'She's been like this the whole time.'

'Just tell us! What's with all the mystery?' Alice examined the painting again. 'Shit, it's intense. And kind of . . . terrifying. What is it, when your parents told you they were getting divorced or something?'

'No.'

'Your first time meeting Jasper?'

'No.'

'Your first time having sex with Jasper?'

'No.'

'The last time you had sex with Jasper, on the weekend?'

'No! How did you know about that? And, by the way, my answer's gonna be the same no matter what you guess.'

Alice chuckled. Then, as she remembered why she was up here, her face darkened. 'Hey, Dill,' she asked, 'want to take a walk?'

'Now?'

Alice nodded.

'But it's dark out.'

'Don't be such a baby.'

Dylan looked hard at Alice. She must have seen something in Alice's eyes, because she put down her paintbrush and took off her smock. 'Let me just wash my hands.'

A few minutes later, the two girls were retracing Alice's steps along the corridor.

'Hang on,' Alice said, as Dylan started down the main staircase. 'Not that way. We're going up.'

'How can we go up? We're on the top floor.'

'That's what you think,' Alice said. Checking furtively behind her, she opened a broom cupboard at the top of the stairwell, stepped through to the back of it, and opened another door. There was a narrow staircase on the other side.

'Whoa,' Dylan breathed. 'I had no idea that was there.'

'Of course you didn't. I doubt even Miss Baskin knows it's there.'

'So how come you do?'

Alice tapped her nose, leading the way upwards. 'When you've explored this school enough, you start to discover its secrets.' At the top of the staircase, she signalled for Dylan to be quiet, then dug her heel into a stiff-looking door. It burst open in a cloud of dust, revealing a long, low attic crammed with broken easels, grimy palettes and old still-life props.

'Welcome to the Grubhouse.' Alice dangled a faded piece of fabric, streaked with dirt. 'I assume there's no need for you to ask what inspired the name.' Stepping over a motheaten stuffed parrot, she pulled up a stool to one of the garret windows and perched in a pool of moonlight. 'Cigarette?'

'No. I'm trying not to.'

'Isn't that mature of you.' Alice's face flared in the spark of the match. She exhaled a cloud of pale smoke. 'Tally and I named this place back in Year Nine, when we first found it. We always come up here. You should feel privileged – I've never shown it to anyone else before.'

Dylan folded her arms. 'So why are you showing it to me?'

'I don't like to smoke alone.'

'Where's Tally?'

'I, uh . . . She's working.' Alice toyed with a length of red velvet curtain. 'We're not joined at the hip, you know.'

'Poor Tally.' Dylan dug another stool out of a pile of fake fruit and sat down. 'I'm surprised she can concentrate after what happened with Rando. I feel bad for her – she really liked him, didn't she?'

'Yeah.' Alice pursed her lips. This conversation wasn't exactly going the way she wanted. 'Anyway, I'm glad the two of us can have a gossip. Let's talk about boyfriends! Ooh, here's a question I've just thought of: have you ever had a boyfriend but fancied someone else?'

Dylan looked at her.

'What?' Alice said.

'You just thought of that question, just now?'

'Yeah.'

'Kind of random, isn't it?'

'I'm only asking theoretically.'

'Right.'

'Don't get all weird on me. Obviously I'm completely in love with Tristan.' Alice twisted the red velvet between her fingers. 'But, I mean, do you think it's normal to fancy someone else at the same time? Do you think it's possible to like . . . I mean, *really* like two people at once?'

For several seconds, Dylan examined her fingernails in silence. Finally, she looked up. 'There's something I have to tell you.'

'What?'

'I saw you. Last night.'

'Well, duh. We were all at supper together.'

'No, I mean, on the train – with Rando.'

'Oh my god.' Alice's eyes widened. She stood up and started pacing. 'What did you see?'

'Everything. You sleeping on his shoulder.' She paused. 'The kiss.'

Alice turned pale. 'Did you tell anyone?'

'No. Of course not. And I'm not going to.'

'Why not?' Alice covered her face with her hands. 'God, you must think I'm such a bitch – why are you even here?'

'Because I figured you might need a friend?'

Alice stared at Dylan as if she'd never really seen her

before. Then, without warning, her face crumpled. Tears ran down her cheeks. 'Oh, shit, I can't believe I did it. I feel so awful.'

'Hey . . .' Dylan stood up and squeezed her shoulders. 'Don't cry.'

'But I'm so c-c-c-confused. I feel like the worst person in the world.'

'You're not the worst. Even if what you did is pretty bad.'

'It was a mistake! I never meant to. I was tired, I hardly knew what I was doing.'

'I believe you,' Dylan nodded. 'But that's not much of an excuse, is it? It won't be to Tally, at least.'

'Thanks a lot,' Alice snapped. 'Is that why you're here – to be the voice of doom? To make me feel even more terrible?'

'Of course not! I'm just trying to be honest. I mean, this is a real problem, and no amount of sweet-talking is gonna change that. Do you really want someone sucking up to you at a time like this? I thought there was a reason you came to me and not to – oh, I don't know – *Sonia*.'

Alice dabbed her eyes. 'I guess.'

'And, yeah, OK, at first I guess I did think you were a total bitch. But since then I've been thinking – this stuff happens. Sometimes you just fall for people – not that you should always act on it. If you ever did this kind of thing to me, I'd kill you, naturally.'

Alice giggled, despite the dire situation, and rubbed her nose on her sleeve. 'You're right – I think I really might be falling for him. Oh my god, that's the first time I've ever said it out loud. I tried to resist it. I never thought anything could ever happen, 'cause he was with Tally and they seemed so happy, and why would anyone ever dump someone that stunning?' Alice rubbed her forehead. 'Up in our room just now I used some stupid excuse to lash out at her. Why did I do that?'

Dylan cupped her chin in her hands. 'I don't know. Maybe 'cause it's easier to feel angry than guilty. Maybe you wanted to push part of the blame on to her – like, in some way, she deserved it.'

'Maybe you're right.'

'So, are you going to tell her?'

'Are you crazy?' Alice cried. 'No way. I'll just . . . I'll never do it again. I'll pretend it never happened, and she never has to know.'

'Is that really gonna work? What if you keep falling for him?'

'Let's not talk about that, OK?'

'Then how about Tristan? Are you still in love with him?'

Alice went pale. 'I don't know,' she whispered. 'He's my first serious boyfriend. He's been my friend my whole life. How do I know if I was *ever* in love with him?'

'Maybe the fact that you're even questioning it means you weren't. My mom always says that if you're in love, you know it. For sure.'

'Have you ever been in love?'

'No. I mean, I don't think so.'

'I guess that means you haven't – according to your mum!'

Both girls laughed. All of a sudden, Alice reached across and squeezed Dylan's arm.

'Hey, by the way, thanks for this. You always seem to come through for me. Even though—' she chewed her thumbnail – 'even though I'm not always the world's greatest friend to you.'

'Oh, stop it,' Dylan scoffed. 'Let's not get all weepy.'

'No, seriously – I knew you were trustworthy – you've kept secrets for me before. I guess I just never knew you were so wise.'

'I guess not.' Dylan's smile seemed to turn somehow sad. She stared out the window, over the moonlit lawn. 'I guess there are lots of things about me that you don't know.'

Chapter 32

Mimah spotted Aidan's head above the crowds of Christmas shoppers as she wound her way along the Hasted street.

'You're here,' she said, finally reaching him. 'What a pleasant surprise – I thought you'd be late.'

'Interesting,' Aidan said. 'Is that why *you're* late?'

'I'm not late! Just because you're early doesn't mean the rest of the world is automatically late.'

Aidan raised his eyes to the sky. 'God, you're easy to wind up.' He shot Mimah a teasing grin. 'Come on.'

'Where are we going?'

'I thought we could get some food before you started bullying me with your Maths knowledge,' he said, swinging round a corner into a quieter side street.

'Oh. OK. Where did you have in mind?'

'Fish and chips, down the chippie.'

'Oh, wow.' Mimah folded her arms. 'You sure know how to treat a lady.'

'That's just the point,' Aidan said, digging his hands into his pockets. 'I do want to treat you. As in, pay for you. But the chippie's kind of all I can afford.'

Mimah stared at him. 'Hang on – why do you want to pay for me?'

'Why do you think? Because you've been such an exemplary tutor.'

'Right. All two times I've tutored you,' Mimah retorted. 'I'm sensing an ulterior motive here.'

'For goodness' sake,' Aidan said. 'I've never known anyone so eager to pass up a free meal. Just think of it as an investment in our tutoring future, OK?'

'Whatever you say,' Mimah grinned.

Five minutes later, she and Aidan emerged from the fish-and-chip shop with cardboard plates of fluffy cod and chunky chips, and wandered towards the playground.

'Are you warm enough to eat outside?' he asked, unlatching the gate.

'Yeah,' she replied, remembering with a flush the way he'd warmed her hands last week. 'I wore more clothes today. So, don't worry, you won't have to come to the rescue again.'

'Good.'

Mimah's heart faltered. *Good*? Did Aidan not want to touch her again? Obviously not. Or maybe she was sending out all the wrong messages – maybe he thought she was trying to brush him off. It probably sounded that way, from the stupid things she kept saying. Mimah sighed. She was so crap at this whole flirting thing. It had been ages since she liked anyone. Everything she said seemed to come out wrong. If only she could stop over-analysing.

There was a climbing frame in the playground, built in

the shape of a castle. Aidan sprang on to its lowest platform, which was shaded by a small turret. Mimah jumped
up after him.

He regarded her, eyebrows raised. 'My, that was athletic.'

'Yeah? And?'

'I didn't know you were so agile.'

'That's surprising,' Mimah snorted, 'since you obviously
know everything else about me.'

She almost kicked herself. See? It sounded like she was
trying to squash Aidan flat, not seduce him. What an idiot.
Spearing a piece of fish with her small wooden fork, she
leaned against the climbing frame. The bare winter
branches looked like cracks in the night sky and the orange
glow of the street lights gave the playground an air of
perpetual sunset. Mimah's legs dangled over the edge
of the platform, tantalisingly close to his.

She looked at him, her black fringe falling across her
eyes. 'I'm glad you asked to see me tonight.' As soon as
she'd said it, she lost her nerve. 'I mean, three weeks seems
like a long time to abandon our tutoring. What are you
up to for the holidays, by the way?'

'Holidays?' Aidan gave a derisive laugh. 'You forget, not
everyone's a good little schoolgirl like you. They're not
holidays for me.'

'Fine.' Mimah hugged her arms to her chest. 'Don't
answer, then.'

'Sorry,' Aidan said, blunting the edge from his voice. 'I
shouldn't be so bitter about being a working stiff. I'm a
dickhead, aren't I?'

'Yes.'

He chuckled. 'That's what I like about you, Jemimah – you never mince words.'

'I could say the same about you.'

'I guess we're two of a kind, then. Not a bad hand in poker.'

There was a silence.

'Oi.' Aidan nudged her. 'Stop hogging all the mayonnaise. Give me a packet.'

'But you already finished yours!'

'So? No self-respecting person eats chips without mayo. You've got plenty there.'

Rolling her eyes, Mimah handed over her last unopened pouch.

'Mmm. Thanks.' Aidan rubbed his hands together. 'This is how fish and chips should be eaten – out in the rough, piping hot when it's freezing cold – not the way posh people do. I've catered at weddings where they actually hand round portions in little paper cones as canapés. I mean, how fucking ridiculous is that?'

Mimah coughed.

'You all right?'

'Yeah. Fish bone in my throat.' She was trying her hardest not to collapse in giggles. Aidan was so right – serving mini fish-and-chips portions at parties was totally the done thing in her set. They'd passed them round at Alice's brother Dominic's eighteenth last year. 'Isn't this a clever little idea?' Alice's mother had remarked, pinching a chip between her elegant, ring-laden fingers.

'So,' Mimah choked, controlling herself with an effort, 'you've worked in catering?'

'I've worked in everything at one point or another,' Aidan said. 'How about you? Go on, tell me your worst ever job.'

'Oh ... Let me see,' Mimah stuttered, scrambling for time. The only job she'd ever had was tidying her own bedroom. Back when her father sill lived at home, he used to pay her to put away her clothes whenever it turned into too much of a tip. She could make ten pounds in five minutes if she worked fast enough. But for some reason, she didn't think Aidan would be too impressed by that. 'I've had so many jobs, I can't think. Tell me yours.'

Aidan chewed thoughtfully. 'I worked at McDonald's once.'

'That doesn't sound so bad.'

'You have no idea. It was repulsive – stuck in a hot, greasy kitchen for hours at a time, dealing with rank so-called "meat"? I feel ill just thinking about it. I'll never eat McDonald's again. And the guys I worked with weren't exactly reputable. We'd finish work and go out slashing tyres.'

'Seriously?'

'Yeah.' Aidan flexed his hands. 'I even had my own knife. It was pretty awful. Working a mindless job was bad enough but, on top of that, I felt like I was letting myself down – like, morally, I mean. And the worst part was, I didn't know how to get out of it. My whole life seemed like a dead end.'

230

'Do you still feel that way?'

'No.' Aidan smiled at her, the planes and hollows of his face sculpted in the orangey light. 'Not recently, at least.'

'Oh,' she said softly. 'Why not?'

He tilted towards her, his mouth soft, beguiling. 'Why do you think?'

'I don't know,' Mimah murmured, closing her eyes as Aidan leaned in and kissed her. It felt amazing, like everything she'd ever wanted. He unbuttoned her coat and slipped his hands inside, sliding her jumper over the small of her back. Mimah fumbled with his trousers, trying to unzip his jeans.

'Wait,' he said, breathing hard.

'What for?'

'I don't think we should do this right now.'

She drew back. 'Don't you want me?'

'Don't be silly,' Aidan said, kissing her again. 'I wanted you as soon as I saw you. As soon as you glared at me with those inky eyes of yours, and told me to fuck off.'

Mimah chuckled. 'So why don't you want to have sex?'

'I do. I just don't want to have sex here, in this playground. Not for the first time, at least.' He tugged at a piece of her jet-black hair. 'I don't know what sort of history you've already got, young lady, but I want whatever's between us to be fresh and new. Not rushed. Not on a park bench, or up against the wall in some public toilet. I want it to be good. No regrets. Don't you agree?'

'I had no idea you were such a romantic,' Mimah smiled.

The truth was, everything Aidan said was making her more besotted by the second.

He brushed his lips over her neck, and she stroked his hair.

'Meet me tomorrow, at my house?' he said. 'We'll do it right.'

Mimah nodded. Aidan kissed her again, knocking their fish and chip wrappings to the ground beneath their feet.

Chapter 33

'I think it's good,' Lauren Taylor said, studying Dylan's painting, which was hanging in the foyer of the Art Block. 'Very . . . intense.'

'Thanks,' Dylan said cautiously. It was the last day of term, and parents and girls were milling all around them, sipping glasses of mulled wine and nibbling mince pies. Eager voices echoed off the brick walls and concrete floors.

'Ohhh,' Lauren exclaimed all of a sudden. She was reading Miss Baskin's description of the Lower Sixth assignment on a laminated page at the bottom of the stairwell. A light had dawned in her face. 'Dilly, I totally know what your painting's supposed to be.'

Dylan grabbed her by the shoulder. 'Well, don't say! OK? Don't you dare say it out loud!'

'Ow!' Lauren yelped, struggling in her sister's vice. 'Calm down.'

'Promise me,' Dylan growled, her eyes flashing. 'Promise right now!'

'Fine! What do you think I am, an idiot? Now let go, you're hurting me.'

'Sorry,' Dylan muttered, releasing her sister and rubbing her forehead as if she had a headache. 'I panicked.'

'I noticed. You scared me.'

'I didn't mean to.' Glancing up, Dylan smiled over Lauren's shoulder as Farah Assadi waved a few fingers in her direction. Farah was standing a few metres away, in front of her own painting, with a dapper-looking couple who were obviously her grandparents.

'But Farah, dear, I don't quite understand,' the grandmother was saying, peering at Farah's artwork through her spectacles. 'It's all swirls and psychedelic colours. What's that supposed to represent?'

'Reema, dear, not everything in art has to represent something else,' her grandfather said in a learned tone. 'Perhaps Farah is harking back to the era of London in the sixties.'

'Hassan, dear, you haven't got a clue,' the woman argued. 'This painting is supposed to represent something emotional. An era that Farah never lived through can hardly be emotional for her.'

'You've got a point, Reema, my dear,' said the grandfather, patting his wife's hand. 'I'll admit, you do have a point.'

Farah shot Dylan a grin over her grandparents' heads. '*See you later*,' she mouthed.

Dylan nodded and walked outside with Lauren, on to the sunny Great Lawn. 'What are you up to now?' she asked. 'I mean, where are your friends?'

'Oh.' Lauren pouted. 'Don't you want to see me?'

'Of course. I'm flattered you wanted to look at my Art project – but it's the last day of term. Shouldn't you be celebrating with people?'

'I guess,' Lauren shrugged. 'Or maybe I'll go write in my diary. I've kind of been neglecting it for the past week.'

'I didn't know you kept a diary,' Dylan said.

'I just started. I thought it'd be a good thing to do, starting at a new school and everything.'

'So true! It'll give you amazing memories to look back on when you're older.'

Lauren sighed. 'Yeah. Actually, I feel like taking a walk by myself. I might go get a snack in the Dining Hall. See you later.'

Dylan waved goodbye and strolled across the Great Lawn, where smartly-dressed parents were wandering arm-in-arm with their daughters, admiring the school in all its stark winter splendour. Just as she was passing the wide brick steps that led from Quad, she spotted Mimah, who waved.

'Oh, hey,' Dylan said. 'Where are you coming from?'

'Meeting with Mr Vicks,' Mimah replied. 'He wanted to know how my tutoring's going. He's going to help me work out a strategy to apply to Cambridge next term.'

'Wow.' Dylan pursed her lips. 'I haven't even thought about university yet. I guess I'll end up back in the States.'

'You never know what's gonna happen,' Mimah said. 'A month ago, I'd never have thought I had a shot at Cambridge.' She grabbed a cup of steaming mulled wine from one of the festive refreshment stands outside the Tuck In Café, and took a sip, peering over the rim.

'Ridiculous. Just look at all these mothers and daughters, arm in arm, so peaceful and friendly. Don't you love it when your mum pretends to be your best mate? By the end of the holidays they'll all be fighting like wolves.'

'Yeah,' Dylan chuckled. 'But at least their moms are here. Mine didn't bother cutting her vacation short.'

'And mine didn't bother leaving her house,' Mimah said. 'This time last year, both my parents were here. Now neither of them is. They wouldn't even be caught dead on the same property. Things change pretty fast, don't they?'

The two girls stood for a moment in silence.

'Mimey! Dill!' called a voice. Alice bounded up to them, arm-in-arm with Tally and Sonia. 'We've been looking for you. Oooh, mulled wine,' Disengaging herself, she swiped a cup and held it up. 'Girlies, I feel a toast is in order: congrats to us for surviving another term. There are now zero obstacles between us and Lucian Scott's Christmas party on Saturday night.'

Sonia downed her wine and clapped her hands. 'Oooh, yes! Let's all go shopping tomorrow to buy gorgeous new dresses.'

'Good idea!' Alice hopped up and down. 'We have to look doubly hot now that the Paper Bandits are playing. Whee!'

Next to her, Tally sniffled.

'Oh, shit.' Alice bit her lip and gave Tally's shoulders a squeeze. 'Sorry, babe. I didn't mean to bring up the boys.'

'I-It's OK,' Tally whimpered. 'I just c-can't stop th-thinking about him.'

'Oh, shoot me now,' muttered Sonia, rolling her eyes. It had been three whole days since Rando had dumped Tally. Was she planning on taking all century to get over it and shut up? 'Personally, I think we've all done pretty well with guys this term.'

'Why do you have to talk about men?' Tally cried. 'I think it's really mean – you know how bad I'm feeling.' She broke away from the group. 'I need to be alone. I'll see you guys later.'

'Hey, wait!' Alice called, but Tally was already striding away across the Great Lawn.

'What's up with her?' Sonia sniffed.

'Sonia Khan, the master of empathy,' Mimah snorted.

'Shut up, *Jemimah*. All I was trying to say is, we've all snogged people we fancy this term. Well, except you.'

'Been keeping tabs, have we?' Mimah shot back.

'Obviously. Only thickos neglect to stay on top of gossip.'

'Actually, Sone's got a point,' Alice said. 'Mime, I can't remember you snogging anyone in ages. Why not? Isn't there anyone you fancy?'

'No. why should there be?'

'Um, because you're a human being?' Sonia scoffed. 'At least, I thought you were. Now I'm worried you're an asexual or something.'

'"*An* asexual"?' Dylan giggled.

'Shut your mouth, Dylan Taylor,' Sonia snapped. 'Who invited you, anyway?'

'No one. It's a communal space.'

'Oh, please – I have no time for your technical terms.'

'Babe, do yourself a favour and shut up,' Alice sighed, tweaking the sleeve of Sonia's cashmere coat. 'By the way, Dill, how's your painting going down?' She grinned at the rest of the group. 'Have any of you seen Dylan's painting? She's refusing to tell anyone what it's supposed to be. Apparently it's something personal.'

'Oh, really?' Sonia said, narrowing her eyes and folding her arms. So, the secret painting cropped up again. She sneaked a glance at her watch. It was two o'clock, and her chauffeur was collecting her from London at eight. She had exactly six hours to crack the mystery, and get the power balance back where it belonged.

Chapter 34

Georgie Fortescue scowled out the window of her dorm room, a dirty sock dangling from her fingers. The front garden of Locke House was crawling with over-enthusiastic parents, slobbering and beaming as their darling daughters showed off all the petty things they'd achieved this term. She chucked the sock into her half-packed suitcase. It felt like everyone's family had shown up but hers. Typical.

'Hi, Georgie!' Her dorm-mate, Portia Mehew-Montefiore, was waving from the lawn. 'This is Mummy and Daddy,' she called, hugging the radiant, attractive couple by her side.

Georgie forced a smile, ducking back into the bedroom just as her phone pinged. She snatched it up. Maybe it was a text from Hugo Rochester – not that there was any reason why it should be but, whenever her phone lit up, she lived in hope that it was him.

It was her mother.

We'll be out when you get home. Let yourself in. I've told Cook to leave supper in the fridge. Don't touch the good cheese. It's for a dinner party. Mum.

As Georgie threw down her phone, her eyes fell on

Lauren Taylor's bed, which was still neatly made up even though all the girls were required to strip their sheets before they went home. She smirked. Maybe Lauren could use a little help.

Dumping the rest of her undies into her case, Georgie crossed the room and yanked at Lauren's duvet. It tumbled to the floor, along with her pile of pillows – and something else, which landed with a thud. Georgie sifted through the bedding, searching. Finally her hands touched something hard and rectangular. A baby-blue book was lying splayed on the carpet. Picking it up, she saw the gold embossed letters on the front – and a slow, triumphant grin spread across her face. Little Lauren Taylor's diary. Jackpot.

She opened to the first page. *Dear Hugo,* the large, curly handwriting said.

Dear Hugo? Georgie's eyes almost popped out of her head as she skimmed down. No. Effing. Way. Could this be true? Yes. Lauren Taylor was actually addressing her journal to Hugo Rochester – a boy who was not only way above her on the social ladder – who was surely destined to become Georgie's own boyfriend – but who she'd never even met. Unbelievable. Did that psychotic, stalking loser actually think this was acceptable?

Georgie read on, phrases leaping at her from the page.

I've never even kissed a boy . . .

Does that mean I'm a loser beyond repair?

What if my teeth get in the way?

Does it help if you lick your lips?

She burst into a cackle. This was too good to be true.

The world had to know. And, more importantly, a certain special someone had to know, too.

Diving into her suitcase, Georgie seized her digital camera and snapped photos of every page of the diary. Then, giggling to herself, she transferred the pictures to her laptop and opened Facebook.

'Knock, knock,' came a voice.

'Wait!' Georgie jumped, slamming her laptop shut.

'Whoa,' grinned Charlie Calthorpe de Vyle-Hanswicke. 'Someone's got a guilty look on her face.'

'Oh, it's only you.' Georgie snickered. 'Charl, come here – you have got to see this.'

'What?' Charlie asked, bounding over to her friend's desk. '*Dear Hugo*,' she said, reading from the photos. 'What is this, a letter?'

'Nope – better.'

'A . . . secret letter?'

'Nope – even better. A diary.'

'Whose diary? Yours?'

'Of course it's not mine, you cretin!' Georgie snapped. 'First of all, why would I post my own diary on Facebook? And, second of all, do you actually think I'd address my journal entries to Hugo Rochester?'

Charlie shrugged. 'OK, it's weird . . . But you do like him. Who knows what lengths you'd go to?'

'Shut up!'

'So, whose is it?'

'Whose do you think?' Georgie said, shooting a significant look at Lauren's bed.

241

'Nooo . . .' Charlie's mouth dropped into an 'o'. 'Oh, Georgie, you can't do that.'

'Of course I can. I've done it already, see? Now, what shall I call the special Facebook group I'm making? *The Stalker Diaries*? No . . . *The Hugo Diaries*? No, I know!' She typed out the words. *Diary of a Loser Beyond Repair. By Lauren Taylor.*

'George,' Charlie said, trying to keep her voice calm, 'do you realise what you're doing here?'

'Yes. I'm creating a Facebook group. And now I'm inviting everyone I know to join it,' Georgie gloated, selecting names from her friends list. There were hundreds of them. 'And now I'm sending Hugo a text. Isn't this fun?' she giggled, showing Charlie her phone.

Hey, Huggy, got a pressie for you. Watch your FB news feed. It'll make you laugh. xoG

Charlie pressed her fingers to her temples. 'No, George, hang on; I don't think you get it. I mean, I know we don't like Lauren—'

'Wrong. We hate Lauren. She's an annoying little creep and I want her out of my hair.'

'But why? What did she do to deserve this?'

Georgie shrugged.

'Those are her most personal and private thoughts, and you're posting them online.'

'Oh, get a grip; it's just a practical joke.'

'Don't you read the papers? Some people commit suicide over this stuff! It's serious. Listen to me.'

'Hmmm? What did you say?' Georgie asked, turning to

242

Charlie with a smug smile on her face. Her index finger was hovering over the *publish* button. She pressed it down. 'Ooopsie! It just went public!' she cried in mock horror, slapping her hand over her mouth. 'Oh dear, oh dear, oh dear. Guess no one can stop it now.'

Chapter 35

Mimah followed the map on her iPhone, her heart hammering as she wound deeper and deeper into Hasted's unfamiliar residential streets. Finally, she turned the last corner into Aidan's road. It was lined with grim, two-storey terraced houses built of sooty brick, so narrow they wouldn't even fit a room the size of Mimah's bathroom at home. They had small, dark windows. Some had dirty old cars outside, parked in the leaf-logged gutters.

Mimah swallowed and rang the buzzer.

'Hey.' Aidan opened the door to the ground-floor flat. He was wearing a red and blue lumberjack shirt and his favourite lived-in jeans. His brown hair was tumbling over his face, as if he'd rushed to get the door. Mimah's heart went into overdrive.

'Hi,' she breathed.

'Come in.' He stepped back. The narrow front passage was littered with junk: a broom was teetering against a pile of yellowing magazines; empty beer bottles were crammed into an old-lady-style shopping trolley; unopened mail lay scattered on the carpet. The place smelled of dog food.

Mimah wanted to cover her nose – but obviously that was the last thing she could do.

'Here, let me take your coat,' Aidan said. 'Glad you made it.' He stood for a second, awkwardly, his face hovering between its normal sardonic expression and something like uncertainty. Mimah cleared her throat. Why did everything suddenly feel so stilted? Maybe coming to Aidan's flat was a mistake. Maybe they were getting way too personal way too fast.

'Come through,' Aidan said finally. He led her into the kitchen, where a cold wind hit her in the face.

'Shit!' Mimah exclaimed, without thinking. 'It's freezing in here.'

'Oh, yeah, I should have warned you.' Aidan pointed to a cracked windowpane above the sink. 'We've got a draught. Sorry.'

'Th-that's OK.' Rubbing her hands together for warmth, Mimah bit her lip. Thank god Aidan didn't know what her real life was like. If he ever laid eyes on her family's Victorian mansion, never mind their country house in Wiltshire or their villa in Spain, he'd run a mile in shame.

'Wow,' Aidan said. He was looking round the kitchen as if he'd only just laid eyes on it himself. 'Guess I should have tidied up, huh?'

'Don't worry.' Mimah forced a grin. 'I had very low expectations of your hosting skills.'

'How reassuring. I did mean to tidy, I swear – but I had to pack.'

'What for?'

'I got a holiday job this morning.'

'Where? Doing what? Is it something to do with engineering? That's so exciting!'

'Oh . . .' Aidan shrugged. 'Yeah, sort of. I'll be helping my cousin out with his business.'

'What does your cousin do?'

'He's . . . Well . . . He's a building surveyor. I'm off to London tomorrow to stay with him in Whitechapel.'

'That's great!' Mimah exclaimed, then stopped herself. She'd been going to suggest that she and Aidan could meet up in London. But she was forgetting one thing: in the lie she'd woven, she lived in Hasted. And it had to stay that way.

'So . . .' She flailed to change the subject. 'This building surveying stuff, what does it involve? Poking round houses to make sure they won't fall down?'

'A little of that,' Aidan replied. 'And, you know, checking out the plumbing and stuff.'

Mimah raised her eyebrows. 'I didn't know you were a plumbing expert.'

'That's because, unlike some people, I don't go round bragging about my talents.'

'I do not do that.' Mimah swatted him. 'My talents speak for themselves.'

'Oh, really? They must speak incredibly quietly.'

'Did you bring me here just to insult me?'

'Of course. Why else would I have invited you?' Aidan's eyes sparkled. 'So, do you want the tour?'

Mimah smiled. 'I suppose.'

'Right, this is the kitchen. That's the garden.' He pointed through the window at a scrubby yard. 'Although, at this point, it's more like a dump for all the things Mum can't be bothered to throw away. I think last year's Christmas tree might still be out there somewhere.'

Mimah giggled. 'Just make sure it doesn't spontaneously combust. I've heard of that happening – dry old Christmas trees suddenly bursting into flames.'

'You're just a treasure trove of useful information, aren't you?' Aidan said. They moved into the corridor, his arm grazing hers. Mimah's breath caught in her throat.

'That's the lounge,' he said, pointing into a room with his thumb as he passed.

Poking her head round the door, Mimah glimpsed a couple of tatty sofas, a TV and a pile of baby toys. 'Oh! Is there a kid here?'

'Not right now,' Aidan said. 'We keep those for my nephew – my brother's baby.'

'Hang on, how old's your brother?'

'Seventeen. A year younger than me.'

'And he already has a baby?'

'Yep. He got his girlfriend pregnant. They moved in together to try to make a go of it.' Aidan shot her one of his cynical looks. 'What's up with your expression of shock, Jemimah? Don't tell me no one's ever got knocked up by mistake at your school.'

'Um, yeah, obviously,' Mimah lied. 'But they weren't my friends. I didn't really know them. So, I mean, what's your brother's plan?'

Aidan shrugged. 'Honestly, I try not to interfere. He's made loads of choices that I don't agree with, but he's trying to be a dad now and I respect that. He and Beth live in a council flat on the other side of the river – which is lucky for me, because it means I no longer have to share –' he opened a door – 'my bedroom.'

As soon as she stepped inside, Mimah felt different from how she'd felt in the rest of the house. Aidan's bedroom was . . . *his*. It was him. She looked round, at the dark-green walls, at the band posters, at the cool, mismatched furniture. The curtains were drawn and the air smelled of incense, making the whole place seem private, intimate.

She ran her fingers over the top of a vintage wooden swivel chair, painted a rusty orange. 'I like this.'

'Thanks.'

'Where'd you get it?'

Aidan sat on his bed. 'I found it on the street. It was a wreck, so I fixed it up. It's kind of a hobby of mine.'

'What? Scavenging?'

'Actually, it's called salvaging,' Aidan retorted. He pointed to a 1950s-style radio with a jumble of wires sticking out the back. 'I found that on the street, too. I think I can make it work again. It's amazing what people chuck away.'

'Yeah, imagine chucking out a broken radio,' Mimah smirked.

She looked at Aidan. There was something about seeing him in his own house that made him seem vulnerable, earnest, naked. Or maybe she was just getting to know him better. Stepping over to his desk, she sifted through his things. Books about engineering lay next to *The Old Man and the Sea* by Hemingway, next to old Michael Jackson CDs.

'Hey, you,' Aidan teased, 'what do you think you're doing, nosing through my stuff?'

'It's your fault. You invited me here.'

'I know,' he grinned. 'But I was only after one thing.'

Mimah giggled. 'Oh. And yesterday you were being all romantic, wanting to wait and take it slow.'

'Yeah, that romantic act works on chicks the whole time.' Rising from his bed, Aidan sloped towards her, a sexy, crooked smile on his face. 'Did it work on you?' he murmured, leaning towards her until their lips were almost touching.

'Of course not,' Mimah whispered. Her knees went weak as he kissed her. He ran his fingers through her hair and tugged her head back, exposing her neck to his soft, warm mouth.

Mimah closed her eyes. A giggle escaped her.

'What? Am I tickling you?'

'No. I just keep thinking about what you said yesterday – about not having sex on a climbing frame or up against a tree. It's funny, because . . . Well, promise you won't hate me?'

'You mean more than I do already?' Aidan smiled. 'Go on – what?'

'Well, it's funny because I lost my virginity in someone's garden. In a shrub.'

Aidan cracked up, laughing into Mimah's shoulder. 'I

knew it – I knew you'd have some funny story about your first time.'

'How?!' Mimah cried.

'I guess it's that gleam in your eye,' he chuckled, stroking her cheek with the backs of his fingers. 'The way you're so determined not to do things by the book – I think it's what I like about you best. Because I really do like you, you know.'

'I like you, too.' Mimah kissed Aidan, abandoning herself to his hands on her body, as he lifted her dress over her head, unclasped her bra and took her to the bed.

If only he knew the truth about her, she wondered, watching the curtains flutter – would he still really like her, then? Hopefully she'd never have to find out.

Chapter 36

Lauren Taylor shivered. The night was as cold as ice. She was standing outside the Chapel, along with the rest of the St Cecilia's student population, waiting to file into the Carol Concert in an orderly queue. Everyone's parents and guests were already inside, in the warmth. Surely this had to qualify as child abuse.

'Oh. My. God,' Lauren heard someone whisper behind her. 'Is this real?'

'How the hell did it get on Facebook?'

Lauren rolled her eyes. Just what she needed – more stupid gossip she wasn't involved in. She wriggled her toes, just to make sure they weren't getting frostbite.

A burst of giggles reached her ears, followed by a gasp of shock.

'No way,' someone murmured. 'This is bad.'

Suddenly, Lauren became aware of a weird rustling stillness all around her, like the stillness in a forest before a storm. She turned. All the girls near her had moved away. It felt like she'd been abandoned in the middle of a clearing. She saw Minky Coombes and tried to meet her eyes, but

Minky lowered her head. So did Tabitha Fitzsimmons. Rosie Westmoreland was staring at her, open-mouthed.

'What's going on?' Lauren asked uneasily.

'N-nothing,' Rosie said, backing off.

A few feet down the queue, someone guffawed. 'Wait, is that really Lauren Taylor's—?' The rest of the sentence was strangled.

Lauren spun on the nearest girl. It was Portia Mehew-Montefiore, her most timid and scrawny-looking dorm-mate. Portia was clutching her phone.

'Hey!' Lauren grabbed her arm. 'Show me what's on there.'

'I can't,' Portia said. Her sweet face was twisted with alarm. 'I swear I had nothing to do with it.'

'With what? Just show me!'

Portia's fingers loosened their grip. Lauren stared at the Facebook page on the screen. At first, she couldn't tell what it was about. Then she saw the heading: *Diary of a Loser Beyond Repair. By Lauren Taylor* . . .

Her heart contracted. She recognised her own hand-writing in the photos.

Dear Hugo . . .

No. This couldn't be happening.

The group had been created by Georgie Fortescue and it already had eighty-seven members – eighty-seven people who'd read her most intimate secrets; eighty-seven people who knew she'd never been kissed, who knew about her crush on— Lauren turned pale. She started to tremble, feeling sick. Black spots appeared in front of her eyes. She couldn't stand up.

And then the black spots closed in and the world went dark.

Portia flapped her arms. 'Oh my god, she's fainted. Help!'

Gasps rose up, then bubbled into panic as the Year Tens broke ranks and crowded round Lauren's body.

Charlie Calthorpe de Vyle-Hanswicke and Georgie Fortescue pushed to the front of the throng.

'What did you do, you idiot?' Georgie growled.

'It wasn't me!' Portia squeaked.

'Whatever. She's probably faking it, anyway. Hey, Lauren, get up!'

'Quiet,' Charlie said. 'Someone get the nurse.' She squeezed Rosie Westmoreland's arm. 'Rosie, you go, you're the fastest.'

Rosie darted away. Over in the Lower Sixth queue, Alice nudged Dylan. 'Hey, what's up with the fourteen-year-old drama?'

'Who knows?' Dylan glanced over. 'Probably just juvenile— Oh my god. Is that my sister?' Pushing past Alice, she raced towards the head of blond hair lying on the ground. 'Lauren!' she cried.

The Year Tens scrambled away.

'*Hey*,' Charlie murmured to Georgie, '*maybe you should make yourself scarce. This could get ugly.*'

Georgie shrugged. '*What can Dylan Taylor do to me?*'

'Oh my god, oh my god, what happened?' Dylan was wailing, kneeling next to her sister. She grabbed Portia's wrist. 'Is she sick?'

'I don't think so,' Portia whispered, clearly terrified. 'I think . . . I think—'

'What? I can't hear you,' Dylan yelled, jumping up and shaking Portia's shoulders. '*What?*'

'I said I think it was this!' Trembling, Portia held out her phone.

Dylan stared at the screen. There was a long silence, as every single girl in Year Ten held her breath. At last, her lips tight and trembling, Dylan's voice came out in a whisper: 'What the fuck is this?'

As soon as the words left her mouth, she felt that old switch flick in her brain. Her vision blurred with rage.

'What the fuck is this?!' she screamed this time, lurching like a crazed animal, thrusting the phone in people's faces. 'Is this my sister's diary? Is it? Who the fuck is responsible?'

'Dill . . .' Alice's cool hand landed on her shoulder. 'Calm down.'

Minky Coombes nudged Isabelle Bruin. '*Oi,*' she whispered, '*did you know Dylan Taylor was friends with Alice Rochester?*'

'*No. I might have been nicer to Lauren if I had.*'

'Come on, Dill,' Alice went on, soothingly. 'No need to lose it like this. Stop yelling and chill till the nurse gets here. Otherwise they'll hear you in Chapel.'

'I fucking hope they do hear me!' Dylan bellowed. 'Someone better come up with a good explanation for this before I really lose it!'

Behind her, someone smirked. 'Before you really lose it?' Sonia snorted. 'Um, yeah, because you're so serene and composed right now.'

254

Dylan wheeled on her. 'Shut up, you little creep! Can't you just be quiet for once in your stupid, meaningless life? Unless you want me to break your perky little nose for you – in which case, by all means, keep blabbing your usual brainless bullshit!'

Sonia stumbled backwards, open-mouthed.

Charlie nudged Georgie. *'OMG. Did you know Dylan Taylor had a temper like that?'*

'Nope,' Georgie giggled. *'She puts on quite a show. Maybe we should give her a round of applause.'*

At that moment, Mrs Gould, the Year Ten Housemistress, ran up with the school nurse.

'What's going on here?' she panted. 'Everyone, stand back, give Lauren room to breathe. Good. Now,' she said, hands on her hips, 'someone explain to me exactly what's going on.'

'Tell them,' Charlie whispered to Georgie. 'You have to. Lauren needs help. And they might go easier on you if you confess.'

'Whatever,' Georgie smirked. 'They'll go easy on me, anyway. They'll never expel me. My parents give too much money to this school. Come on, let's go for a fag.' Turning on her heel, she walked off towards the rear of the Chapel.

Charlie stared after her, suddenly feeling the cold. She didn't follow. Perhaps she'd never follow Georgie again.

Chapter 37

Sonia crept down the corridor outside Nurse Reynolds' suite. She'd changed out of her usual heels and put on trainers (which she wore about as often as Dylan wore training bras) so no one would hear her footsteps. There was a grim frown on her face. She was still fuming from Dylan's vicious attack outside Chapel – which was exactly why she was here.

'Don't get up,' came a hushed voice from one of the rooms.

Sonia stopped short. Score. She'd found them. And the door was ajar.

'Nurse Reynolds says you have to lie down for at least another half hour. And drink lots of juice.'

'Will you stay with me, Dill?' came Lauren Taylor's voice.

'Of course, sweetie.'

'I don't want to go back out there. Do you think Mom will let me leave?'

Sonia peeked through the crack in the doorway. Dylan was stroking her sister's hair like some kind of busty blonde saint. Vomit.

'I don't know,' Dylan said. 'You've only been here for a

few weeks. And this is one of the most elite schools in England. You know what Mom's like. You know how much she wanted us to come here.'

'But I hate it. I hate my dorm-mates. The only one who isn't a horrible bully is Portia.'

'Trust me, sweetie – it'll get better.'

'How can you say that?'

'Because I saw the looks those girls had on their faces – they all thought what that Georgie Fortescue monster did was wrong.'

'That's not the point! The point is, all those things they know about me now . . .' Tearfully, Lauren shook her head. 'How did I end up the laughing stock of the universe, when you ended up friends with the coolest people in school?'

Dylan gave a bitter laugh. 'Believe me, it wasn't always that way.'

'What do you mean?'

'Alice Rochester and her friends – they all hated me at first.'

Out in the corridor, Sonia dug her nails into her palms. She practically had to gag herself from shouting, '*We still do!*' Instead, she pressed herself flat against the wall like a Bond girl on a stake-out.

Dylan chuckled ruefully. 'Do you remember when my costume came off at the school fashion show?'

'Yeah. So?' Lauren said.

'So, that wasn't an accident.'

'Wait, what are you saying?' Lauren stammered. 'That it was—'

'Sabotage? Absolutely.'

'Are you serious?'

'Dead serious.'

'But how did you get through it?' Lauren cried. 'How did you force yourself to stay?'

'I had to stay,' Dylan said. 'Mom didn't give me a choice. And maybe she was right. Because everything's better now. Well, except for Sonia – my bitch room-mate. She's still coming up with pranks to get rid of me. Luckily, she's too stupid to do any real damage.'

Outside the door, Sonia clenched her fists. How dare Dylan insult her behind her back?

'But why am I talking about myself?' Dylan was saying. 'I don't understand – I had no idea how Georgie and people were treating you. Why didn't you tell me they were bullies?'

There was a silence. Sonia inched forwards and peeked through the doorway again, just to make sure the terrible Taylors hadn't suddenly both dropped dead.

Unfortunately, they hadn't. She saw Lauren looking intently into Dylan's eyes.

'You know why I didn't tell you,' Lauren said. 'If I'd told you, you would have lost your temper with those girls. I mean really lost it. And let's face it, we both know what happened the last time you did that.'

Sonia went as still as a cat about to pounce. What had happened? What had happened?!

'OK,' Dylan whispered. 'Don't bring that up.'

'But you still think about it all the time, don't you?' Lauren said. 'That's what your painting was about.'

'Yeah. So? The painting was just therapeutic. All that stuff's just a memory now.'

'Really?' Lauren said. 'Because, from what I overheard the nurse saying, you went pretty crazy outside Chapel.'

'You'd fainted, for fuck's sake! I was worried.'

'Promise me you'll be careful, Dilly? If anything like what happened in New York happens here, you'll be done for.'

Sonia was listening so intently that she almost didn't hear the footsteps approaching along the adjacent passageway. If she was caught here, *she'd* be done for. She darted down the corridor and back in the direction of Tudor House. She had some digging to do.

Dylan's suitcase was sitting on her bed. She'd already packed most of her things, Sonia saw – which was annoying, because it would be impossible to unpack her bag, search her stuff for secrets, and then repack everything in an acceptable order before Dylan reappeared. By Sonia's calculations, she only had about twenty minutes to find something incriminating. And then it would be the holidays and her chance would be gone. At that moment, her eyes fell on Dylan's computer. This time, Dylan hadn't logged out.

Quick as lightning, Sonia shoved a chair in front of the door so no one could get in. Then she opened Dylan's first email. Admin. Boring. More admin. She scrolled down. An email from Jasper:

Hey cutie, trying to work but can't stop thinking about you. Kisses on all your pink parts. Jxx.

Sonia clapped her hand over her mouth. *Kisses on all your pink parts?* Scandalous. But not destruction-worthy.

The next email was from Dylan's mum. Sonia skimmed it, just out of nosiness – and suddenly, she sat bolt upright.

This was it. And it was better than she ever could have imagined.

My dear Dylan,

I know I'm far away in Berlin and not, perhaps, where I should be: with you and your sister on your last day of term. But I want you to know I'm proud that you've stuck it out at St Cecilia's this autumn. Proud, and I must admit, a little bit surprised. I know it hasn't been easy for you.

Despite what you might think, I love you and care about you very much, and I'm hoping that these last three months in England have done you good. I know you hate me for dragging you over there. I know you blame our entire move on Victor, but that's only the partial truth. I couldn't stand to see you ruin your life in New York.

What you did at Mary Whittaker's house party at the end of the summer was a disgrace. I know it was a raucous night. I know you didn't mean to push that poor girl through the plate-glass window. And I know you didn't mean to verbally abuse the police when they arrived. But all these things are what happens when you lose that terrible temper of yours – especially when there's alcohol involved.

Getting arrested and spending that night in jail (yes, I know we agreed as a family never to speak about that again, but I'm writing it down, because I never want you to forget

*it) helped teach you a lesson. And it helped you grow up.
But I'm glad I brought you to England for a fresh start.
You needed one. Not everybody has the chance to start over
again, and I hope you've made the most of yours. I'm looking
forward to seeing the evidence, not only in your report cards,
but in your attitude towards me.*

*You know I've always believed in tough love. Just because
I've been spending a lot of time with Victor recently doesn't
mean I haven't been thinking about you. But there comes a
point in every girl's life when she needs to grow up and take
responsibility for herself.*

*I'll see you tomorrow, darling. Victor won't be joining us
until Christmas Eve. I'm looking forward to spending some
time with you and Lauren alone.*

Love,
Mom

Sonia read the email three times, just to be certain
she wasn't making it up. Then, her fingers trembling, she
forwarded it to herself. She wasn't going to use it now. Oh,
no, she was going to use it at the best possible moment,
for maximum impact.

What was it Dylan had said about her in the nurse's
suite? She was 'too stupid to do any real damage'? How
wrong that was. And soon Dylan would be wishing with all
her heart that she'd been right.

Chapter 38

'Watch out for the ice!' Alice gasped. She grabbed Mimah's arm, giggling as the two girls wobbled up the steps to the front door of Sir Lucian Scott's huge house in Hampstead.

'Disaster,' Mimah groaned. 'My Louboutins totally weren't made for this weather.' She looked down at her black pumps, which were embellished with crystals all round the edges. The flaring torches outside the Scotts' front door made them glitter like icicles.

'Ooh, I'm excited!' Alice said, trying to ignore the butterflies in her tummy. Tonight was going to be her first time seeing both Rando and Tristan since that fateful train journey, and she wasn't sure she was ready.

'Me too,' Mimah said. 'I always love Sir Lucian's Christmas party. Doesn't it look gorgeous?' She was gazing up at the Scotts' house. A giant wreath was hanging on the front door and every window was flickering with candlelight and buzzing with laughter and music.

The sound swelled as a butler swung open the door.

'Welcome, ladies,' he said, bowing Alice and Mimah inside. 'Happy Christmas. May I take your coats?'

'Champagne?' jumped in a hostess, swinging a silver tray in their direction.

'Absolutely.' Alice swiped a glass and, sliding her phone out of her Marc Jacobs clutch, cast a glance at the screen. The Rando–Tristan scenario wasn't the only thing on her mind. She gave a worried frown.

'Everything OK?' Mimah asked.

'Yeah. Fine.'

'Good. Because this is totally the party of the year.'

It was true. The Scotts' gigantic front hall looked breathtaking. Hundreds of crystal snowflakes hung from the double-height ceiling. Sprays of winter branches popped out of glass urns. In the middle of the hall shone a Christmas tree, trimmed entirely in hand-blown silver spheres, and, on the first landing of the grand staircase, a string quartet was playing Christmas carols. Through a pair of French doors, Alice glimpsed the crowded living room and beyond that the garden, where the party continued into a marquee.

But, still, the most impressive thing was the crowd. Famous faces were everywhere.

'Is that Keira Knightley?' Mimah whispered.

'OMG, maybe she's here with Rupert Friend,' Alice said. 'He is so adorable.'

'No way. He's too scrawny. Bella said Daniel Radcliffe was coming. Let's try to spot him.'

'He's so short we probably won't be able to see him.'

Mimah giggled and grabbed another glass of champagne.

Glancing at her phone again, Alice sighed. 'You know who I'd really like to spot?'

'Orlando Bloom?'

'No. Tally.'

'What on earth are you talking about?'

'I can't get through to her.' Alice pursed her lips. 'I haven't heard from her since the last day of term and I've rung her about twenty times. She was really upset at the Carol Concert. God, I hope she's OK.'

'Do you want me to try her?'

'Yeah.'

Mimah rang Tally's number. She hung up. 'It's going straight to voicemail.'

'See? I'm worried.'

'Shit. Maybe there's something wrong with her phone?'

'She'd have got it fixed by now. I mean, come on – Tals without a phone? It's like a fish without water. I've never gone three whole days without hearing from her.'

Mimah squeezed her friend's shoulders. 'I'm sure she's OK. She'll turn up tonight – she wouldn't miss this party.'

'Fish and chips?' asked a waitress, holding out a silver tray full of mini paper cones.

'Thanks,' Mimah said taking one. She bit her lip, sharing a secret smile with herself at the thought of Aidan – at the thought of his arms around her, only a few days ago. He'd be in London now, too. She missed him already.

Mimah glanced across the room. 'Look, Al,' she said, 'there's Seb. Hi, Sebbie!'

Over near the Christmas tree, Seb waved. He pinched a honey-mustard chipolata off a tray of hors d'oeuvres, then turned back to his new acquaintance.

'So, do you enjoy acting in films?' he asked. The boy he was talking to was about nineteen, with red hair and light blue eyes. He'd introduced himself as Will. And he was seriously cute.

'I do, but there's so much sitting around, killing time in your trailer,' Will said. He had an earnest, enthusiastic manner. 'Not that I've been in loads of films or anything – I'm only just starting out. I actually prefer stage acting.'

'Really? I love theatre.'

'Me too. I have an audition for this Tennessee Williams play at the National Theatre next week. I so want to get it – the director's amazing. I've worked with him before.'

'Wow, that's so cool,' Seb said. He had no idea why this glamorous Will character was bothering to talk to him instead of all the gorgeous girls here – but he wasn't about to complain.

'Do you act at all?' Will said.

'No. I do a bit of singing, though,' Seb added bashfully. 'Our band's playing later, actually.'

'Dude, that's awesome.'

'Yeah. I mean, I'm only the backing singer, but whatever.'

'Don't do yourself down.' Will grinned a knockout, white-toothed grin and brushed Seb's hand. 'You might be the backing singer, but I bet everyone's attention's on you.'

Seb's heart was suddenly in his throat. His hand throbbed where Will had touched it. Was the boy actually flirting with him? Or was he just being nice?

'Hey,' Will said, 'I was wondering – do you have plans for later?'

'I . . . don't know. Why?'

'Well, a bunch of us are going to this club, out east. Dalston Superstore – do you know it? It's kind of a gay night tonight. You should totally join us.'

Seb stared. He seemed to have lost the ability to speak.

'I mean, I know we just met and everything,' Will said. 'You don't have to decide now. Just give me a call if you want to come.' He slipped a card into Seb's palm. 'My number's on there.'

Seb felt like his entire face had turned as red as the ribbons on the Christmas wreath. Will was gay? And Will knew *he* was gay? How?

'Oh, I think I'm, uh, busy tonight,' he said, wondering how the hell he was managing to speak coherently. And why the hell he was turning down what could be the invitation of his life.

Will smiled. 'That's a shame. Give me a call another time, then. Maybe in the new year?'

'Um, yeah, OK. That sounds nice,' Seb said. He stuffed Will's card in his pocket before any of his friends could see it.

'Will!' A hysterical woman was suddenly yelling at his new friend's shoulder. 'I've been looking for you all over. There's someone I simply must introduce you to. He's a very important producer! Come on, come on.'

'Sorry,' Will mouthed. 'My agent.' Giving Seb an adorable shrug, he downed the rest of his champagne and ducked into the crowd.

Still dazed, Seb wandered over to Alice, who was

hanging out by the Christmas tree, chatting to Dylan and Jasper.

'OMG,' Alice laughed, 'who was that random guy you were talking to?'

'Dunno,' Seb said. He realised his mouth was dry, and grabbed a glass of champagne off a pasing tray. 'He's called Will. He's an actor.'

'He's hot,' Dylan said.

'Yeah,' Jasper cackled, 'and a total homo.'

Seb swallowed. Was he the only one at the entire party who hadn't realised?

'Who's a homo?' said a voice.

Alice drew in her breath. Tristan was standing at her side – with Rando in tow. Her heart pounded as Rando's eyes met hers. Quickly, she looked away.

'That guy Seb was just talking to,' she said. 'Jasper thinks he's gay.'

'Oh, the ginger guy?' T said. 'Super gaylord. Obviously.'

'Yeah, total battyman,' Rando smirked.

The others guffawed.

'Hey!' Dylan interrupted. 'Shut up.'

'Who yanked your chain?' Jasper grinned.

'You guys. I can't believe how immature you are. Who cares if the guy's gay? What's wrong with being gay?'

'Come on,' Jasper smirked. 'It's a bit gross. It's unnatural.'

'I can't believe I'm hearing this,' Dylan said. 'Have we regressed fifty years?'

'"Regressed"? Oh, sorry, I didn't realise we were back at school again. I should have brought my uniform.'

'You should have brought a straitjacket, you mean,' Dylan huffed, storming away.

Jasper's swagger deflated.

'Hey, babe, wait,' he called, chasing her towards the garden. 'Let's not fight. I didn't mean it.'

'Back in a sec,' Seb said, rushing for the bar. He definitely needed a martini after that conversation.

Tristan grinned. 'Dylan and Jasper – you've gotta love them. The warring couple.'

Alice didn't reply. She wasn't listening – she was too busy trying not to meet Rando's eye again.

'Speaking of warring couples,' Tristan went on, 'where's Tally tonight? I haven't seen her anywhere.'

'I wish I knew,' Alice said. 'We haven't spoken in a few days. She must be busy Christmas shopping, or something.'

'I hope so,' Rando said. 'I feel terrible that we had to break up right before the holidays.'

His voice sounded normal. Alice risked it – she looked up, right into Rando's clear, beautiful, blue-green eyes. He smiled at her, as if nothing was weird between them at all. She blinked. How could he be so calm? Was it possible she'd imagined their kiss? No. It was too vivid in her mind.

'T, Rando,' Seb said, reppearing with a half-drunk martini, 'we'd better get ready – that string quartet's packing up. The Paper Bandits are on.'

Tristan gripped Alice's hand.

'Shit,' he said. He'd turned pale. 'I'm not sure I can do this – I've never been so nervous in my life.'

'Me neither,' Rando said. 'I think David Bowie's here.'

'Give me that,' T said, grabbing Seb's martini and polishing it off.

'Good luck, guys,' Mimah cried, materialising by Alice's side. 'Here, babe, I got us top-ups of champagne.'

Ding ding ding ding.

The girls looked up. Sir Lucian Scott was standing on the grand staircase, pinging his champagne glass with a fork. Gradually, the party fell silent.

'Thank you, my dear guests,' Sir Lucian said. 'I'm reluctant to interrupt the drinking and merriment, even if only for a moment—'

'So you should be!' heckled someone who looked suspiciously like Guy Ritchie.

Sir Lucian chuckled. 'But I'd like to raise a glass,' he went on, 'to a simple toast: Happy Christmas to all my friends and family. Thank you for braving the cold to be here tonight. Cheers. Here's to the world achieving great things this coming year.'

'Happy Christmas!' the rest of the party echoed.

'And now, for those who are interested,' Sir Lucian said, 'we have a few rather special bands playing in the garden marquee. The first is called the Paper Bandits, and I'm assured by my very hip teenage daughter that they're going to be the next big thing.'

The crowd laughed and whistled.

'Did you hear that?' Mimah punched Alice's arm as they squeezed through the crowd to the marquee. 'The next big thing!'

The tent was swarming with people. The girls elbowed

their way to the front, where T was leaning into the mic. For a second, Alice's eyes slipped past him, to the drum kit – to Rando. He was adjusting his seat. His lips were pressed nervously together. He was gripping the drum sticks he'd bought that Friday night in town.

She forced her gaze away.

'Thanks for coming to listen, everyone,' Tristan said. 'We're the Paper Bandits, and this first song is called, "Too Cruel For School".' He paused, then grinned. 'And, just so my girlfriend knows, it's not about her.'

The audience laughed.

'Have you heard this one?' Mimah whispered.

'What?'

'I said, have you heard this song?' Mimah gave Alice a sharp look. 'What were you just thinking about?'

'Nothing. Shhh. They're starting.'

Tristan played the opening riff.

> *I see her walking past my classroom,*
> *Killer pout, killer shoes.*
> *She doesn't blink.*
> *She doesn't care.*
> *There's no one here she wouldn't use.*
>
> *She's hard as nails.*
> *She's super cool.*
> *She's irresistible.*
> *Too cruel for school.*

Too Cruel for School

She crushes my heart an like eggshell.
She shoots her friends down with a glare.
Her name is Helen;
I am Troy.
Sometimes I wonder how she dares.

She's cold as ice.
She breaks the rules.
She's irresistible.
Too cruel for school.

Her eyes, oh they are made of diamonds.
Her heart is made of Swiss cheese.
She's got a smile.
She's got a bite.
She's got the whole school on its knees.

You burn for her.
And she'll burn you.
She's irresistible.
Too cruel for school.

The crowd cheered.

'They're doing really well, aren't they?' Mimah cried over the applause. 'They don't look nervous at—'

Suddenly, she stopped speaking. She was gaping in horror at something – or someone – a few feet away.

'What's wrong?' Alice cried. She followed Mimah's eyes – and saw nothing but a tall, dark-haired waiter holding a tray.

'Oh my god,' Mimah whispered. 'This can't be real.'
'Well, what a pleasant surprise,' the waiter sneered.
Mimah's champagne glass crashed to the floor.

Chapter 39

Spilt champagne seeped into Mimah's fifteen-hundred-pound shoes, soaking her feet. But she couldn't move; she was as frozen as an ice sculpture.

'Aidan . . .' she whispered.

'Oh? So you recognise me?' the waiter said. 'So it is you. Because I wasn't sure, under all that expensive lace.'

'Aidan, I . . .'

'Fish and chips?' Aidan snapped, holding out his tray. 'The way posh people eat them. Just how you like.'

'Aidan—'

'What's the matter, Miss? Not hungry?'

'Please—'

'Please what?' Aidan's voice came out as a snarl. He had a twisted, sardonic sneer on his face. 'Please what, Jemimah? If that's even your real name.'

'What are you doing here?'

'I could ask you the same thing.'

'Now, wait just a minute,' Alice cut in. 'Mimey, how do you know this person?'

'Ha!' Aidan spat. 'I think the more relevant question,' he said, turning on Alice, 'is, how do *you* know her?'

'What on earth are you talking about?' Alice cried indignantly. 'She's one of my best friends. We grew up together. We go to boarding school together. I think I know her better than some rude second-rate waiter. How dare you attack a guest at Sir Lucian Scott's—'

'Alice,' Mimah gasped. 'Stop.'

'What do you mean, "stop"? Who is this creep?'

'He's not a creep. He's my . . . my pupil. I tutor him – in Hasted.'

Aidan laughed. 'Yeah, Hasted, where she lives? You know, with her poor, hard-working grandmother with the posh accent? Oh, don't tell me you haven't met her *grandmother*? Well, then, maybe you've heard about her mother – the cruel drug-addict mother who abandoned her when she was a baby?'

'Mimah, is this guy insane? Do you want me to call security?'

But Mimah wasn't listening. She was shaking, with grief and anger. 'How dare you, Aidan,' she began, screwing up her eyes to keep from crying. 'I told you those things in confidence—'

'Hmmm . . .' Aidan cut in sarcastically. 'Does it still count as a confidence if it's a lie? Because they are lies, aren't they, *Mimey*?'

'Not lies. Just—'

'Why did you do it?' Aidan clenched his jaw. 'Do you think I'm a complete moron? Just wanted a bit of rough, did you? A rough-and-ready working-class boy to show you a good time?'

'It wasn't like that!' Mimah choked back her sobs. 'I liked you. But you were judging me – you thought you knew all about me and I wanted to prove you wrong.'

'By lying your arse off?'

'You lied, too! You said you were coming to London to be a surveyor. But you weren't, were you? You're just a waiter.'

'Did you hear the way you just said "waiter"?' Aidan scoffed. 'It sounded like you were eating shit. You're right; I did fib. I wanted you to think I was gonna be a success. But I lied about a *job*. You lied about your whole life!' He was shouting now. Guests were staring. 'You have no clue how this feels, do you? I thought I liked you. I thought I'd met someone incredible, who was going to change everything. Turns out I don't even know who you are!'

'What the hell is going on over here?' Bella Scott broke through the throng in a floor-length green silk dress, followed by her tall, glamorous mother. 'Alice, Mimah, are you OK?'

Alice said nothing. She was gaping at Aidan.

'We – we're fine,' Mimah stammered. 'Sorry for the noise. Sorry, Bella. Sorry, Regina. There's been a . . . misunderstanding.'

'You can say that again,' Aidan sneered.

'Just one minute, young man,' Lady Regina Scott interrupted, turning on Aidan. In her spike heels, with her upswept hair, she was almost as tall as him. 'How dare you speak to one of my guests that way? Clean up that champagne and take it back to the kitchen. You're being paid to serve people, not to stand around talking back to them.'

'Actually,' Aidan said, 'I'm not being paid at all. Because I quit.' He dropped his tray of fish-and-chip hors d'oeuvres with a crash. 'You can take your posh finger food and shove it up your arse, lady. Because I'm done with you people. Done!'

Lady Regina pressed her hand to her heart. 'Well, I never—!' she gasped, as Aidan ripped off his black bow tie.

'Congratulations, Jemimah,' he said. His eyes, which had been so soft and laughing and tender the last time Mimah had seen him, were hard as flint and glinting with rage and humiliation. 'You got what you wanted – you proved me completely and utterly wrong about you. Happy Christmas.' He turned on his heel and stalked away through the gaping crowd. 'And, by the way,' he hurled over his shoulder, 'make sure you stay away from me. For ever.'

'Oh my goodness,' Lady Regina said. 'Oh my goodness, gracious me.' Fanning her face with her manicured hand, she looked up at her guests and forced a smile. 'I'm terribly sorry, everybody. Just an unfortunate incident with the staff. Please, have more champagne. Cheers, everybody. Cheers!'

Alice laid her hand on Mimah's shoulder. 'Sweetie, are you OK?'

Mimah said nothing. She was shaking, her eyes bloodshot and her as skin as white as chalk. She looked down at her expensive lace dress and crystal shoes, and tears welled from her eyes.

'Come on, let's get you out of here,' Alice said. 'We'll

head to Shoreditch House and get you a stiff drink. Why don't you go get our coats? I'll tell the others we're leaving.'

Mimah gave a mute nod.

As Alice headed towards the Paper Bandits, who were still playing, oblivious to everything, her phone beeped.

It was Tally – at last.

Hi Babe. I can't face New Year knowing Rando will be there. Have gone away. Don't ask where. Don't look for me. I need time to find myself. Love you. Tals

Alice stared at the text. Two thoughts raced through her mind. One: she hoped with all her heart that Tally was OK. The girl had always been a drama queen, but she'd never pulled anything quite like this before. Two: spending New Year around Rando was going to be a lot more complicated, now that one distraction was out of the picture.

Chapter 40

'I'm never getting up that early again,' Sonia grumbled, tearing off her purple fur hat as she walked through the chalet door. It was nine in the morning on 30 December and the gang had just arrived at the von Holstadt's compound in Val d'Isère. 'My poor eyes. I bet there are massive bags under them. I bet I look like a raccoon. Do I? Do I?' She thrust her face into Alice's.

'Personal space!' Alice ordered. 'And please shut up about your eyes. It's nothing a bit of Touche Éclat can't fix.' She glanced towards the front door. 'Put them in the red room, please,' she called loudly, as the von Holstadts' chauffeur hauled her suitcase and skis inside.

She flopped on to a couch covered in woven blankets and deep, cashmere cushions. 'I am so glad Christmas with my family is over. Too much family time drives me insane.'

'Me too,' T said, throwing himself down beside her. He wrapped his good arm round her waist. 'Mmm. Your hair smells amazing.'

'Whoa.' Dylan had come inside and was stamping her snowy feet on the mat. 'This place is gorgeous.'

She gazed round the chalet's main room. It was huge,

built of antique beams and full of candles, flowers, rugs and carved Alpine furniture. A pair of antlers hung above the mantelpiece and a log fire crackled in the grate. Through a door, Dylan glimpsed a games room kitted out with a pool table, video games, a film projector and shelves upon shelves of DVDs.

'And we have this chalet all to ourselves?' she asked, grabbing Jasper's hand.

'Yep. My parents have their own, across the grounds. Theirs has an indoor swimming pool and a separate sauna hut. It's so unfair.'

'OMG, I can't believe I'm actually in the Alps,' Dylan said. 'This place is like a winter paradise.'

Jasper kissed her. 'And you haven't even seen the outdoor hot tub yet. Our bedroom leads right to it – through here.'

'I think Alice and I might go check out our room, too,' T grinned.

'Hold your horses,' Mimah said, jumping up from the armchair she'd claimed. 'Before all you smug couples disappear for a marathon shag session, can we please get some skiing in?'

'I second that,' Seb said.

'Me too,' added Rando. 'Otherwise us single people are going to feel terribly left out.'

Alice coiled her hair over one shoulder. 'Fine. Let's ski.'

'Seriously?' Tristan said. 'You're just planning to leave me here while you go enjoy yourself on the slopes? What am I supposed to do all day?'

Alice broke away from him. 'Babe, you knew that was the deal. I thought you were bringing books and stuff to keep yourself entertained. You can't expect me not to ski just because you're in a sling.'

'I guess,' Tristan said moodily.

'What do you mean, you *guess*? Why are you acting like such a child?'

'I'm not. It's all right for you,' Tristan retorted. 'You don't have to sit around for four days with nothing to do while all your friends have the time of their lives.'

'Come on; you're exaggerating.'

'And you're being selfish,' Tristan snapped.

'Why? For wanting to ski on a ski holiday? Oh, yeah, how selfish and unreasonable of me.'

'Now, now, lovebirds,' Sonia cut in. 'No fighting. Don't worry, T – I'll keep you company.' Sonia never skied – she hated it: the frozen toes, the wind-burned cheeks, the bulky clothes. She only came to Val d'Isère for the après ski – that, and the fact that missing a group trip would be lethal for her social standing. 'You should consider yourself lucky that you're stuck on level ground,' she declared. 'Why anyone would want to slide down a mountain on two sticks is beyond me. We're not cavemen anymore.'

'Hold on,' Dylan said. 'If you don't like skiing, then why did you come?'

'Because,' Sonia said, with a saccharine smile, 'I'm a sociable person. I like to spend time with my friends. Unlike you, I've actually known these people for longer than five minutes.' She turned to Tristan. 'Anyway, darling, don't worry; I have the perfect plan for our day. First, we'll check out the boutiques in town. Then we'll have a lovely long lunch and drink delicious coffees with hot creamy milk. Then we'll curl up by the fire and watch romcoms.'

Tristan rolled his eyes. 'Sonia, just because I'm injured, doesn't mean I've turned into a girl.'

'Or a poof,' Jasper chortled. 'Look, why don't you two come meet us in a couple of hours for lunch in the café at the top of the ski lift?'

'Fine.' Tristan nodded, even though he still looked annoyed. 'I guess I can at least eat bratwurst and look at the view while everyone else has fun.'

Ignoring this, Alice stood up.

'So, Dill, are you good on the slopes?' she asked, lifting her ski boots out of their case.

'I'm OK,' Dylan said. 'My dad used to take us to Aspen every year. I like going off-piste best – making tracks in the virgin snow.'

'Me too!' Alice squealed, taking her arm. 'This is gonna be wicked. I'm so glad you're here.'

Sonia scowled. Stupid Dylan Taylor and her stupid sporty suck-up comments – not that she'd be around for much longer. Dylan's downfall was just a matter of time. Her dirty secret was waiting to be unveiled.

Chapter 41

Up on the mountain top, the snow glittered like cement. Alice flung out her arms, pausing before she followed the others down the final steep plunge to the café for lunch. Below, Alpine villages stretched across the valley and along the river, smoke from their chimneys blending with the icy mist. The fresh, freezing air burned in her lungs. She turned away, her eyes bright and her cheeks flushed with cold – and saw Rando staring at her.

'Oh!' she blurted out. 'I thought you skied down with the others.'

'No. I thought I'd wait for you.'

'Oh. Right. Thanks.'

Rando blinked.

'What?' Alice said. She touched her hand to her face, suddenly self-conscious.

'Nothing. You just look so . . . happy. It's nice.'

'Oh. Thanks.' She swallowed.

Wind gusted across the slope, rippling Rando's messy brown hair. He pulled up the collar of his ski jacket and, for a moment, they were both silent. When they spoke, their words came out in a jumble.

'Are you—' he began.

'I'm sorry that Tally—'

'– OK skiing without T?'

'– bailed on the trip.'

They both laughed.

'Conversation obviously isn't our strong suit,' Alice said. 'Race you down to the restaurant?'

'You're on.' Rando snapped on his goggles.

Alice grabbed her poles. 'Ready, set, go!'

They pushed off, their skis shaving the snow like blades, crunching and grinding, and sending fine mists of powder glinting into the air. Alice felt weightless, gleeful, as if all her worries were flying out behind her and evaporating into the sky.

'Can't catch meee!' she yelled, beaming as she swerved on to a wide, steep run.

'Wanna bet?' Rando shouted. Rounding the corner fast, he drew level with her, then ahead. 'Take that!'

'No way!' Alice cried. Bending low, she shot past him, took the final curve and skidded on to the flat snow near the café. 'I win!' she cried, sticking both her poles in the air as she scraped to a stop. 'Whoa!' she squealed. Rando was racing towards her at full speed. 'Don't hit me, don't hit me. Help!'

At the last possible instant, Rando braked, his skis halting inches from hers. 'Had you scared, didn't I?' he grinned.

'You loser,' Alice laughed. She flung her arms round his neck. 'Ohmygod, that was so fun. Just what I needed.'

'Good.' Rando hugged her back, squeezing her tightly.

Suddenly, Alice pulled away. 'We . . . We should go inside,' she said. She turned away to unsnap her skis, hoping Rando couldn't see how fiercely she was blushing.

Still breathing hard from the race, they stomped their way into the café.

'Where have you two been?' Tristan demanded.

'Nowhere,' Alice smiled. 'Just taking our time coming down. It's so gorgeous out there.'

'Thanks for rubbing it in,' T said. Folding his arms, he directed a cold look across the table.

'Sorry,' Alice muttered, sinking into a chair. All the joy she'd felt on the slopes seemed to seep through her feet into the floor. She reached for the menu with a sigh. 'Let's just order, OK? I'm starved.'

Chapter 42

The centre of Val d'Isère twinkled like a jewel in the black night. Strings of lights decked the fir trees, reflecting off the snowy ground. The moon shone through silvery clouds. And the sign outside Dick's Tea Bar, the town's oldest club, flashed like a beacon.

'Get ready, people,' Jasper shouted above the music as he slipped the bouncer a twenty-euro note and led the way inside. 'We're doing some serious drinking and dancing tonight. No losers allowed.'

'But I can hardly move,' Sonia groaned. 'I think I ate a whole vat of fondue at dinner. Ali, do I look fat?'

'Yeah – obese.'

'Nooo!' Sonia squealed. 'How could you guys have let me gobble all that cheese? I feel like my intestines are made of Gruyère.'

Dylan rolled her eyes. 'Wow, Sonia, you know what? The longer I know you, the more charming and varied your conversation gets. How do you manage it?'

Alice laughed, as the DJ started spinning a hip-hop remix of 'Strawberry Fields'.

'Let's dance,' she cried, grabbing Mimah and Dylan.

The others followed them on to the floor. Green and blue disco lights flashed overhead, and champagne sprayed down from the bottle Jasper had just popped. Nearby, two girls fell on each other in a sloppy, drunken kiss. The group around them exploded in cheers.

'That is so hot!' wolf-whistled a boy with shaggy blond hair.

'Take pictures!' shrieked another guy, practically climbing on people's heads to get a better view of the action.

Alice rolled her eyes. 'OMG, that is so lame,' she said in Sonia's ear. 'As if fake lesbians are so exciting.'

'Agreed,' Sonia sniffed. 'They're just snogging for attention. Hey, babe, are you sure I don't look fat?'

Before Alice could respond, her stomach tightened. A few feet away, a girl wearing a slutty minidress was closing in on Rando, gyrating against him, her boobs practically bursting out. She snaked her arms round his neck. Alice tried to ignore the jealousy surging inside her. But she couldn't tear her eyes away.

'Hey,' Sonia shouted in her ear, 'are you OK?'

'What? Yeah. Why?'

'You didn't answer my question. What are you looking at?'

'Nothing. Ugh. I hate this place. Why is it such a meat market?'

'It's always been that way. That's why it's fun. Oh, god,' Sonia groaned, 'look who's here.'

'Hey, Al,' Dylan said. She pointed at the group surrounding the kissing girls. 'Those guys are ridiculous. And, by the way, is it just me, or is everyone in this place English?'

'Duh,' Alice said. 'This is the Brit hangout. If you're a Brit and you come to Val d'Isère, then you come here.'

'But why?' Dylan insisted. 'What's the point of being in France and surrounding yourself with the same people you can meet at home?'

'Oh, didn't you know?' Alice gave a sardonic smile. 'It's the English custom. Wherever we go, all around the world, we always manage to find two things: each other, and Irish pubs.'

'So true!' Tristan said. He'd been dancing near them and had caught the last part of the conversation. 'You know what I like best about this place?'

Alice shrugged. 'The champagne?'

'Nope. The fact that it never, ever changes.'

'You can't be serious,' Alice scoffed, raising an eyebrow. 'What's so great about that?'

'Come on.' Tristan lit a cigarette, even though smoking inside Dick's was banned. 'We've been coming here since we were barely thirteen, and the place is the same as it always was: the same music, the same drinks, the same décor, the same crowd. You know exactly what you're getting. Are you saying that's not comforting?'

'Yeah,' Alice retorted. 'That's exactly what I'm saying. It's boring. Change is good.'

Tristan clenched his jaw. 'Hey, can I talk to you for a second?'

'Fine.'

'They walked to a quieter part of the club, near the door. Tristan wheeled on her.

'Listen,' he growled, 'why do you keep disagreeing with everything I say? What's your problem?'

'*My* problem?' Alice snarled. 'You're the one who's being a dick.'

'That is so unfair! How? Please, tell me, because I have no idea what you're on about.'

'The whole time we've been here, you've been guilt-tripping me about having fun. You've been complaining about everything I do.'

'Oh, right. Because I'm supposed to be happy that you obviously don't want to spend time with me?'

'What the hell are you talking about?' Alice cried.

'Oh, please. Don't pretend you don't know. How about today? We could have hung out together; it could have been awesome. We've got this great room, this awesome king-size bed, a hot tub. I mean, you're my girlfriend, for fuck's sake – but no, all you want to do is ski with your friends.'

'They're your friends, too! And how many times do I have to tell you – this is a *ski trip*. What part of that don't you understand?'

'See?' Tristan threw up his hands. 'You keep completely missing the point. It's like you've suddenly turned into a massive bitch and—'

'Hey!' Alice shouted. 'Don't you dare call me a bitch.'

'Excuse me, sir,' said a bouncer, tapping Tristan on the shoulder.

'What?' Tristan shouted.

'Calm down, please. There's no smoking in here. You need to put that out.'

'For fuck's sake,' Tristan snapped, 'it's just one cigarette. Can't you see I'm having a crisis with my girlfriend?'

'Sir, I really don't care about you and your girlfriend. You need to follow the rules of the club.'

'How dare you speak to me like that?' Tristan demanded. 'You'd be out of a job if it wasn't for people like me.'

The bouncer grabbed his arm. 'That's it. You're out of here. Now.'

'What? Get off me.'

'*Now,*' the bouncer ordered, tightening his grip.

Tristan rolled his eyes. 'Fine. This place is shit, anyway. Come on, Alice – we're going.'

Alice shook her head. 'No way. I'm not going anywhere with you. You're obviously in a ridiculous mood.'

'Seriously?' Tristan widened his eyes. 'I'm getting kicked out, and you're just gonna stand there and let me go home all by myself?'

'It's your own fault,' Alice shot back. 'You shouldn't have called me a bitch. Anyway, I think a few hours apart will do us both good. We obviously both need to cool off – especially you.'

'Fine,' Tristan spat. 'I can see where your loyalties lie – with yourself. I hope you're happy,' he called over his shoulder as the bouncer led him away. 'I'll be expecting an apology when you get home.'

Alice shut her eyes, fighting for breath. She needed a moment alone. She needed to cool off. She pushed her way towards the toilets, shoving at anyone who got in her way.

'Ow!' cried a voice, as her elbow thudded against someone's ribs. 'Alice?'

'What?'

'It's me.'

Alice looked up. Rando.

'Oh. Sorry. Hi.' She dabbed her face with her fingertips, trying to compose herself. 'What are you doing all the way back here? I thought you were with that girl.'

Rando rolled his eyes. 'No. I managed to escape her.'

'Oh, really?' Alice tried to suppress the ridiculous relief welling in her chest. Suddenly, it all just felt like too much – Tristan, Rando, the horrible fight, the confusion. She turned away, her lower lip trembling.

'Hey.' Rando touched her arm. 'Are you OK?'

She shook her head.

'What happened?'

'Nothing . . . Just, Tristan and I had a fight. A big one. He went home. And I don't know what to do.'

'Oh.' Rando bit his lip. 'I'm sorry. What was your fight about?'

'Nothing. Just stupid stuff. God, I feel so awful about it.' Alice wiped her eyes. 'Do you think . . .' She suppressed a sob. 'Do you think you could give me a hug?'

Without answering, Rando wrapped his arms around her. He held her close – even closer than outside the café. Alice stayed very still, willing him not to break away. Just then, the music slowed and the lights dimmed to red. The disco ball above them sprinkled the world with diamonds.

'Dance with me?' Rando murmured.

'Of course.'

They swayed back and forth, cheek to cheek. Rando smelled of soap and shaving foam and fresh mountain air.

'Hey,' Alice whispered, her voice muffled by his shoulder.

'Mmm?'

'About the other day – on the train. We should never have done that.'

'I know.' Rando pulled back and touched his forehead to hers. 'I'm sorry. It was wrong.'

'It's just . . . Tristan's my boyfriend.'

'Right. And he's my friend. We owe him more than that.'

'Exactly.' Alice brushed her hand against Rando's cheek. 'I'm glad we got that out of the way,' she murmured. 'So, friends?'

'Friends.'

They danced. She felt the length of his body against hers. She felt the swaying of his hips and the press of the clubbers around them. Despite her words, her heart was beating like a baby bird against her ribs.

The song ended. They broke apart. Alice tried not to look into Rando's eyes. She felt like someone trying not to look into the sun.

'Come on,' she whispered. 'The others will be wondering where we are.'

Chapter 43

'Where have you two been?' Sonia squawked, practically jumping out of her seat as Alice and Rando materialised from the crowd.

Alice shrugged. 'You guys got a table – nice,' she said, ignoring the question. 'How'd you swing it?'

'Aha,' Jasper winked, as Rando sat down by his side. 'That's my little secret. I have my ways with the bouncers around here.'

'Uh, did you mean that to sound dodgy?' Alice smirked, slipping into a chair next to Dylan. 'Because it totally did.'

'Hey, sweetie, wait,' Sonia interrupted from the other side of the table. 'Why are you sitting so far away? I saved you a seat over here.'

'Thanks, but I'm fine where I am.' Alice grabbed an empty champagne flute and filled it with the dregs of a bottle. She didn't care if it was flat; she needed a drink.

'You OK?' Dylan said quietly.

'Yeah,' Alice murmured. 'I'll tell you about it later. God, why does everything have to be so complicated?'

'You're telling me. Tristan texted Jasper and said he got kicked out. Did you guys—'

'Ahem,' Sonia barked. 'It's rude to whisper. What are you two talking about? I demand that you share it with the table.'

'Right. And I demand that you shut up, get a better personality, and develop a higher IQ,' Dylan said. 'But it's not gonna happen, is it?'

'Excuse me?' Sonia stammered. 'I'm-I'm-I'm *speechless*.'

'If only,' Dylan muttered.

'Did everyone hear that?' Sonia cried. 'I hope everyone can hear the insults Dylan keeps flinging at my poor innocent head.'

Before anyone could respond, a girl with bleached-blond hair and bee-stung lips swayed over to the table.

'Hey, hottie,' she slurred, draping herself across Jasper like a feather boa. 'You're a tasty muffin, aren't you?'

'Um, yeah.' Jasper rolled his eyes and turned back to his conversation with Rando and Seb.

'Tee hee. I bet you've got a smokin' hot body under that baby-pink shirt. How about we go to the toilets and you show me?' She scraped her talon-like fingernails across Jasper's chest.

Chuckling, he pushed back his chair. 'Excuse me, darling, but I've got a girlfriend.'

'Yeah,' Dylan added, 'and she's sitting right here. So watch it.'

'Another bottle of bubbly for the table, people?' Jasper said.

'Excellent!' Seb cheered drunkenly. 'Bubbly, bubbly, rah rah rah!'

'Coming right up.'

'Hey, fittie,' the girl called, stumbling after Jasper as he headed for the bar, 'wait up.'

'No, you wait up.' Dylan slammed down her empty champagne glass. 'I warned you, that's my boyfriend you're hitting on.'

'Oh, really?' the girl sneered, looking her up and down. 'Not for long, 'cause I'm here now, and you're punching above your weight.'

'Fuck you!' Dylan yelled. Jumping to her feet, she grabbed the girl's shoulders and glared into her face. 'If you think I'm gonna sit here and watch someone trying to steal my boyfriend in front of my face, then you've obviously never met me. So you can take your Botoxed lips and your tacky hair-extensions, and go drool on some other guy. Slutty bitch,' she muttered, as the girl stumbled away.

Sonia cleared her throat. 'My, my, my,' she drawled. 'Someone's got a bad *temper*. Don't you think Dylan has a bad temper, babe?' She turned to Alice with what was supposed to be a significant sneer, but Alice was shaking with laughter.

'OMG, Dill,' she giggled, 'hilarious. Sometimes you remind me of a guest on Jerry Springer.'

Dylan snorted. 'That girl was a joke.'

'Hmmm, I don't know,' Sonia sneered. She leaned across the table and put her lips to Dylan's ear. 'She did have a

point. You are punching above your weight with Jasper.'
Dylan recoiled. 'What did you just say?'

'You heard me. I mean, everyone knows Jasper only likes
you for one thing – or should I say, two things.' Sonia cast
a smirk at Dylan's boobs.

'Look, you snake,' Dylan snarled, 'I've had enough of
you. Why do you always have to say such bitchy things?
We're on vacation, for goodness' sake. And, anyway, what
did I ever do to you?'

'Oooh, sorry,' Sonia smirked. 'Don't lose your temper.
I don't want you to throw me out the window.'

'Excuse me?'

'Oh, nothing.' Sonia examined her purple-painted
fingernails.

'Champagne, everyone!' Jasper said, reappearing at the
table. He popped the cork. Everyone cheered. Dylan held
out her glass to catch the overflow.

'Careful, Dylan,' Sonia said loudly. 'You wouldn't want
to drink too much and get violent.'

Dylan ignored her.

'I'm only looking out for you,' Sonia went on. 'I hear
the French police aren't as lenient as the American ones.
But you'd know better than me, naturally. Are the American
police lenient, Dylan? Are they?'

Dylan grabbed Sonia's delicate silk top. 'What the hell
are you talking about?'

'Ow!' Sonia squealed, with a manic, delighted smile on
her face. 'You're hurting me. At least there aren't any plate-
glass windows in this club. So I'm probably safe.'

Dylan turned pale. She dropped Sonia's shirt.

'Sone!' Alice said. 'What are you on about? You're not making any sense.'

'Oh, but I am.' Sonia smoothed her hair. 'Just look at Dylan: she knows what I'm talking about. Don't you, roomie?'

Dylan was shaking. Her cheeks were hollow.

'What?' Alice said. 'What on earth *are* you talking about?'

'Tell us,' Rando pressed. 'This is weird.'

'Spit it out,' Mimah nodded. 'Now I'm totally curious.'

'Me too.' Jasper was starting at Dylan, holding his champagne flute mid-air. She met his eye.

'No!' she suddenly cried. 'Sonia, just shut up.'

'I will not shut up!' Sonia shrieked triumphantly. 'People have a right to know who they're dealing with. Jasper has a right to know who his girlfriend really is. Alice has a right to know the truth about her new BFF. And it's this –' She pointed a finger in Dylan's face. 'The person in our midst is a common criminal. She came here because she was running away from her history. In New York, she threw a poor defenceless girl through a window and spent the night in jail! That's who your new friend is.'

Mimah gasped.

Seb's eyebrows shot towards the ceiling.

Dylan covered her face with her hands. This was it. Her new, happy life was over.

'Is this true?' Jasper whispered.

Dylan nodded miserably. 'Yes.'

'This is what you didn't want me to find out from your

notebook, isn't it? You've been keeping this secret for months.'

'I wish I could deny it,' Dylan said. 'But I can't.'

There was a long silence around the table. Then, out of the blue:

'Awesome!' Jasper guffawed.

Sonia snapped her head round.

'What?' she and Dylan both burst out together.

'Dill . . .' Jasper was choking with laughter, 'were you really arrested?'

'Yes, I was. And that's not all. I spent the night in a cell.'

Jasper took Dylan's hand. 'My girlfriend's a badass! OK, so you obviously have a bit of explaining to do, but seriously? That's kind of sexy.'

'I can't believe I'm hearing this,' Sonia spat. 'Al, surely you don't find Dylan's moral shortcomings amusing?'

Alice's face was set. 'No,' she said. 'I don't.'

'I knew it!' Sonia cackled.

'But,' Alice said, looking Sonia in the eye, 'that doesn't mean I'm turning my back on her.'

Sonia's jaw dropped.

'We all have secrets,' Alice said. 'At our age, you can't expect people to be totally innocent and squeaky clean.' She swallowed. It was taking all her willpower not to look at Rando. 'Dylan's obviously trying to make a new start, and I respect that. And you know what I don't respect? You, Sonia – for dragging her name through the mud. Now, if you'll excuse me, I need some fresh air.'

Sonia watched Alice go. Then, shoving back her chair,

without meeting anyone's eye, she stalked off in search of her coat. She was fed up of Alice Rochester's ingratitude. And she was fed up of being kicked to the curb like a mutt. Next term, things were going to change. She'd been Alice's lapdog for long enough.

Chapter 44

Mimah sat curled in the corner of the sofa, wishing she felt more like joining in with the New Year's Eve festivities and less like crawling back into bed. She looked around the chalet's living room, where the gang was gearing up for a big night out. Candles glimmered on the coffee table. Lady Gaga was blasting out of the iPod dock. Seb and Tristan were smoking a huge joint. Rando, Jasper and Dylan were attempting to breakdance. And Sonia was guzzling wine straight from the bottle, every now and then casting evil looks at Alice, Dylan and anyone else who happened to cross her line of sight. Soon, according to tradition, they'd all be heading to the centre of town to see in the new year under the church clock.

Mimah sighed. For the hundredth time that evening, she slipped her phone out of her pocket. Nothing. She'd sent Aidan half a dozen texts in the past few days, but she hadn't heard a word from him since Lucian Scott's party. She bit her lip. No one liked a downer, so she was trying to put on a brave face around her friends. But she felt awful. Christmas had been the worst. Not only because her mum had been bedridden, her dad had been absent and

Charlie had been in a weirdly guilty mood – but also because Aidan's silence had made her feel desolate. *I don't even know who you are.* His words tolled over and over in Mimah's mind, like a death knell. How could he say that, when he knew her better than anyone in the world?

'Hey, mopey.' Alice was stumbling towards her, carrying a glassful of poisonous-looking orange liquid. 'Would you like to sample Jasper's amazing fruit-punch-whisky cocktail?'

'Um, I don't think so.'

'You OK?' Alice asked, flopping down on the couch.

'Yeah.'

'Still thinking about that stupid waiter?'

'I guess. Except he's not really a waiter. And he's not stupid.'

'He seemed pretty dumb to me,' Alice snorted. 'What sort of idiot causes a scene like that at the most important party of the season? He'll never work again.'

'Like I said, he didn't want to be a waiter, anyway.' Mimah shut her eyes. 'Shit, I wish I'd done things differently.'

'Aw, babe,' Alice said. 'I know how you feel. Boy-trouble sucks.'

'Are you still not talking to T?'

'You could say that,' Alice scoffed. 'No way am I forgiving him this quickly – not after he called me a bitch. And I don't think Sonia's talking to me, either.'

'Oh, really?' Mimah smirked. 'What gave you that impression? The fact that she keeps shooting death stares in your direction? Or the fact that she snorts as loudly as a walrus whenever you say anything?'

Alice giggled and rested her head on Mimah's shoulder. 'Oh, god, we're a pair, aren't we? Sometimes I hate hanging out in a group.'

Mimah looked at her friend in surprise. What was she on about? Alice had thrived on groups ever since Mimah had known her. She was like a queen bee, lost without her hive.

'This corner looks cosy.'

The girls glanced up. Rando was standing near the couch, holding a joint. 'Mind if I join you?'

'Of course,' Mimah said, budging over so he could sit between her and Alice. 'As long as you share some of that.'

'Naturally.'

Alice ran a hand through her hair as Rando settled into the cushions. She tried her best not to think about how close he was, even though his thigh was pressing against hers. *Friends*, she recited to herself. *We're friends. Just friends.*

'By the way,' she said out loud. 'Thanks for making dinner. I didn't know you could cook.'

Rando chuckled. 'I can't. Stir-fries don't count.'

'They do in my book,' Alice said. 'Most guys I know consider themselves heroes if they can fry an egg and toast some bread. As if making breakfast the morning after is some amazing seduction technique.'

Mimah giggled. 'Totally. I can't count the number of guys I've dated who brag about their fry-up skills. It's like,

301

learn to make a meal that involves non-brown food, and then I'll get excited.'

'Whoa,' Rando grinned. 'Hang on, let me get my note-book. I should be writing these tips down.'

Peering across the room, Alice heaved a sigh. 'Guys, is it just me, or is Tristan drinking way too much? I mean, not that I care right now, but look at him – I think he's put away half that bottle of vodka.'

'Well, it is New Year,' Mimah said.

'So? Is that any reason to drown his liver?'

Rando squeezed Alice's arm. 'He's probably trying to forget about your argument last night. He's been in a foul mood all day.'

'You're telling me,' Alice mumbled, trying to ignore the thrill that ran through her at Rando's touch.

At that moment, Tristan lurched over to the couch. 'Hey, homies,' he slurred. His eyes were bloodshot. 'Hand over the weed.'

'Hold your horses,' Mimah said. 'I'm not done yet.'

'Leave it, mate,' Rando added. 'I think you've had enough.'

'I'll be the judge of that!' Tristan shouted, lunging for Mimah's fingers.

'Watch out!' Alice cried, as he stumbled into the coffee table, lost his balance and landed on a cluster of tea lights.

'Ouch!' T bellowed. 'My bum – it's burning!'

'Are you OK?'

'OMG,' Mimah giggled, 'his jeans are singed.'

'Owww,' Tristan moaned.

'For god's sake,' Alice muttered, rolling her eyes.

Rando dragged Tristan across the room. 'Come outside and sit in the snow,' he said. 'That'll cool you off.'

'What's going on?' Seb asked, as everyone crowded out the door and into the garden. 'Is T OK?'

'Fuck, it's freezing out here,' Mimah cried. 'It's got to be at least minus twenty.'

'I'm getting another jumper,' Sonia shivered. 'I've never been so cold in my life.'

Alice jogged in place, her teeth chattering.

'Uuurgh . . .' T rolled in the snow. 'I feel sick.'

'That's because you're an idiot,' Alice said. 'I told you not to drink so much.'

'Blaaargh!' Tristan vomited.

'Gross,' Mimah cried, running backwards. 'Frozen vom.'

'Wonderful,' Alice groaned. 'The height of romance. This is exactly how I imagined spending New Year's Eve – watching my boyfriend who I'm not talking to sick his guts out in the snow.'

'Ali, I'm sorry,' Tristan gurgled. 'I'm sorry for every-thing. I'm sorry for last night. And tonight. And . . . And forever. Go on without me – go with the others – it's almost midnight. Blaaargh!' He hurled again. Then he started shaking with cold.

'Come on,' Rando said, 'we'd better get him inside. Seb, Jas, help me.'

Thank you,' Alice mouthed, catching Rando's eye as the boys dragged Tristan into the chalet.

'Do you think he'll be OK?' Dylan shivered, rubbing her hands together for warmth.

'Yeah, he's just gotta puke it up.' Mimah wrapped her scarf tighter round her throat.

'Poor Al,' Dylan frowned.

'Humph,' Sonia snorted.

'Right,' Jasper said, emerging from the house, 'let's go. We've parked T next to the toilet with a bottle of water. He'll be OK.'

'Are you sure?' Alice said. 'Shouldn't someone stay with him?'

Jasper shrugged. 'Sure. If you want to spend New Year watching your boyfriend barf, be my guest. Otherwise, come on – the crowds are gathering. If we don't hurry up, we won't get a good spot for the fireworks.'

'I've got the champagne,' Seb said.

'And I've got the sparklers,' Dylan added.

Jasper scooped up a handful of snow. 'And now you've got a wet face,' he laughed, chucking it at her.

'Ow!' Dylan cried. 'I'll get you.'

The gang took off across the snowy garden, throwing snowballs as they ran.

'Take that!' Seb shouted, rubbing powder in Mimah's nose.

She shrieked. 'Dill, Alice, come on – let's get the boys!'

Alice bit her lip, hovering between the house and the game. Maybe she should stay and nurse Tristan. After all, he was her boyfriend – even if they weren't speaking. More than that – he was her friend.

Then she shrugged. It was his own fault if he'd drunk too much, not hers. And it was New Year, after all. Gathering an armful of snow, she ran at Rando and dumped it over his head.

'Argh! You're asking for it!' Shaking the powder off his curly brown hair, Rando bolted towards her.

'No!' Alice squealed, dashing across the snow. 'I'll do anything! Please!'

'Ha!' he laughed. 'You should have thought of that before you attacked me.'

Catching her round the waist, he picked her up and tossed her into a pile of snow. Then he fell on top of her.

Alice laughed, her chest heaving against his. Rando's face was centimetres from hers. Their eyes met. They lingered. Alice could pick out each freckle on his pale face, each tiny fleck of snow on his skin. She wanted so badly to reach out her tongue and lick one off.

But no . . . It was wrong. They were friends. They'd promised.

Rando must have thought the same thing, because he scrambled off her and held out his hand. 'Come on,' he said.

Alice gave him a suspicious look. 'Why should I trust you?' she giggled. 'You're going to drop me, aren't you?'

'No! No tricks. I promise,' he said, hauling her to her feet.

'Oh, n-n-no,' she shivered. 'My leggings are s-s-soaked.'

'Let's see?'

Alice's teeth were chattering. 'It's m-m-my fault. I'm not wearing anything w-w-w-w-waterproof.'

'Shit,' Rando murmured, touching her cheeks. 'You're freezing.'

'It's OK-K-K; let's go. I'll warm up while we watch fireworks.'

'Don't be ridiculous – it's below zero. We'll be standing in the cold for ages. You'll get ill.'

Alice shivered wildly. 'Maybe I should g-g-g-go back to the chalet and change. I just want to get warm. You go on without me.'

'No, hang on,' Rando said. 'I have a better idea. I know a place that's even nearer than the chalet. This way.'

'But . . .' Alice hesitated.

'Do you want to catch your death out here? Trust me. Come on.'

Alice cast a glance back at the others. Then, taking Rando's hand, she followed him into the night.

Chapter 45

'I hope the key's still here,' Rando said, as he and Alice approached the cabin. It was built of rough-hewn mountain logs and lay on the edge of the von Holstadts' chalet complex. Behind a line of snow-covered trees, Alice could hear groups of revellers making their way into the centre of town. Jasper and Dylan and Mimah and Sonia and Seb must be way ahead of them by now.

'What is this place?' she shivered.

'It's Aunt and Uncle von Holstadt's spa hut.'

'Seriously? We can't just go in. What if they're using it?'

'Oh, yeah, valid point,' Rando retorted, rolling his eyes. He flashed his cheeky grin. 'I'm sure Jasper's parents are spending their New Year naked in the sauna. Or maybe they're getting special midnight massages?'

Alice giggled. 'OK, hurry up then – I'm dying of cold. I think my leggings are frozen to my skin.'

Reaching up, Rando felt about under the overhang of the roof. 'Jasper and I used to play in here when we were younger, even though we were totally forbidden. They used to keep the key under the eaves . . . Aha!' he said, as his fingers hit metal. 'And they still do.'

'G-g-good,' Alice shivered.

Rando unlocked the door. Inside, the hut was modern, with an open glass-and-steel fireplace in the middle of the room, a thick sheepskin rug and a low-slung couch. The air was scented with aromatherapy oils and pinewood. Two doors led off the main room – one into a sauna, the other into a massage suite.

'Mmmm, warmth,' Alice said. 'Quick, let's light the fire.'

'I'll take care of that.' Rando tossed her a cashmere blanket from the couch. 'Here. You get out of your wet clothes.'

Alice slipped into the dark massage room, leaving the door ajar to light her way. She stripped off her jumper, her lace top, her leggings – and stood for a moment, naked except for her pants and bra. Her heart was fluttering. She could hear Rando in the next room, piling logs in the fireplace, boiling the kettle, opening a cupboard.

Wrapping the blanket around her shoulders, Alice peered into the mirror above the sink. Her hair was rumpled and damp. Her skin was rosy from the cold. But she hardly bothered with that. She stared into her own eyes in the glass, as if she might find all the answers to all her questions there.

Back in the main room, the fire was crackling, throwing shadows over the walls.

Alice laid her wet clothes on the hearth and settled on the rug, right up close to the heat.

'Tea?' Rando called.

'Mmm, yes please.'

'What sort? They only have weird herbal ones. Green? Ginger? Lemon? Some super-healthy looking thing called "Bancha"?'

'I'll have whatever you're having,' Alice said.

'OK – green. Here.' He handed her a steaming mug, which she cupped between her hands. Then he sat next to her.

Alice drew her knees to her chest and stared into the blaze. The firelight licked over their faces. Outside their circle, the hut was dark.

'Feeling better?' Rando asked.

'Yes. Thanks.' Alice sipped her tea and watched a trail of steam rise from her clothes. 'They're going to take ages to dry,' she said.

He didn't reply.

'Rando?'

'Yeah?'

'It wasn't quicker to come here than to go back to the chalet, was it?'

He looked at her. The flames played in his eyes. 'No,' he said. 'But I think we both knew that.'

Alice swallowed. He looked so gorgeous in the firelight. She'd never wanted anyone so much in her life. Not even Tristan. She'd never felt like this before.

'I wanted to be with you,' he said. 'Alone. I know we said we wouldn't. But I can't stop thinking about you. We have this connection. I feel it – you must feel it, too?'

Alice put down her tea. She was shaking a little, but it wasn't with cold.

'Stop talking,' she whispered, reaching out and touching his arm. It was like reaching across a bottomless mountain chasm. The vertigo closed in.

Rando cupped her face with his hand, and she sighed softly as he kissed her.

'You're beautiful,' he breathed, unwrapping the blanket from her shoulders and letting it fall around her waist. They peeled off the rest of each other's clothes and lay down on the rug, and she held him, and closed her eyes.

In the distance, the first chimes of midnight struck. Fireworks exploded outside the windows, red and green and yellow and silver and blue. Alice watched them burst and disintegrate, their embers smoking in the black sky.